PRAISE FOR
THE UNLIKELIES

"This unlikely story is likely to be a hit." —*Kirkus Reviews*

"A memorable blend of the serious, madcap, and romantic."
—*Publishers Weekly*

"Carrie Firestone weaves together humanitarianism,
friendship, love, heartbreak, and good old-fashioned
summertime fun in her exquisite novel.... Odds that this will
be a YA favorite? Likely."
—*Shelf Awareness*

"*The Unlikelies* is the summer read that'll remind you how
much good there really is in the world, and of how much
impact even the smallest acts of kindness can have."
—*Bustle*

THE LOOSE ENDS LIST:

★ "A poignant and important story about compassion, love,
and the decision to live life on your own terms—right up to
the very last minute." —*Kirkus Reviews* (starred review)

"Filled with equal amounts of laugh- and tear-inducing
moments, this debut novel will be impossible to put
down...With its fresh, original plot and thought-provoking
themes, this title will have a high teen appeal." —*SLJ*

The
Unlikelies

The Unlikelies

CARRIE FIRESTONE

LITTLE, BROWN AND COMPANY

New York Boston

Copyright © 2017 by Carrie Firestone

Excerpt from *The Loose Ends List* copyright © 2016 by Carrie Firestone

Cover design by Karina Granda. Cover background pattern © by elyomys/Shutterstock.com. Cover ice cream illustrations © by mart/Shutterstock.com. Cover copyright © 2017 by Hachette Book Group, Inc.

Little, Brown and Company
Hachette Book Group
1290 Avenue of the Americas, New York, NY 10104
Visit us at LBYR.com

Originally published in hardcover and ebook by Little, Brown and Company in June 2017
First Trade Paperback Edition: June 2018

Little, Brown and Company is a division of Hachette Book Group, Inc. The Little, Brown name and logo are trademarks of Hachette Book Group, Inc.

The publisher is not responsible for websites (or their content) that are not owned by the publisher.

The Library of Congress has cataloged the hardcover edition as follows:
Names: Firestone, Carrie, author.
Title: The Unlikelies / Carrie Firestone.
Description: First edition. | New York ; Boston : Little, Brown and Company, 2017. | Summary: "Sadie Sullivan's pre-senior year summer changes for the better when she and four other teens band together to right local wrongs, but the Unlikelies and their heady new friendships soon face obstacles that could tear them apart"—Provided by publisher.
Identifiers: LCCN 2016034374| ISBN 9780316382861 (hardback) | ISBN 9780316382854 (ebook) | ISBN 9780316382885 (library edition ebook)
Subjects: | CYAC: Heroes—Fiction. | Friendship—Fiction. | Summer—Fiction. | Hamptons (N.Y.)—Fiction.
Classification: LCC PZ7.1.F55 Un 2017 | DDC [Fic]—dc23
LC record available at https://lccn.loc.gov/2016034374

ISBNs: 978-0-316-38289-2 (pbk.), 978-0-316-38285-4 (ebook)

Printed in the United States of America

LSC-C

10 9 8 7 6 5 4 3 2 1

For the unlikely friendships,
the ones that inspire us,
the ones that change our lives

A FEW MINUTES before the incident, I noticed a tuft of dune grass stuck to a discarded strawberry crate. A honey jar had fallen from the shelf, but I didn't feel like picking it up. Daniela, my farm stand coworker, had a crusty cold sore on her mouth. I wondered if it was herpes.

I was twelve hours into downsizing my life and just beginning to be more aware of my surroundings.

The incident happened on a Tuesday, early summer, so the heavy Hamptons weekend traffic hadn't started yet and we had only a few customers. Old Mr. Upton and his aide, Sissy, were on a quest for unbruised peaches. A couple of women from the city, probably there to get their summer houses ready for the kids and their nannies and the investment banker husbands, were talking near the buckets of wild-flowers. A tourist family loaded up two baskets. The mother told me she and the kids were going to have a picnic at the Montauk Lighthouse.

I stood near the register, my hands tucked in the pockets of my unflattering farm stand apron, disappointed that it was only ten four-teen and I still had six hours and forty-six minutes left in the dim shed with the horseflies and Daniela's cold sore.

Maybe I'll run home for lunch, I thought.

ONE

I SPENT TWO months assembling care packages for my friends. It was my way of thanking them for being awesome. Nobody had ever seen such a tight senior class, united by over a decade of friendship and compulsive thrill seeking, and a chemistry my own dysfunctional junior class would never have. The inseparable seniors were about to disband, bound for summer camp jobs and sports clinics and European vacations—and then college.

I wanted to do something special before they left.

The boxes, lined up in neat rows on my window seat, were all the same size and shape. I had scoured the shops and flea markets in town, adding online items that reflected the recipients and what they meant to me. The care packages cost me all my birthday money, but as I tucked in the notes, wrapped each small box with brown paper, and tied it with gold-flecked garden twine, it felt right.

I passed out the boxes at the Night of a Thousand Good-byes, held every year after all the graduation parties and drawn-out family dinners.

"Thank you, thank you, thank you, Sadie," Ellie said as we sat on the log and she took out the contents of the box: A snowflake-shaped cookie cutter to represent Ellie's annual cookie exchange. An elephant figurine carved out of a giant nut to represent Ellie's love of elephants. A miniature bobblehead of our assistant principal to represent her strange crush on Mr. Wilson.

"I will cherish these," Ellie said, "like forever." Ellie had only a few more hours of freedom before her family volunteer trip to Mongolia.

Parker was one of the few not leaving right away, but I gave her a care package anyway: A tiny plastic Wonder Woman figurine because Parker was the spitting image of Wonder Woman on Halloween. A box of Thin Mints, her favorite cookie since our Girl Scout days. A temporary tattoo collection to help her finally decide if she wanted a real one.

Parker hugged me so hard I thought I might bleed internally.

The care packages were a big hit. I even made Seth a care package, because he had been a damn good boyfriend while it lasted. I saved his until the end of the night, which was probably a mistake, because he was drunk by then and very handsy.

"Sadie Cakes, come here," he said, pulling me toward him and leaning down to kiss me. Our original breakup had happened via text during spring break, in the middle of his trip to Cabo. We had mutually decided it was impossible to sustain a relationship when he would be spending the summer at his dad's in Israel, then going to college in North Carolina. But mutual and amicable didn't mean fast or easy. It was easier to hook up than not hook up. It was easier to go to a movie with Seth than stay home and watch HGTV with Mom. It was easier to go to senior prom together than to mess up the whole plan.

The first breakup never sticks anyway, so it was good we'd started in March.

"Stop, we're broken up," I said unconvincingly. "Here, I made you a care package."

"Aww. You're the best ex-girlfriend ever." He laid his hand on the small of my back. I didn't move away, but I didn't move any closer to Seth's lips either.

I was going to miss Seth and all our history and our chair, the chair we sat in at every Shawn Flynn party, the chair in the middle of it all. And I would miss the bonfires and the football games and the movie nights in Seth's basement. But I had to stay strong.

Seth tore open his box. He took out each item and studied it. A bobblehead of my deceased cat, Lucy, Seth's favorite pet. I had gotten a little obsessed with the custom bobblehead site. A bag of hand-cut potato chips, Seth's favorite snack. And a printout of the first text Seth ever sent me—*Do you like sushi?*—rolled up in a tiny scroll.

He was quiet.

I hadn't wanted to get too sentimental. As much as I had loved being Seth's girlfriend, we both knew there wasn't enough between us to transcend time and space.

"You suck," he said, rubbing his eyes. I hadn't planned to make him cry.

I left him standing there, holding the care package. One last hookup wouldn't be good for either one of us.

Between the care package distributions and handing out Woody's Ice Cream hats to everybody—compliments of Dad, who always gave out hats to his graduating customers—I barely talked to Shay. When it was time to go, I pried the fine-tipped Sharpie out of her yearbook-signing hand and waited on the edge of the sob-fest for her drawn-out good-byes.

Shay and I took one last best-friend drive home in Mom's Prius, which I had basically taken over, forcing Mom to use Grandma Hosseini's Buick. Shay had to leave for California the next morning to teach at a tennis camp before starting college at Pepperdine. I dug into a bag of tortilla chips and listened to Shay go over her packing checklist one more time.

"Should I just wait until I get there and see what shoes California people are wearing?"

"Yes. It's humanly impossible to fit another pair of shoes into that suitcase."

Shay turned to me. "Is this happening?" she said. "Because it feels like a normal night."

"It *is* a normal night." I reached over and squeezed her hand.

Shay was a steaming hotbed of emotion. If she started reminiscing about all the things we'd been through together and how awesome our friendship was, she would blow. I wanted her to remember her graduation night as fun and happy.

We pulled into Shay's driveway and I turned off the car.

"I have a little something for you," I said, reaching behind the seat.

"A Sadie care package?"

I grabbed my last Woody hat and set it on her head. Shay adjusted it and said, "I'm going to miss him. If it weren't for the Woodster, there'd be no Shay and Sadie. Isn't that crazy to think about?"

When I'd met Shay, we had just moved to the East End from Queens and Dad wanted to take me out on the maiden voyage of the Woody's Ice Cream truck. Shay chased us down the street barefoot and, after ordering her Nutty Buddy, promptly invited me to the birthday party she was having that afternoon.

"Should I open it now or wait?" Shay said, taking the care package.

"Open it now."

She carefully untied the gold-flecked twine and pulled off the paper and the box lid, revealing:

A tin of peppermint drops in honor of the fourteen-act play we'd written, acted in, and directed called *Peppermint Drop City: The Fairies Take Over*.

A berry fusion lip tint and a berry nice lip shimmer (because I always stole hers).

A purple condom (because...college).

A framed photo of Shay and me taken the day we met, when I actually showed up at her tenth birthday party that afternoon.

Twin bobbleheads of Shay and me holding hands. (I had treated myself to a matching set of Bobblehead Shay with the long blond hair and bulging blue eyes and Bobblehead Sadie with the thick wavy black hair and sharp nose.)

"Wow, my bobblehead has a huge rack," Shay said, running her fingers over the bobblehead's plastic chest.

"I thought you'd appreciate that."

"There's nothing I can say to do justice to this care package, so I'm just going to hug you," Shay said, leaning over to pull me in. I hugged my best friend and pressed my face into her wild blond mermaid hair. She smelled of the lavender essential oil she rubbed on her temples when she was stressed.

We let go at the same time and said what we said on any normal night.

"Later, Shay-Shay."

"Later, Sader."

The next morning I woke at six, still on school time, and reached for my phone to text Shay. It took me a few seconds to remember it was over, that she was probably already on her way to the airport.

I hugged Flopper, my stuffed harp seal, and tried to go back to sleep, but Mom's kitchen clanging and television sounds put an end to that.

"What are you doing up?" Mom looked over from her perch at the kitchen island, where she sat sipping tea and reading the headlines as the Hamptons forecast blared from the TV above the sink.

"My brain thinks it's a school day." I foraged through the fridge. "Can you make pancakes?"

"Chocolate chip?"

I nodded, then sat at the counter, hands folded, waiting for my pancakes.

"What's on the agenda?" Mom asked, setting a glass of milk in front of me.

I stared up at her and then reality set in.

"I have no idea."

I welcomed my first official shift at the farm stand. I knew work would be hot, and full of horseflies and sawdust and some of the world's most irritating customers, referred to by year-round Hamptons residents as *cidiots* (city idiots). But I would get to eat a lot of peaches and strawberries, and I needed the paychecks for school clothes and college savings.

The first morning, Farmer Brian reminded Daniela and me how to work the register and do the tally sheets, and we got a refresher on the difference between ripe and rotten. After Farmer Brian left,

Daniela spent most of the time on her phone, or dozing off because her three-year-old exhausted her, but I didn't mind. Work gave me something to focus on.

I lingered awhile in the back of the wooden building, with its three walls painted dark green and its open, awning-covered front that faced the road. I unloaded crates of vegetables, avoiding the picky locals and the overeager city people and the tourists who drove all the way to the Hamptons to take pictures for their Facebook pages.

The cidiots were back.

That night, Mom and Dad took me for pizza to celebrate the beginning of summer. They had promised not to bring up college until I'd had a chance to adjust to my new normal. College had been a family sticking point since Shay got into Pepperdine, mostly because I had no idea where I wanted to go or what I wanted to do.

Two bites into my calzone, Mom sent Dad to the bathroom to wipe the Parmesan off his mustache. "I picked up the *Guide to Northeast Colleges* at the bookstore," she said casually. "It's on the dining room table. I earmarked a few that look interesting."

"Thanks, Mom." I knew better than to remind her of her promise.

I reached under my bra line and scratched the hot, clammy skin. I needed a shower. And sleep. But halfway through my calzone, Shay texted me. Hannah S. and Chelsea want you to escort them to Shawn's tonight.

As much as I'd told Shay I was happy hanging out on our porch with my parents and our neighbor Mr. Ng, she worried about me. She had been trying for months to play friend matchmaker with Hannah S. and other people from my dysfunctional class.

Oh, come on, I replied. The gadflies?

I told them to pick you up at nine.

Shay, I don't feel like socializing.

Come on, give them a chance. Otherwise you have the potential to turn into one of those agoraphobic people.

No I don't.

Please?? I want to know what's going on. I'm already out of the loop.

Damn it, Shay. FINE.

Hannah S. and Chelsea were part of the *gadfly* faction of my dysfunctional junior class. Shay titled them gadflies because they hung around like insects, buzzing in tightly drawn circles, gossiping and side whispering and basically being petty, drama-slinging troublemakers. Shawn Flynn was having another party because Shawn Flynn was addicted to the moment when a rush of freshly showered people rounded the back bend of his hedgerow to fill the empty spaces of his parentless mansion.

Hannah S. and Chelsea pulled into our driveway just as I was throwing on shorts and my leprechaun T-shirt. I put my wet hair in a bun and found my overaccessorized classmates on the front porch with Dad and Mr. Ng.

"Have a blast," Dad shouted as we climbed into Hannah's car.

"I feel so bad that Shay has to miss this summer," Hannah S. said, acting like Shay was her lifelong friend.

"She's in California. I'm sure her summer will be better than ours," I said, texting Shay from the backseat. So bored. Wish I was in bed right now.

We drove around awhile and parked down the road from Shawn's massive mansion. Chelsea cracked open a warm screw-cap bottle of wine she must have clipped from a hotel minibar. They bombarded me with questions about the Night of a Thousand Good-byes and who'd hooked up that night and was it true D-Bag fell in vomit?

Hannah swallowed another mini bottle of zinfandel and smacked her lips.

"Let's do this," she said loudly, tossing the bottle out the window.

Hannah is littering, I texted Shay.

Just give them a chance.

I flung open Shawn's front door and ushered in Hannah and Chelsea.

"This house rocks," Hannah said, giggling awkwardly.

"I'll be back." I scanned the crowd of sunburned faces and found Parker on a lounge chair playing a game on her phone, probably counting the minutes until college.

"Parker, slide over." I crawled up next to her and sighed heavily.

"The juniors have moved in," she said. "This is bullshit."

Shawn's back deck teemed with drunken ruffians (also Shay's term): the assholes who made everyone loathe my class. In true clichéd form, the ruffians targeted the weak kids, the smart kids, the robotics kids, the loner kids, the theater kids, and anyone else they could get away with harassing.

"Filling the void with assholes," Parker said.

I spotted Hannah and Chelsea side whispering near a potted tree. "I'm going for a walk," I said.

I wove through the shot takers and pool poseurs to the beach path and made my way over to the hump of sand a few feet from the surf. I sat down, brought my knees up to my chest, and planted my chin on my stubbly kneecap. The party sounds blended with the waves under the sliver of a moon.

Loneliness set in like thunderclouds.

When I got home, I sent Shay a long-winded text about how I was better off removing myself from the Shawn Flynn party scene and how I really was looking forward to reading books on the porch. I wanted to downsize my social life and just hang out alone for once.

She responded with: Parker told me Shawn's was a shit show. I don't blame you.

To which I replied: Good. You can stop pimping me out to the gadflies. I've got my Flopper. He's all I need.

❧ TWO ❧

ON DAY TWO of work, the family of tourists stood in line behind old Mr. Upton, who swatted at a mosquito on his cheek, leaving a crush of black and blood the size of a dime on the rosy area to the right of his bulbous nose. He held a quart of peaches and I noticed his nails were long and yellow. I tried to tell him there was something on his face, but his hearing aids weren't in. "What?" he kept saying, until I mouthed *Nothing* and walked away. His aide, Sissy, wandered up to the farm stand counter. Sissy held two bunches of flowers and a head of Swiss chard. Sweat beaded on her dark Caribbean skin. She wore teal mascara, and her loose-fitting rust-colored T-shirt had a purple stain near the collar. I wondered if it was plum juice.

The car barreled through the gravel parking lot so quickly a few rogue pebbles flew up and hit Mr. Upton's Lincoln. We all stopped where we were. Mr. Upton and Sissy. Daniela. The two women near the wildflowers. The family shopping for their Montauk picnic.

The car made that much of a commotion.

A guy jumped out and slammed the door. He called somebody a *fucktard* on the phone as he pushed past the berry display and into the building where we all stood, staring.

"What are you looking at, rich bitches?" the guy slurred.

I hadn't seen someone so angry drunk since a kid from Watermill had had to be transported out of Shawn Flynn's snow day party in an ambulance to have his stomach pumped.

"Eat shit and die," the guy yelled into the phone before he shoved it into the pocket of his faded jeans. He clumsily wove around the vegetables and opened the cold case. He grabbed a fistful of cheeses and threw them into a basket. His face, mottled with acne scars and covered in patches of salt-and-pepper facial hair, was almost purple, probably because he was wearing a flannel shirt and work boots in ninety-degree weather.

Sissy shook her head and raised her eyebrows. Mr. Upton fumbled with his wallet. A noise came from the parking lot. At first it sounded like the guy had left the car radio on. But then the noise revealed itself.

Herself.

She was a crying baby.

I stepped away from the counter and walked out to the guy's burgundy sedan. The tinted windows were up tight, except for the baby's window, which was down only an inch or two. The baby's shape moved frantically as the wailing sounds got worse.

"What the hell?" His voice hurtled toward me from behind. "Get away from my car, you little A-rab." He was talking to me.

I whipped around. The stink of liquor and B.O. hit me in the face. His eyes were wild, the whites stained yellow. Some sort of valve opened inside me and adrenaline shot through my body. It was massive and electric and, in a weird way, calming.

My voice was measured when I said, "Sir, why don't you take out the baby and get her some cold water? She's probably really thirsty."

"She's fine."

"I don't want to offend you, sir, but I think you've had a bit to drink and maybe it's not a great idea to drive right now."

His face purpled even more. "I don't want to offend you, but you're a twat."

The crying got louder.

The guy hurled the plastic basket onto the ground. Cheese bricks, strawberries, and jars of honey scattered. One of the jars smashed and honey oozed into the gravel. He reached into his pocket for his keys and stumbled around to the front of the car. I tried the back door handle. It was locked. I ran around to the driver's side, where he was climbing in, and I dove on top of him, trying to grab for his keys.

I was not going to let him put his key into that little slit.

Sprawled across his foul-smelling body, I felt his hand grab my ponytail and yank my head upward. For a split second, I was angled toward the backseat and noticed the baby's face, bright red and tear streaked, brown eyes fixed on the guy's hand pulling me up by my hair.

For another split second we were all suspended in silence.

The grip tightened on my ponytail and forced my head downward. My face collided with something hard on the passenger seat. He yanked up and forced my face down again. The cold metal of a toolbox cut into my forehead. I cried out before reaching again for the keys.

In an instant, he let go of my ponytail and grabbed a nearly full bottle of liquor. The amber liquid swished upward before he struck me on my back. My body curved instinctively. Blow after blow, he pummeled the bottle into my torso. I cried out from the crushing pain of each blow as my own guttural sounds blended with the staccato cries coming from the backseat.

It was only after the sirens were surrounding the car that I noticed the police. A cop reached in to pull me out. I resisted at first, because I still hadn't gotten the keys.

"It's okay, Sadie." I heard Daniela's voice echo through the pounding in my head. I stumbled and collapsed onto Daniela, who couldn't handle the weight of my body, and we fell to the ground. The gravel tore into my knees as the cop who'd pulled me out and several others wrestled with the guy until they finally got him down. He landed inches from me, his face stuck to shards of glass and honey. I looked up and saw another cop carefully unbuckle the baby. She had stopped wailing, as if she knew she was safe.

For a single moment, it all shifted into slow motion.

I noticed the two city women had never left the wildflower stand. One clutched the other, and they stood with their hands over their mouths. I noticed the family talking to the cops over by the willow tree.

I reached up and felt the blood seeping out of my head.

The blood from my head gash felt sticky, more like Jell-O than juice. The paramedic pulled out my ponytail holder and released a matted knot of hair. They covered me with a thin white blanket, and I fell in and out of sleep.

"Sadie, I'm going to need you to wake up." The words floated somewhere beyond the deep, pulsing pain in my head and my back. I looked up, only for a second, and saw a woman's face, blue eyes with deep half-moon bags underneath.

"What's up?" My mouth tasted like metal and dried leaves.

Every time I fell asleep, somebody bothered me awake.

"Sunshine, it's Daddy." I opened my eyes, strained hard to keep them open. Dad's face hovered above mine, his gray eyes ringed in red. He forced a smile.

"What's wrong, Dad?" The pain tore through my side. "Ow. My back."

Mom appeared from behind Dad and took my hand. Her hand was freezing.

"Sadie, you've got some injuries from the incident back at the farm stand. I don't know how much you remember, but it doesn't matter. You're okay, sweetie." Mom's voice sounded like it was echoing through a tunnel.

"Can you turn the lights off?" I said as they wheeled me toward the CT scanner. My head hurt more than anything else, like a terrible, unrelenting, migrating toothache.

A guy in green scrubs tried to talk about normal things as he searched for a vein plump enough to stick a needle into.

"Do you know what happened to the baby? In the car?" I asked him.

"No, dear, I don't. I'll try to find out."

"I need to use the bathroom," I said.

I had a concussion and a deep monster of a gash on the side of my head. A doctor with the voice of a radio DJ talked to my parents behind the curtain. "Sadie has two fractured ribs, displaced inward. There's some blood around the spleen, but I don't think we're going to need to intervene surgically. We'll keep her here for observation."

I fell asleep again.

A nurse shined a bright light into my face.

"Hi, Sadie. I'm *blah, blah, blah.*" I didn't hear what the nurse was saying.

"I can't breathe."

The panic rose up toward my throat. "I can't breathe!" I yelled.

"You can breathe, Sadie. It's just uncomfortable." She held up a plastic thing with a thick tube hanging out of it. "I need you to suck air through this tube every few minutes. It's going to hurt. But just breathe through the pain. This will prevent you from getting pneumonia."

I sucked air from the tube while my parents hovered over me, trying not to lose their shit.

A newswoman wanted to interview me from my hospital bed, but Woody the ice cream man told her to *Please get the hell out*. I was still in and out of sleep the next morning, still breathing into the plastic thing, waking for vital signs and questions about what number my pain was on a scale from one to ten. The pain traveled from my side to my shoulders to deep inside my head to my badly skinned knees.

I hadn't eaten in a day and a half, but I wasn't hungry. The doctor wanted me to get up and pee on my own. A new nurse with a platinum-blond weave kicked out my parents so she could remove the catheter and walk me to the bathroom.

"It's burning," I said to the nurse, who stood in front of me while I tried to pee. I took small, shallow breaths to avoid the searing rib pain.

As the nurse helped me up, I glanced down at the plastic tub attached to the toilet seat. It was full of blood.

"Um. Okaaaaay. Uh." I froze and studied her face, wondering if I was dying.

"It's totally normal with a spleen injury," she said, helping me to bed.

I had no idea what a spleen was.

Dad talked loudly on the phone in the hallway, and I tried to shush him but my breath was too shallow to make sounds. Mom worried I might get addicted to the painkillers. My grandmothers prayed to Jesus and Allah in the waiting room. They wandered in periodically to make sure I had enough blankets. At some point, I was awake enough to check my phone. I had hundreds of texts. From Shay. From Seth. From the seniors. Daniela. Some of the people in my class.

Shay had taken it upon herself to organize a get-well origami-crane project, so people were texting me images of badly made origami cranes while I tried to piece together what had happened. I remembered it in fragments: the man barreling through the farm stand, the liquor breath, and the baby girl.

The baby girl.

I couldn't get her terrified, wailing little face out of my head.

A woman named Officer Estrada sat in the upholstered chair and asked me questions. Her pinched face and irritated tone coupled with Mom's "Think, sweetie. Tell her exactly what happened" paralyzed me.

"Can you tell me what's going on with the baby?" I stared blankly at the officer.

"I'm not at liberty to talk about the case," she said.

"Aren't we talking about the case?" I said, confused.

Finally, Dad had the doctor kick Officer Estrada out.

After a liter of water, my second attempt at peeing was more successful. I winced as I leaned forward to try to wash my hands. That's when I saw my face in the mirror. I had a blue-black jellyfish-shaped tumor spilling out around the tight white bandage. It looked like my eyes had been hollowed out and smeared with wet charcoal.

I smiled. It hurt to move my face, but I still had all my teeth. And for that, I was grateful.

❧ THREE ❧

WHEN THEY FINALLY released me, I slumped in the wheelchair while an aide paraded me through the brightly lit hallways and into an elevator, where a couple tried not to stare. Mom carried my plastic breathing thing and my blood-spattered shoes. Dad ran ahead to get the car, which my grandmothers had already filled with the get-well flowers.

The wait in front of the hospital, in the heat and bright sunshine, made me nauseated. I started to dry heave, and the guy pushing the wheelchair handed me a pink barf bucket. I had never felt so awful.

That was when a woman came out of nowhere and took my picture.

"Do you need me to come home? Because you know I will," Shay said. She called or texted me hourly. "I feel so bad I'm not there."

"I'm okay. Just sore. It's not like you could do anything if you came home. I'm sitting around with ice on my ribs, trying to take deep breaths and listening to my mother tell the story to the relatives over and over again. If you want to help, send me really good noise-canceling earbuds."

"Do you like the cranes?"

"I love the cranes."

The origami cranes had taken over the house. People were dropping cranes on our porch with notes, with chocolates, with magazines, with flowers. Shay was the ringleader, the crane queen. It didn't matter that I was pretty sure I was supposed to make the cranes myself for the healing to happen, or that I wasn't on the brink of dying, or that it was all so melodramatic. Shay wanted to deliver a grand gesture, and I loved her for it. But I was uncomfortable with all the attention. I didn't want people worrying about me.

The local newspaper published the horrible picture of me with my bandaged head holding a barf bucket on the front page with the headline GOOD SAMARITAN TEEN SAVES BABY FROM FUGITIVE FATHER. I sat on the living room couch, propped up on pillows, reading about the Alabama man who had fled his estranged ex-wife's house with their baby girl to get back at the mom for leaving him. He had a history of domestic violence and drunk driving. There was a nearly full bottle of Southern Comfort in the passenger seat. I assumed that was the bottle he had used to beat me in the spleen.

There was a shotgun in the trunk next to a stuffed owl wrapped in a pink box.

I watched the whole thing, which had been recorded on a tourist kid's iPod. It was all a blur of sounds, mostly—head-cracking sounds and baby cries and sirens. Watching it over and over again was strangely comforting. I didn't have to work so hard to remember.

It turned out there were many things I hadn't noticed the day of the incident. I hadn't noticed Daniela calling the cops or Sissy and old Mr. Upton banging on the back window of the car with a rock, trying to get to the baby. I only noticed those things the fifth time I viewed the video on YouTube. The first four times I was focused on the bizarre kicking motion my legs made while *he* drove the base of the bottle into my back. And then there was my ass crack hanging out when the cops pulled me from the car by my shorts.

I clicked on the TV news story that aired the night of the incident. The newspeople speculated the guy might have been planning to drive his baby off a cliff. They speculated he might have been gearing up to go on a shooting spree. People online said I was a hero. They said I was stupid. They talked about me, Sadie Sullivan, the girl named after her paternal great-grandmother, an Irish seamstress who saved seven children from a fire and burned the bottoms of her feet so badly they had to be amputated.

"Where the hell did they find out about that?" Dad said, leaning in to watch the video.

"I'm surprised the news didn't say something about your thumb," I said, referring to Dad's missing thumb, a casualty of an accident he refused to discuss that happened when he was a New York City cop.

I wanted to stop watching, especially when they zoomed in on the blurred ass crack. I wanted to stop looking at the pictures online, especially the one of me in the wheelchair looking like a deformed larva. But I couldn't stop. For two days straight, I watched and read and searched for more stories.

There was one story out of Alabama. A dark-haired newsman with a deep chin dimple told the story of the seventeen-month-old baby who was saved by the New York farm stand worker. They cut to a blurry photograph of the baby, with wisps of sandy hair and apple cheeks and a wide, drooling smile. "Thanks to that Good Samaritan, baby Ella is home safe with her mother and doing well."

Her name was Ella. And according to my laptop, baby Ella was home safe and doing well.

I spent a week on the couch, sleeping, texting, reading online comments about baby Ella and me, fielding visits from family, from the remaining seniors (even Shawn Flynn and D-Bag stopped by with flowers), from my food-pushing grandmothers, who didn't understand I was drinking all my meals through a straw.

Seth sent a few more *How's it going?* texts before returning to his vacation. I was surprised by how little I thought about Seth, how I didn't need him during such a stressful time. Shay called whenever she could, until I promised her I was really, really, truly fine and she should use her breaks to find some California friends. By the end of the week, the flood of origami cranes dwindled to two or three a day.

I was relieved.

Mom went back to work designing window treatments and Dad resumed his twelve-hour shifts, leaving me with my laptop and the online East End troll mill.

Nobody knew who had started the school slam pages or how they had blown up all over Long Island to the delight of the gadflies. But they were full of horrible comments about people's appearances, and mental health, and family crises. The slam pages were pure evil. Everyone walked on eggshells, afraid one wrong move would make them slam-page targets.

The incident made me an instant target. And every comment, even the nice ones, caused my heart to race and my stomach to sink, but I couldn't stop myself from reading.

If that were my daughter, I'd kick her ass a second time for pulling that stunt.

The world needs more heroic people.

She's hot. I'd hit that.

Yeah, if you like Al Qaeda looking bitches.

"Very original," I said to Shay, who was going through the slam page with me on her lunch break.

"At least they didn't say your ass was fat." Somebody once called Shay a fat-ass on the slam pages, which was ridiculous because Shay's entire body was tiny. That one comment made Shay eternally ass-obsessed.

"I just remembered the guy called me an A-rab right before the incident," I said.

"You get that a lot," Shay said. "Somebody should write a 'Geography for Dumb Racists' book."

"We could send it to him in prison. A Sadie care package." I was half serious.

"Is he going to prison?"

Until that moment, I had assumed he was going to prison for a long, long time. A wave of anxiety swelled inside me. "I hope so."

Lucky for me, the Hamptons Hero story was soon overshadowed by the Hamptons Hoodlum story about a local teen Meals on Wheels volunteer who had been caught stealing from elderly people to feed her shoe-shopping habit. I preferred to be me—ass crack, larva face, and all—than the shamed Hamptons Hoodlum.

Mom woke me up early for my appointment. I couldn't wait to get rid of the itchy bandage. I had never been so excited to shower and hopefully smell like a human being again. I shuffled out to the back porch and stood there for a long time with my face up to the sky, grateful to be breathing better. I wandered through the neatly groomed rows of flowering vegetables, then climbed up the back porch steps and sat on the cushioned wicker chair in the shaded corner next to Mom, who was having her tea.

My swollen face changed color every day. One day it was purple, like the inner petals of a crocus flower, then it faded to hyacinth blue until it settled on the brownish-gold hue of a smashed sunflower. Each time it changed, Mom took a picture.

"In case they need it for the trial."

"I'm sure they don't need to know how my bruise changes color."

"They might, Sadie." She dropped a pinch of rose petals into her teacup and set it on the saucer. "Are you able to do with just the ibuprofen today?"

"Yes, Mom. I'm not addicted to painkillers. Stop worrying."

"I'm not worrying."

"Mom?"

"Yes, hon?"

"I think I'm ready for pancakes."

Farmer Brian had cleaned up the parking lot and hosed it down. As far as I could see, there were no remnants of blood or glass or honey. I eased back into work, handling the customers while Daniela did the stacking and rearranging. During break, I sat on a wooden crate under the willow tree and ate a quart of strawberries while the weekend traffic crawled by like a long, impatient caterpillar looking for a sea bath and some steamers with butter.

Sissy and old Mr. Upton wandered in during the afternoon lull.

"How are you feeling, Sadie?" Sissy asked while Mr. Upton examined snap peas like a jeweler studying diamonds.

"I'm okay. Thank you for the flowers, by the way."

"I'm still shaken up. I can't imagine how you're doing it, being back here." Sissy walked around to the side of the counter and put her hand on my shoulder. I felt a tickle inside, like there was a cry trying to surface. "Take care, dear," she said.

Mr. Upton nodded and gave me a wink before he took Sissy's arm and shuffled toward the old Lincoln.

City people came in to load up on corn and watermelon and cheese and honey to drizzle on the cheese. After the farm stand, they would stop at Citarella for baguettes and Tate's cookies, and then they'd cozy up on their rental porches, taking in the sea air and dressing fancy for casual dinners.

The city people probably didn't know me or what had happened in the parking lot.

But the locals knew.

"Sadie, wow. You look so good." Hannah S. blindsided me while I was bent over a shipment of cherries.

"Thanks, Hannah. And thanks for all the cranes." I wiped cherry juice on my apron. "You're really good at origami."

Hannah flashed me a smile. "So...I'm guessing you'll be at Shawn's white party?"

I had forgotten about Shawn's white party, a variation of his usual Fourth of July tradition. By the look on Hannah's face, she was going. And I assumed all the gadflies and ruffians would be there.

"Not sure. I'll keep you posted."

Did you know that there are over a thousand causes of vaginal itch? Shay texted randomly.

I laughed out loud as I waited on my willow crate for Dad to pick me up.

If it had been last summer, Shay and I would have met at her house before the party. Shay would have been wearing a white strapless pantsuit with funky white hair feathers and red lipstick. We would have shown up fashionably late, and Shawn's new girlfriend would have given us jealous looks because we'd known Shawn since he was a bucktoothed kid with ADHD and a huge Pokémon collection. We would have eaten marshmallows and vanilla milk shakes and whatever else people ate at white parties, and watched Seth and those guys do vodka shots off ice sculptures until they dove backward into the pool, messing up their crisp white linen shirts. And Shay and I would have left fashionably early to get pizza before the pizza place closed. We'd have sat on the curb in the middle of town in our dirty white clothes, eating and laughing and making fun of the people who took white parties too seriously.

But it wasn't last summer. Shay was in California. And I'd been through an incident.

Shawn's white party would be all lameness and emptiness.

It would be white noise.

When Dad and I pulled up in the ice cream truck, Mom was on the porch frantically waving a piece of paper.

"Maybe Grandma finally won the lotto," I said.

"Sadie." Mom bent to catch her breath. "You've been invited to be an honoree at the Rotary Club Homegrown Hero Award Luncheon." She handed me a red-edged invitation. "This is fantastic."

I stared at the letter.

You have been nominated for this special honor... Please join us... Lunch... Homegrown Hero... Other young community leaders nominated from local junior classes...

"Mom, I can't go to this. I'm not a community leader. I did one thing."

Her smile disappeared. "Of course you're going to this."

"Dad, please don't make me go. I helped a baby for, like, two minutes. This is for people who do real community service."

Dad studied the letter. "I gotta go with your mother on this one, Sadie. They selected you. It's an honor! We have to go."

We went back and forth over our rice and kebabs and vanilla pudding, and in the end, honor won over *Please don't make me do this.*

At least I had an excuse to miss the white party. Two events in one day would be more than my spleen could handle.

❧ FOUR ❧

EARLY MORNING ON the Fourth of July, the day of the dreaded homegrown hero luncheon, I lay in bed searching Facebook for pictures of baby Ella. It had become a habit, something I did when I was feeling anxious. Ella's grandmother had plastered her page with pictures, one with baby Ella holding her fingers, one with baby Ella on a swing, her sparkly pink shoes kicking up toward the sky. I clicked on every friend, every family member. The only one of *him* was on Ella's mom's page, buried in the sea of well wishes and prayer GIFs. He was standing in front of a bonfire, holding a beer, turning away from the camera. It made me cringe to see him there, looking like any guy on Facebook.

Ella's grandmother had started a crowd fund on NeighborCare.

She called it *Help Tammy Make Ends Meet. Pray for Ella.* They had raised only $120. It didn't seem nearly enough.

❧❧

Mom made sure we got to the luncheon nice and early. Dad dropped off my grandmothers and Mom and me in front of the main door of the country club and we walked into the lobby, which was bursting with flowers in giant vases on dark wood tables. Three women greeted us from a welcome station.

"It looks like we have an honoree here," one of the women said loudly. "You must be Alexis."

The woman next to her raised her eyebrows and grabbed the name tag out of her hand. "No, Linda. She's the young lady who saved the baby. Alexis is the one who will no longer be attending."

"Oh. I am so sorry. I just realized I didn't make up a new name tag." Linda smacked herself on the forehead.

"It's okay," I said. I glanced quickly at Mom.

The other woman printed my name on the back of the ALEXIS AHERN name tag with a Sharpie and slid the makeshift name tag into the plastic sleeve. "We are so glad to have you here, Sadie," she said with enthusiasm.

Mom and I made our way into the dining room, where most of the crowd was gathered around the bar, sipping martinis and chardonnays. We scanned the bar area for my grandmothers.

"I can't believe I'm a fill-in for some other girl who couldn't make it. This is so mortifying," I whispered.

"Let's try to make the best of it." Mom was obviously embarrassed, too.

Dad came in and ordered us all club sodas, except Grandma Sullivan, who wanted a highball. We stood awkwardly among throngs of red, white, and blue balloons and mini flags as bald guys with red faces patted me on the back. "Thank you for all the great stuff the Rotary Club does," I said, trying to deflect.

"Are you going to have to face that evil man in court?" an elderly lady asked me. She talked with a side whisper, and I imagined she had been a lifelong gadfly.

"I have no idea," I said. I didn't want to think about facing *him* again.

"Sadie?" I turned to see a familiar face standing behind me. I glanced at her gold-starred name tag.

"Oh my God! Alice! I haven't seen you in forever."

Alice had been in my Girl Scout troop all the way through seventh grade, when our whole troop decided Girl Scouts would not be happening anymore.

"Troop one eighty-six," she said with a wink and a thumbs-up.

"You look awesome. I love the lip ring," I said. She was tall and thin with long white-blond braids tied back with beaded elastics. Her skin was vampire pale, as if her face had never seen a drop of Hamptons sunshine. "You're still hanging out with the puppies, huh?" I pointed to the dog rescue T-shirt she wore over a long floral-print skirt. Alice had been obsessed with rescuing dogs since Brownies.

"I still love my puppy friends. Now I do photography for the shelters."

"That's so cool. I'm here by default."

"Hell no. You're the Hamptons Hero." She smiled.

A guy with bushy white eyebrows, also wearing a dog shelter T-shirt, tapped Alice on the shoulder and asked her something about the number of hours she spent at the shelter every week.

I texted Shay, Alice from Girl Scouts is a homegrown hero and she has multiple piercings. She looks good, though, before Alice turned and led me to the table with the giant gold-star balloon centerpiece.

A girl with straight shoulder-length black hair pulled back with a headband sat reading the program. Her name tag said VAL RAMOS.

"Hey, honoree table, I'm guessing?" Alice said.

"Yes," she said. "I'm glad you're here. I was feeling a little awkward sitting alone."

I sat next to Val and took a sip of ice water. "I'm Sadie, fill-in for somebody named Alexis Ahern."

"You're the baby saver. Well done," she said.

"Thanks. Some prefer to call me the damn fool." I took a quick bite of the dinner roll on the plate in front of me. "Sorry, I'm starving."

I immediately liked Val, who told us her entire family had come to Long Island from El Salvador. She talked quickly, smiled a lot, and was very animated with her hands. And she seemed passionate about collecting school supplies for migrant workers' children, which made me feel even less deserving of the award. Alice and I told her we knew each other from Girl Scout days, and she said the Haitian guy in the middle of a crowd by the bar was also an honoree from her school named Jean. She described him as the kind of guy who talked to everyone but didn't really hang out with anyone except the art teacher. She said he was an amazing artist.

"How does a kid our age have a full beard?"

"Who knows? He's had that for a while."

Alice buttered a roll. "So are you guys nervous?" she said.

"For what?" I asked.

"The speeches."

My stomach dropped. "I thought we were just going up to get the award and shake some hands."

"I wish I hadn't known. I've been freaking out for days. I hate talking in public," Val said. She unfolded a piece of yellow lined paper.

"Don't worry about it, Sadie. People will understand you didn't have time to prepare," Alice said. "Do you know who you're filling in for, by the way?"

"No?"

"The Hamptons Hoodlum. You know, the one who stole the money from old people and used it to buy shoes."

Somehow the fact that I was a substitute for the troll mill's current favorite subject made me feel even worse about being there. I searched the room for anyone else I knew. I was getting more self-conscious by the minute and desperate to go home and eat franks and beans and watch Mr. Ng screw up the street fireworks.

A guy in a seersucker suit cleared his throat into the mic and tapped a glass with a knife. "Can you take your seats, please, folks? We're about to begin."

Jean made his way over to the honoree table. "There she is. The Hamptons Hero. You're totally famous." He held his hand up for a high five. "That took some balls."

I high-fived him and laughed. "Yeah, that's me. Big Balls Sullivan," I joked.

He sat next to Alice and guzzled water.

"Jean, this is Sadie and Alice. Sadie and Alice, Jean," Val said.

"Pleasure," he said, nodding. "Dude, this place smells like golf bag. Can you guys smell that? Like, leathery or something."

"It's so friggin' noisy in here I can't hear anything," Alice said loudly.

"My mom brought everyone she knows. And they're all loud," Jean said, motioning toward the table of women behind us. "I tried to get out of it, but they're pumped to be eating lunch at the country club."

"I actually wanted to come. It's good exposure for my cause," Val said. "Your mom is really dressed up for this, huh, Jean?" We all looked at the table of women wearing fancy suits and oversize hats.

"She's Haitian. She dresses up for bed."

Just as the guy was tapping the glass with the knife again, Gordie Harris rushed in and sank into the seat on the other side of Val.

"Gordie? You're a homegrown hero?" I said, surprised.

"Yes, I appear to be." He fumbled with his gold-starred name tag and pinned it to his navy polo shirt. Gordie was rich, preppy, and the smartest kid in my class. He sailed. And he played the saxophone. Those were all things I learned during my massive middle-school

Gordie Harris crush phase (which ended when the ruffians, of all people, saw him hooking up with a guy and I realized I probably didn't have a chance).

Gordie nodded at Jean. "Man, that is some impressive facial hair."

Just then, a Rotary guy took the mic and spoke about community service and civic responsibility. Through the clinking and scraping of people inhaling their dry chicken and soggy asparagus lunches, the guy called up Rotary members to talk about their nominated honorees.

A school principal walked to the podium, held up a red-white-and-blue ribbon, and called Val to the stage. Val's hand trembled as she slid past me and walked slowly in her knee-length khaki skirt, tucked-in pink button-down, and ballet flats.

"Thank you so much for this esteemed award," Val read from her yellow paper. "Migrant children move often and—"

"Can't hear you," some lady yelled from the back.

She leaned closer to the mic. "Migrant children face many struggles. I encourage you all to donate school supplies to my drive this summer. With your help, we can prepare more children for school. And school means so much to these families. Thank you." Val hurried off the stage.

"You did good, babe," Jean said, squeezing her shoulder.

"I was so nervous. I skipped half my speech." She held up her shaking hands.

My phone buzzed in my lap. Shay responded to my text with **Pooch and Neigh?**

I almost spit out my water. "Oh my God. I forgot about Pooch! Remember, you made us all call you Pooch? Is Neigh here?" I whispered to Alice, referring to her best friend, Izzy. A fancy lady in a white hat and otherwise head-to-toe Lilly Pulitzer announced Jean's Artist Guild Young Creator's Award.

"Uh, yeah. My friends still call me Pooch," Alice said. "And no, Izzy's not here."

The lady called Jean up and put her arm around him. "How many other young men take it upon themselves to start programs that revolutionize the way children view art?" She called three adorable kids up to give Jean the award honoring the Tiny Art Camp he started.

Jean squatted down for a photo with the kids before jumping up and saying, "Thank you for this award and for recognizing the importance of art in kids' lives. This is the second summer of the Tiny Art Camp and we have twice as many kids this year. Much appreciated." He held up his ribbon and fist-bumped the kids.

Next up was Alice, who talked about her efforts photographing shelter dogs to give them a better chance at getting adopted. The bushy-eyebrowed guy from the dog rescue played a slide show of pit bulls dressed in pink bandannas and smiling for the camera.

"I'm available to photograph events for free, but only if you adopt a shelter dog." People laughed and Alice smiled. "Thanks for this. It means a lot."

"Badass," Jean said when Alice came back to the table.

"And now I'd like to introduce a young man who has dedicated countless hours to working with developmentally disabled folks. Gordie Harris, come on up."

The man talked about Gordie's volunteer work at the Turtle Trail Recreation Center. Gordie stood on the stage with his hands in his khaki pockets, smiling at the crowd. "Thank you," he said into the mic. Then effortless, perfect public speaker and debate champion Gordie told a story about the time he took a Turtle Trail group on a camping trip. He got sick and the Turtle Trail people took care of him. The moral of Gordie's story: He gets more than he gives.

I was shocked to find out old Mr. Upton from the farm stand had nominated me and that he couldn't be at the luncheon because he had been rushed to the hospital.

A collective gasp filled the room.

Mom and Dad and my grandmothers stared at me as the guy read Mr. Upton's nomination letter.

"I was there that day at the farm stand. This young lady showed presence of mind. She showed quick reflexes. She showed great courage. As a lifelong Rotarian, it is my honor and privilege to nominate Sadie Sullivan for this most deserved award."

I made my way to the podium.

Mom dabbed her eyes with a napkin, and I stood still for a moment, not quite sure if the man was finished, or what I was supposed to do.

I so wished somebody had told me I needed to write a speech.

I stared out at the back wall of the country club and uttered the only thing that came to my head. "Thank you so much. And remember, if you see something, say something."

The crowd applauded. I rushed off the stage to where my

tablemates were blatantly laughing at me. Even Val, who seemed to be the sweet one.

"I think you ripped off the New York subway slogan," Alice said.

I sat back in the chair, shook my head, and covered my face with a red napkin. I felt a twinge of pain as the starched fabric rubbed against my scar.

"I am such a loser," I moaned into the napkin.

Gordie Harris was laughing so hard tears streamed down his face.

The only thing that would have made my Fourth of July Rotary Club Homegrown Hero Award Luncheon acceptance speech more humiliating was if my skirt had flown up and my ass crack had made another appearance.

The clinking sounds erupted again after the staff served coffee and slices of an enormous patriotic sparkler cake.

"In my defense, I bet the Hamptons Hoodlum wouldn't have done any better," I said.

"Yes, but she would have been wearing fabulous shoes," Alice said.

The Rotary MC came over to congratulate us and ask how we were enjoying the cake. "Such upsetting news about Stewy Upton," he said. "He was darn proud of you, Sadie. We're all rooting for him."

I hoped it was nothing, just a run-of-the-mill old-man ailment. I had just seen Mr. Upton, just watched Sissy buckle him into the passenger seat and drive away in the old Lincoln after they'd bought peaches and snap peas and cucumbers.

"Are you done laughing at me, Gordie?" I said after the Rotary guy left.

"So you guys know each other?" Val said.

"Yeah, Sadie's in all my classes. But she's too cool to actually hang out with the lowly juniors."

"Excuse me." I held up my hand. "Our entire class is a bunch of assholes. Am I wrong?"

"Oh, no. They're a bunch of assholes. That is true."

"My best friend and I call them gadflies and ruffians," I said. "They seem to get even more obnoxious when exposed to technology. And sugar. I think sugar's a trigger. Because, lunchroom."

"We have a lot of assholes in our class, too," Alice said. "Did somebody drop asshole pills in the water the year we were born?"

"Speaking of assholes, where's your boyfriend, Val?" Jean said, grinning.

"Stop, Jean. He's not feeling well." She shook her head and looked at Alice and me. "He has lupus, so it's tough for him to get out."

"In your boyfriend's defense, who the hell would come here of their own volition?" Gordie said.

"Did he just say *volition*?" Alice said.

"Gordie's really smart," I said. "Ignore him."

Val turned to Gordie. "Where would you rather be, Gordie?"

"I can't tell you that," he said, smiling cryptically.

"Let me guess, coding or talking about history with Reid," I said.

"No. Nope. It's way more scandalous than that."

"I would do a topless beach," Jean said. "Or like a topless artists' cruise."

"You guys are entertaining. We should hang out," Alice said, taking her phone out of her giant satchel. "Give me your numbers."

43

We joined the mob of Rotary luncheon guests pushing toward the front door of the country club, fielding countless exclamations of "Congratulations" and "Keep up the good work."

"Hey, Sadie," Gordie whispered into my ear as we waited for our parents.

"Yeah?" I said, looking up at his grinning face. He pulled back, then leaned in again.

"If you see something, say something."

❧ FIVE ❧

THREE PEOPLE TEXTED me on our way home from the luncheon to ask if I'd pick them up for the white party. Not going. Have fun, I texted back. WTF? —from Parker. Spleen acting up. That had become my go-to excuse.

When we got home, Dad hung the American flag and got started with the block party preparations while I sat on the porch worrying about poor Mr. Upton and aimlessly watching Mr. Ng set up the Slip 'N Slide for the neighborhood kids.

"Dad, can I take the Prius? I want to run over to the hospital to check on Mr. Upton."

"That's a nice idea. Go for it."

I wrapped some of Grandma Hosseini's sugar cookies in waxed

paper, tied them with a ribbon, and walked past Mom, who had changed into a red dress with blue stars like she had every year since the Iranian Revolution scattered her family around the world.

It was surreal to be back at the hospital, this time as a visitor. The overly air-conditioned lobby reminded me of being wheeled out wrapped in a head bandage.

When I got to the room, I grabbed a squirt of hand sanitizer from the wall dispenser and gently knocked on the half-open door. Sissy stuck her head out.

"Sadie, hello. What a nice surprise."

"Hi, Sissy. I was just at the luncheon, and I wanted to check on Mr. Upton. I was worried about him. I hope it's okay I'm here."

"Of course. He'll be thrilled." She leaned toward me and whispered, "He's on a lot of meds, so he's a little loopy."

The room was identical to my hospital room: the same watery pastel curtains, the same antiseptic smell, the same pink barf bucket.

"Stewy, look who's here." Sissy picked up a needlepoint of a bright blue cross. "Here, let me turn up his hearing aids." She leaned over and gently manipulated Mr. Upton's hearing aids.

Mr. Upton squinted his eyes. His face lit up when I moved closer to his bedside.

"Hi, Mr. Upton. I brought you some cookies," I said loudly.

"Sadie Sullivan, our hero," he said in a weak voice. "Come sit on the bed here. Give me the scoop." Two delicate tubes hung out of his nose. "Don't be shy. You can't catch heart failure, I don't think. Can you catch heart failure, Sissy?"

Sissy laughed. "Nope. Broken hearts maybe, but not heart failure."

I sat on the edge of the bed.

"Thank you so much for nominating me, Mr. Upton. It meant a lot to me and my family."

"That was a no-brainer. You're a special kid." He nodded toward the wrapped package of cookies. "How about a cookie?"

"Stewy, you're on a liquid diet," Sissy said, not looking up from her needlepoint.

"Oh, pshaw. I'm ninety-seven. My ticker is just about out of juice. If I want a cookie, I'm eating a cookie. Open that up."

Sissy rolled her eyes but smiled, and I put a cookie in Mr. Upton's frail hand. He couldn't quite find his mouth, so I guided his hand to his lips. He bit and chewed slowly. "That's a damn good cookie."

He stared up at my face as he ate, studying me like he studied the peaches and snap peas.

"Sissy, go take a break. I want to visit with Sadie."

"Actually," I said, "I should probably go soon. I just came to say thank you and see how you're feeling."

He coughed for what seemed like a full minute and held his hand up. "No, don't go. I need to talk to you." He grabbed my arm. *In private*, he mouthed.

I glanced back at Sissy, who was still focused on her needlepoint, and wondered if he was going to unload some horrible secret about her.

"Hey, Sissy, I'm not in a big rush if you want to go for a walk. Seriously. It's fine."

She looked up. "I think I'll take you up on that. I'd love some coffee. Can I get you anything?"

"No, I'm good." My stomach churned.

"You better not ask her to smuggle in chewing tobacco, Stewy. I'm on to you," she said on her way out the door.

Mr. Upton stared at me. His eyes widened. "You've been the one all along."

"Uh. What one, Mr. Upton?"

"Listen, go to the locker over there and get my wallet out of my pants."

"Oh, Mr. Upton, I hope you're not trying to give me money. I really don't need any money." I thought about my grandpa Hosseini before he died, always handing me twenty-dollar bills.

"I'm not giving you money. I'm too damn cheap for that." He laughed. "I need to get something from my wallet."

It felt like I was doing something Sissy wouldn't approve of.

I opened the locker, felt around Mr. Upton's deep pants pocket, and brought him his thick, weathered wallet.

"Here, give it to me." He stuck his finger deep inside an inner pocket and pulled out an old brass key.

"This is for you." He shoved the key in my face. "Now give me another one of those cookies."

I put another cookie in his hand, and he took a bite. "What is this key for, Mr. Upton?"

He stared at me for a second, chewing slowly.

"Everything…" He stopped. "Everything I have, the whole fortune, is blood money." His eyes narrowed. "It's disgusting."

"Um. What do you mean?"

"I mean my father was a vile man. He was a hardened criminal disguised as a dapper gentleman. He was a lizard. Even had lizard eyes."

I nodded. I was used to my grandmothers going off on tangents. "What kind of criminal?"

"Oh, my father did things I can't say in the company of a young lady. He was a bootlegger and a gambler. He preyed on wealthy widows, used his good looks and charm to woo them, and then robbed them blind with his lizard claws. Left them sobbing in the streets."

He closed his eyes and shook his head slowly. I could sense his urgency, his need to confess.

"And prostitution. He was involved in that, too," he whispered.

"Wow. That's awful, Mr. Upton. Did you have a…What about your mom?"

"She died when I was five, bless her heart." He stared up at the ceiling, his lips covered in crumbs. I reached over and wiped his mouth with a tissue.

"All the money I have came from his evil deeds. And I took it and played with it, instead of finding a way to make it right somehow."

"It wasn't your fault, Mr. Upton. Whatever your dad did."

"No. But I could have done something big with that money, something noble and good. I mean, I gave to charities, was active in the Rotary and such, but I always wanted to find some real way to redeem his evil acts and never did figure out how. I almost felt paralyzed by the whole damn thing."

"I'm sorry." I didn't know what to say.

"Sadie, you're a special kid. I saw that firsthand. You're not a wimp like I was."

Again. Didn't know what to say.

"You're an angel."

I tried to distract him with another cookie, but he turned away.

"Listen." He lifted a finger and pointed his long yellow fingernail at the key I was holding. "I need you to do something for me."

"Sure, Mr. Upton."

"I'm about ready to die."

"Don't say that. You're not going to die."

He held his finger up again. "I need you to do what I could never do, and find a way to make it right again. Find a way to redeem the lizard's evil deeds."

"Uh. Mr. Upton, I can't—" But he ignored me, continuing on.

"There's an old suitcase buried under a tool table in the shed near my house. Inside, you'll find things he left behind."

My curiosity got the better of me. "What things?"

He started to cough hard until liquid rattled in his throat. I poured water from a pink plastic pitcher, but he refused it.

"I have never been so sure of anything. You're the one I've been waiting for all these years."

"Wait. You're not even telling me what's in the suitcase?"

"I'm not going to get into it here. This place could be bugged, for all I know." His eyes narrowed. "You'll know when you see it."

"Don't you think Sissy would be a better fit? I'm just a farm stand worker."

"Sissy's the best. She's been my family for fifteen years. I've willed her the whole estate. Shh. Don't tell her. I don't want her gushing all over me. But you're the one for this job. You'll do it right."

I rolled the key between my fingers. "So, you want me to get an old suitcase from the shed behind your house and open it with this key?"

"Yes. It's covered with Nova Scotia stickers. God only knows what the lizard was doing up in Nova Scotia, but yes."

"And you want me to find a way to make up for your father's bad deeds by doing something with the contents of the suitcase?"

"Yes. Do something noble."

"That's a lot of pressure, Mr. Upton."

"No pressure, kid. Do what feels right, that's all. You got this."

"I'm going to need more direction here."

Sissy came in, balancing two coffees and a carryout container.

Mr. Upton's eyes got wide again. *Don't tell Sissy*, he mouthed, before shooing me away. I squeezed Mr. Upton's arm and took a few steps back.

"You're going to want to rip Andy's legs off!" he called out.

"What, Stewy?" Sissy glanced at me.

"I'm talking to Sadie. You need to rip off Andy's legs. Don't forget."

"Wow. It looks like the medicine's kicking in," Sissy said.

"You probably need to rest, Mr. Upton. I'll stop back in a couple days. How about I save you the best peaches from Tuesday's harvest?"

He smiled. "That would be terrific."

Sissy followed me out to the hallway. "What was that all about?"

I almost kept it from Sissy, but I went with my gut.

"He gave me a key to an old suitcase in his shed. He wants me to have it."

"Lord, he's giving everything away. I had a dozen Rotary Club men at the house last week, picking through Civil War memorabilia. He gave my son his tractor mower." She folded her arms across her chest. "That's part of dying, you know. Purging earthly possessions." Her eyes filled with tears. "Go ahead and take it. You can go over whenever you like. The gate's open."

I left Sissy standing in the hospital hallway and walked out to the car thinking about the key and the suitcase and how sad it must be to spend a lifetime wanting to make up for a father's evil deeds.

On the way home, I passed three carloads of white-clad people en route to Shawn Flynn's.

Dad handed me a mini flag when I got back to our neighborhood, which was buzzing with families grilling and blasting music and setting up illegal fireworks.

"How was Stewy?" he said.

"Not good. He's got heart failure."

"Oh, that's too bad. I bet he really appreciated you visiting him. You're a good kid."

"Thanks, Dad."

"Do you want to help me get the limbo going?" He hoisted the limbo stick over his shoulder.

Dad saw life as one big carnival. His favorite words of wisdom were "Yeah, sure, you might find some creeps at the carnival, and a couple broken rides, and a scam game or two, but for the most part life's all sugar on a stick and music and good times."

"I think I need to pass this year." My mind was still spinning.

I sat on the porch with Grandma Sullivan, eating beans and hot peppers on rolls off paper plates. She told me she was proud of me. The rowdy patriotism and highballs must have gone to her head. Grandma Sullivan was not one for compliments.

Shay texted a picture of herself looking disheveled and tired as her tennis campers warmed up for their first tournament. I texted Shay a picture of Mr. Ng on the Slip 'N Slide. I went to my room to hide the suitcase key in my jewelry box and looked at myself in the mirror. My scar was there, pink and plump and ugly, like a monster's tail.

For a quick second, I considered showering and throwing together a white outfit. But all I wanted to do was lie down. The street fireworks were just getting going when the text came from Alice, now saved in my phone as *Pooch*.

Esteemed honorees: Let's meet tomorrow night at the duck pond at eight. I'm bored.

❦ SIX ❦

BETWEEN THE FIREWORKS sounds, the constant group texts documenting the most epic party Flynn has ever had, the enthusiastic responses to Alice's text from the other luncheon honorees, and the burning curiosity to know what was inside that suitcase, I barely slept at all.

In the morning, as soon as I finished helping clean up from the block party, I tore through the East End streets toward the Stewy Upton estate.

I turned onto the gravel driveway that snaked upward through a grove of birch trees and led to Mr. Upton's house, or, should I say, his *manor*. It wasn't as obnoxious as Shawn's, but it was grand, and old, and slightly run-down, just like Mr. Upton. I parked in front of a redbrick carriage cottage and quickly walked up a path toward the back of the house.

The view came out of nowhere, a vast and brilliant and unobstructed expanse of open sea. *Wow*, I thought. *Just wow.*

Someone had left the shed door slightly ajar. It took a while to wade through the clutter. I squeezed past rusted tools, rows of brightly painted ceramic vases, a giant toboggan standing on its hind legs, a horse's head with dead black eyes that looked like it had been sawed off a carousel, a rusted dressmaker's form.

It took a half hour in the antique land mine to finally reach the suitcase. It was more like a trunk, large and bulky and covered—as promised—with vintage NOVA SCOTIA stickers.

I pulled. I wiggled. I yanked. My spleen ached. I finally conceded that I didn't have the strength to move that suitcase. I had to leave it until I could bring reinforcements.

That night I arrived early at the duck pond. Val was already there, sitting on a bench, writing in a notebook.

"Hi, Sadie. I'm so glad Alice summoned us."

"Me too. What are you writing?"

She closed the notebook and turned toward me as I sat next to her.

"Oh, it's inventory for the school-supply collection. I got a big pledge yesterday after the luncheon."

"That's awesome."

She looked down at a text. "And...my boyfriend is pissed at me. Great."

"Why?"

"He wanted me to stay home and hang out with him and his friend. He's kind of needy," she said, tucking her hair behind her ears.

"Because of the lupus or in general?"

"In general."

"Was he sick when you started seeing him?"

"Yes. But we didn't know it was lupus. He just had all these weird symptoms."

"It must be hard." I didn't want to harass her with more questions, but I didn't exactly know what the symptoms of lupus were.

"We've been together a long time. He has his fun moments."

Alice texted, on way.

"So you and Alice were in Girl Scouts together?"

I nodded. "She was obsessed with dogs even back then. And her friend was obsessed with horses. They called themselves Pooch and Neigh."

"Oh my gosh. That's so cute. And what about Gordie? What's his story?"

"He's like Mr. Everything—musical, academic, he's really good at sailing. He always hung out with this kid Reid until Reid started dating a girl in our class. She's one of the catty assholes."

"Gadflies, right?" she said.

"Yup. Gadflies."

"He's cute," Val said.

"Gordie?"

"Yeah."

He was definitely cute. I had to give him that.

Alice parked her Subaru Outback next to Val's tiny blue car, jumped out, and hoisted her satchel over her shoulder. She was wearing the same long, flowery skirt as the day before, now paired with a turquoise tank top.

"You showed up," she said, sitting down on the grass next to me.

"Of course we showed up," Val said.

"What about the boys?"

"Who knows?" I said. "Gordie Harris is notoriously late."

"Soooo, did anyone see fireworks last night?" Alice rummaged through her bag and pulled out her phone.

"No," Val said. I told them about my block party and the unimpressive but loud bootlegged fireworks display.

"I had hoped to go see good ones with my best friend, but she ditched me, so I ended up playing Pictionary with my parents and my eight-year-old neighbor," Alice said.

"Why'd she ditch you?" It was strange looking at Alice. She still looked like Pooch from Girl Scouts, except that she had an angular, more grown-up face.

Alice played with her silver rings. "Well, Izzy has sort of gone heroin chic on me."

"As in fashion?" Val said.

"As in heroin. She's been doing heroin pretty much every day, and it's getting worse. There's not a lot of quality friend time going on."

"Oh my God. That sucks, Alice," I said. I had a vivid memory of baby-faced Izzy playing tug-of-war in her riding boots and braids at one of our jamborees. I couldn't believe she was doing heroin.

"Yes, yes it does."

A black Range Rover pulled into the parking lot and Gordie Harris jumped out, late as usual.

"Is that your car?" Alice said. "Sweet."

"Yeah. Don't judge," Gordie said, wiping something off his khaki shorts. His tan looked even tanner in a white polo shirt.

"I'm stuck driving my parents' old Subaru," Alice said.

"I have to beg my mother for her Prius," I said.

"I have to beg my mother for her ninety-three Civic," Val said, laughing.

"Somebody text Jean," Alice said. "We need all the homegrown heroes here."

Val texted Jean while Gordie threw a crumpled half-assed origami crane on my lap. "Here. I got the origami crane memo." He smirked at me.

"What's the origami crane memo?" Val said.

"Sadie's friends organized an origami crane project after the farm stand Hamptons Hero thing."

"Wow. It's nerdsville over in your town, huh?" Alice said.

"Jean says he's already here. Near the bridge," Val said, craning her neck toward the forested area.

"Let's go," I said. "Gordie, help me up."

Gordie reached over and grabbed my hand.

"Ow. Don't yank me." My back still ached from the incident. I let go of Gordie's hand and stuffed his origami crane into my pocket. We followed Alice to the path on the edge of the grassy hill and found Jean in the forest, which was thick with insect sounds. The sun was just beginning to set, and pops of fireflies dotted the humid air.

"Hey, heroes," Jean said, sketching furiously in a red leather-bound sketch pad. "The sunlight here is perfection."

The four of us leaned over the wooden bridge and watched the swollen stream flow over smooth stones.

"Are you going to show us when you're finished?" Alice said.

"I'm finished." He held up the pencil sketch of a tree bending over the stream.

"That is amazing," I said. "Like professional level."

"I wouldn't go that far." He stood up and wiped his hands on his faded jeans. "So what's the plan? What do do-gooders do for fun?"

We sat on the edge of the bridge, five people who barely knew one another, kicking our legs and trying to think of something to do.

I couldn't stop obsessing about Mr. Upton's suitcase.

"So, can I ask you guys a favor?" I didn't tell them about the promise to redeem the lizard's bad deeds. I just told them Mr. Upton wanted me to have his suitcase, and I needed help prying it out of a creepy shed.

They followed me in a caravan of mismatched vehicles, all the way up the bumpy driveway of the Upton manor. The whole ride there I thought about Izzy and our Girl Scout days. My heart ached for her and Alice.

It was dark by the time we reached the shed.

"This place is huge," Val said.

"You should see the view. It's all ocean." I pulled the door open and we shined our phone lights into the cluttered space. It stank of mothballs and decay.

"What the hell was that?" Jean jumped back.

"What?" we all said.

"It sounds like a creature's nesting in there, like an owl or something."

"So?" Alice said.

"Okay, I hate birds. They scare the shit out of me. That's why I was in the woods earlier, safely away from those predatory ducks."

"Is he serious right now?" I said to Val.

"We go to school together; I don't know him intimately," she said. "Jean, get it together."

It took a lot of effort to assure Jean there were no owls hiding in the shed. But then, literally everything in the shed creeped us out. Gordie held up a faceless porcelain cat. Jean pointed out a box of freakish Civil War soldier dolls.

"Old men are obsessed with Civil War stuff," Alice said. She picked up a bearded doll in a blue uniform and dangled it in Gordie's face. "Hello, little boy. Would you like some sassafras?"

"That's Ulysses S. Grant," Gordie said, laughing. "In case you were wondering."

It was a struggle to dislodge the suitcase. But we did it. And we dragged it out to the driveway. When we finally accepted it wouldn't fit into the back of the Prius with Dad's golf clubs and Mom's fabric samples, we opened the back of Gordie's Range Rover.

"What the hell, Gordie? Are you a hoarder?" I said. His car was full of crap.

"No. I'm well prepared." He grabbed the suitcase's handle. "Clearly we don't have space back here. Here, help me get it into the backseat."

"I want to open it," Jean said. "Why are we waiting?"

I reached into both shorts pockets and felt only the crumpled origami crane. "And...I don't even have the key. It's still in my jewelry box."

We squeezed the suitcase on top of a blanket in the backseat of Gordie's car and decided we'd just leave it there until the next night to avoid explaining the entire situation to my parents and Mr. Ng.

"I want ice cream," Val said.

"Good call," I said, wiping a cobweb off my face. "Let's go to Carvel."

Our five-car caravan made it to Carvel just before it closed. We ordered cones with sprinkles and sat on the curb. The Southampton streets were eerily quiet.

"Cheers to the honorees. Here's to you for making a difference," Alice said, tapping her cone against each of ours. I wasn't sure if she was being serious.

"Sadie Sullivan's over there," a voice behind me shouted. "She's from my school."

"It's Greg O.," Gordie whispered.

Greg O.'s mom quickly ushered him away, probably afraid I was one of the many people who had been horrible to her son.

"I feel so bad for that kid," I said. "With that whole Mayan blog thing."

"What's the Mayan blog thing?" Alice said, sticking a spoon into Jean's cone.

"Hey, get away from my ice cream," Jean said, pulling his cone away. "I barely know you, woman."

"Greg O. is obsessed with Mayan civilization, so he spent, like, forever making a website about the Mayans and tried to get everyone to visit it," I said.

"Yeah, so the pricks at our school left asshole comments and Greg ended up hitting himself in the middle of the cafeteria, which made the pricks roll around laughing. It was awful," Gordie said.

"That's so upsetting. I feel like crying," Val said. "Is the site still up?"

Jean pulled his phone out of his pocket and we crowded around, scrolling through Greg O.'s Mayan blog. It was littered with comments.

Did the Mayans have sex with Greg O.?

Did Greg O. have fun eating dried-out Mayan feces?

Almost worse than the asshole comments was the fact that nobody, not one single person, had posted a nice word on Greg O.'s blog.

We clicked on the many tabs, in awe of Greg O.'s meticulous volume of work.

"This is heartbreaking," Val said. "He added all the photos and maps. Look, he updated the part about astronomy this morning."

We sat there dejected, tired, and sad.

Gordie took a deep breath. "I think we should fix that."

"How?" Val said.

"Let's post some uplifting shit on the site. Greg O. will love it," Gordie said, tossing a clump of napkins into the trash can.

"I'm in," Val said.

"Man, you guys really are a bunch of do-gooders," Jean said before the homegrown heroes left in our caravan of cars, full from the ice cream and armed with a mission.

Later, I snuggled under my quilt and logged on to Greg O.'s Mayan blog. KINKY 3 had written: **Just found this cool Mayan site. Mayans are awesome!**

PIERRE wrote: **Dude! I love this site. I want to know more about how Mayans sacrificed people.**

I signed in as CAKES and wrote: **What kinds of things did the Mayans wear?**

Great site! CECIL wrote under my comment. And under that, HERMANITA wrote: **My friend told me about this site. I'm especially excited because I might have some Mayan blood.**

In between Greg O. posts, we hypothesized via group text about what might be in that suitcase.

Jean: **What if it's human remains? It smelled funky in that shed.**

Gordie: **That was mothballs.**

Alice: **I bet it's Confederate money.**

Gordie: **Could be a dead Confederate.**

Alice: **Or a dead Canadian. Because . . . Nova Scotia.**

Val: **I'm sleepy.**

I woke up in the middle of the night, my sheets drenched in sweat, my head throbbing deep below the scar. I sat up, confused, and tried for hours to get back to sleep, but a sense of dread hung over me. I finally gave in and made my way down to the alcove in my parents' room, where I curled up with my blanket and my Flopper and finally fell asleep.

SEVEN

I HONORED MY promise to Mr. Upton—one of them, at least. After work, I had Daniela wait in front of the hospital while I ran up to deliver the pint of perfect peaches and, I hoped, get more information about how he wanted me to redeem his dead lizard-father's evil deeds.

The room was dark and quiet, except for the steady beeping of a machine hooked to a sleeping Mr. Upton. Sissy was asleep in the chair, with a thin white blanket draped over her. I tiptoed in and set the pint of peaches on the table next to the pink barf bucket and Sissy's needlepoint. The cross was nearly finished.

Alice agreed to pick me up after dinner so we could go to Gordie's and find out what was in that suitcase. She jumped out of the Subaru and greeted Dad, who was hosing down the truck.

"Woody! It's me, Pooch, from Girl Scouts."

"I know you, Pooch from Girl Scouts. Mills Town Road, white house." Dad had an uncanny memory. He remembered all his customers, past and present. "How's your buddy?"

Alice shrugged. "She's okay."

As we drove toward the main road, she said, "Did you remember it?"

"Yes." I pulled the key out from under my leprechaun T-shirt. I had attached it to my silver chain.

"I have to do a quick drive-by first." Alice checked her rearview mirror and pulled out in the opposite direction of Gordie's. "I'm still trying to find Izzy."

"Can you elaborate?"

"Since Izzy's become a nasty smackhead, she keeps disappearing. I know that sounds harsh, but I'm friggin' furious right now."

"How did this even happen?"

"Well, let's see, Izzy had a riding accident last spring and ended up getting hooked on Oxy. When the Oxy ran out, she started hanging out with this dealer named Hector, who got her hooked on heroin."

"Alice, I don't even know what to say."

"There's nothing to say. She's gone, Sadie. Like a zombie. For a long time, I was taking care of her and protecting her from getting caught. I figured she would eventually get sick of living this way. But it's just getting worse. When I finally threatened to tell her parents a few days ago, she disappeared."

"Did you tell her parents?"

"No. Her parents are not cool people. They'll make things worse—trust me." Alice stopped the car abruptly in front of a run-down house on the corner near the gas station. I'd passed that house a million times and never noticed it. "Wait here."

She marched up to the front door in her long lime-green skirt and combat boots and pounded on the door. Nobody answered.

"I tried," she said. "That was the last trap house I could think of. Let's go to Gordie's."

"What's a trap house?" I turned to look at the house.

"A dirtbag drug house," Alice said. "Damn, you're sheltered."

"Why do they call it a trap house?"

"I don't know. Because they trap people in misery for the rest of their lives?"

On the way to Gordie's, Jean texted us, Do I have the wrong address or does Gordie live in a mansion?

Nope. That's Gordie's house, I texted back.

We parked in front of the towering hedgerows shielding the Harris estate from the rest of the world. I was used to excessive wealth framing the edges of my town. But it never really affected the way we lived. Yes, Parker's mom was a socialite, and Seth's stepdad was a movie producer, and Shawn Flynn's dad ran a hedge fund, but my dad drove an ice cream truck, and Shay's dad was a tennis coach, and Ellie's parents were teachers, and D-Bag's parents were chiropractors.

"Yup. It's a mansion, all right," Alice said, staring out at the manicured gardens that stretched past the guesthouse and the pool house and the tennis courts.

Jean and Gordie had just extracted the suitcase from the Range Rover and were hauling it down to the house's basement entrance. We entered through the sliding doors into a velvet-curtain-lined movie theater with leather reclining chairs and a fully functional popcorn machine.

"So will your butler be joining us?" Jean said, staring at the row of stocked candy jars.

"Can you guys not judge me for having excessively materialistic parents?"

"No judgment here," Jean said, dumping a scoop of chocolate-covered nuts into his hand as Gordie knelt down in front of the suitcase.

"I'm dying to know what's in this thing."

"I think we should wait for Val. Right?" Alice had a point.

"Let's check out Greg O.'s blog." Gordie pointed a remote at the movie screen and a search-engine window appeared. Gordie had somehow figured out how to optimize Greg O.'s blog, and random people were starting to log on.

"KINKY 3? Really, Alice?" I said, flinging off my sandals.

"I'm not KINKY 3. I'm CECIL, after my first dog," Alice said.

"I'm PIERRE, after the rest of my name," Jean said with his mouth full of candy.

"I'm CAKES," I said. "My ex used to call me Sadie Cakes."

"Aw. How endearing. My ex used to call me KINKY 3." Gordie smiled at me and scrolled through Greg's blog.

I was curious to know if Gordie's ex was from our school. The only guy I ever saw him with was Reid, and Reid was straight. I knew so little about Gordie Harris since I'd stopped stalking him.

"Why are you staring at me?" Gordie said. "Do I not look like a KINKY 3?" His smile was much straighter since he'd gotten his braces off.

"Look, somebody wrote 'OMG! I'm obsessed with the Mayans. Can you PM me? Kaycee from Seattle,'" I read.

"Our little plan is working," Jean said.

Val finally showed up well after eight. "Sorry. I had to entertain Javi so he didn't get pissy."

"Okay. TMI," Jean said.

"Not that kind of entertain, you pervert." Val went over to Jean and flicked him on the arm. "This is the most amazing house I've ever seen, including in magazines."

"Okay, Val is here. Come on. Let's do this," Gordie said.

I unhooked my necklace, pulled off the key, then paused. When I'd asked them all to help me, I had welcomed the moral support, but now I almost didn't want to open the suitcase. It meant sharing the contents with four people I barely knew. It also meant unleashing a promise I had no idea how to keep.

"Open it, open it," they all chanted.

I slid the key into the rusted metal keyhole and turned it to the right until we heard a click. Gordie grabbed the leather handle and pulled upward. My heart pounded.

We stared down at a pile of neatly stacked items: a men's pin-striped suit, a satin robe, a wooden umbrella with a metal tip, an ancient pack of cigarettes, a leather shaving kit.

"So you said the old dude was adamant about you getting this suitcase?" Jean said.

"Yes. But he's ninety-seven years old and hooked to a morphine drip. Clearly, he's a little delusional."

We sat on the floor and removed the items one by one.

Alice pulled out the suit and rummaged through the pockets. She found a striped handkerchief and a book of matches from a restaurant on Thirty-Fourth Street in New York.

"Handkerchiefs are gross," Alice said.

"Nice suit, though," Jean said.

I picked up a small metal box tucked between the robe and a folded cloth garment bag and opened it quickly. "What the hell is this?" I sifted through dozens of hairpins like the ones the Gatsby women wore. There were silver ones, gold ones, ones shaped like feathers, like flowers, adorned in pearls.

I dumped the hairpins onto Gordie's thick beige carpet.

"Why would a guy have a tin of hairpins?" Val said, examining a long, pearl-studded one.

I shivered. "I don't want to know. I. Don't. Even. Want. To. Know." It was as if these simple objects were channeling the evil-lizard energy.

Jean held up the folded cloth garment bag, the last item in the suitcase. Alice undid the leather buckles and pulled open the bag.

An oversize rag doll with button eyes and red yarn hair tumbled out.

"Okay, this is too disturbing. I can no longer deal with this level of creepiness." Jean dropped the bag.

I took a deep breath. "Okay, well. I'm glad I'm now the proud owner of vintage men's clothes, hairpins, and a freakish doll." I was sort of relieved that the contents of the suitcase hadn't been more insidious. I still intended to honor my promise to Mr. Upton. Maybe I'd donate the suitcase to the Smithsonian or something.

Gordie stored the badly repacked suitcase in his furnace room behind the Christmas boxes. I needed some sea air to get the lingering smell of mothballs out of my nose.

I took another breath. "Anybody want to go to the beach?"

It was Jean's idea to build a Mayan temple out of sand and post a picture of it on Greg O.'s blog. He announced that sand castle building was his domain and we needed to follow his instructions. We dutifully obeyed and, upon unearthing a hardware store in the back of Gordie's Range Rover, we got to work.

"Shovel," Jean yelled. Gordie went to get it.

"Bucket," Jean yelled. Val went to get it.

We couldn't stop until our temple was immense and perfect.

The sky was white with stars when we finished digging the moat.

Jean wouldn't let us look at the front of the temple until he had finished it.

"Done," he said as the rest of us scavenged in Gordie's car for snacks.

Jean revealed the incredibly detailed, smiling Mayan face he had carved into our temple with just a pencil and an eyebrow brush.

"Genius" was all we could say.

I took pictures and posted the best one on Greg O.'s website with the caption **We built this for you. Hope you like it.**

I took another picture of the five of us smiling in front of the moonlit sea and sent it to Shay with the caption **Portrait of Randomness.**

Gordie stood over the sand temple shaking his head. "I'm sorry, people, but I really want to roll on this."

"No way. You can't roll on our masterpiece," Val said.

Jean and Gordie exchanged glances.

"It's either we roll on it or the ocean rolls on it. Somebody's going to flatten this thing. It might as well be us," Jean said.

In a split second, Jean and Gordie face-dived into the temple. Alice followed. I looked at Val and shrugged. We dived and punched at the sand and rolled over the damaged structure. Alice started to sing, "*Roll, roll, roll your boat, gently down the stream.*" We all laughed and sang and rolled until there was hardly a trace of our sand temple left.

We collapsed on our backs and stared at the sky.

"Ow." I turned on my side, wincing from the battering I had just inflicted on my tender rib cage.

"Sooo, is anyone thinking what I'm thinking?" Jean said, sitting up.

"You mean, naked in the ocean?" Gordie said.

"Precisely."

"Not happening," Val said. "No way. No how."

"Oh, come on, Val, let's do it." Alice stood up. "It'll be invigorating."

They all looked at me. I had to think fast. Did I want to be naked in front of these people? I had skinny-dipped before, with Shay in her pool, and with Seth in his pool, but never in the ocean with strangers.

"I'll go in my underwear."

Alice already had her clothes off and was running toward the water in her bra and underwear. Gordie threw off his LIFE IS GOOD T-shirt and khaki shorts and ran after her in his boxers.

"Come on, Val." I grabbed her hand and pulled her up.

"Javi will kill me, Sadie. He's really possessive. He'll lose it."

"Javi will never know."

She stood alone as I followed Jean, already stripped down to his black boxer-briefs, toward the sea. I looked back and she was behind me, flinging off her blue-flowered sleeveless blouse.

It felt like the start of a whirlwind five-person romance, like we were running into something deep and exciting, something magnetic and abnormally comfortable.

"Let's do it as a round," Alice shouted when we were all in, neck-deep, fighting the pull of the cold, exhilarating Atlantic. *"Roll, roll, roll your boat..."*

"Roll, roll, roll your boat..."

In the morning, Greg O. responded to **We built this for you. Hope you like it** with **Yeah! That's pretty good.**

It was pretty good.

Shay, on the other hand, hadn't responded at all. When I texted her **How's it going? Did you like my picture?** she wrote back immediately. **Yes. So cute. Sorry! Camper duty. Xoxo**

Her response seemed fake, like she wasn't interested in my picture or my story.

❧ EIGHT ❧

MOM DROVE UP in the middle of my shift. The wind had picked up and sheets of rain pelted the farm stand roof. Daniela and I had spent the morning dragging things inside, and my entire body ached. I was wet and cold and hungry for tortilla soup and hot chocolate.

"Mom, are you the best mom ever? Did you bring me soup?" I called out as she hobbled through the muddy parking lot in her gold high-heeled sandals.

"No. I don't have any soup. Sorry." She shook her umbrella. "Sweetie, I got a call from a Barbara somebody this morning. She's a victim advocate. She wants to talk to you about the case."

"Like what about the case? I already told the officer everything."

"She didn't say." Mom picked up a melon and sniffed it. "But I suspect it's pretty standard for her to check in. She suggested it might be a good idea to type up the story as soon as possible, just so it's clear in your mind."

It wasn't clear in my mind. It was a wet, stuck-together nest of smells and sounds. I didn't want to deal with any of it, not the incident, not the thoughts of *him* getting out of jail and going after baby Ella again.

Or coming after me.

"Fine. I'll start writing it tonight," I said, knowing full well that would not be happening.

A few minutes after Mom left with a canvas bag of strawberries and peaches, Farmer Brian and Daniela arrived with fresh eggs.

"Did you hear about Mr. Upton, Sadie?" Daniela said.

I stopped and turned. "No?"

"He passed away this morning. Poor old guy," Farmer Brian said.

"Oh." That was all I could say. I stood there wondering if Mr. Upton had had a chance to eat any of the peaches before he died. And then I started to cry. Farmer Brian and Daniela had no idea why I was so upset, but for ten minutes straight I was inconsolable.

I would have texted Shay, but it dawned on me that Shay had no idea who Mr. Upton was. I hadn't told her anything about him or his suitcase.

So I texted the homegrown heroes.

I'm sad. The suitcase guy died this morning. Can we meet at Gordie's basement tonight?

They all said yes.

"It's not like he was my grandfather or anything," I said when we were sitting in a circle on Gordie's basement floor, eating pizza and talking about Mr. Upton. "I don't know why this is bothering me so much. He was just a customer who happened to bequeath me his weird suitcase."

"We can't help where our feelings take us," Val said.

"Wow, Val. That's profound," Alice said sarcastically.

We helped Val come up with comeback texts after Javi called her a bitch for leaving him alone again.

"How about *It's over*?" Alice suggested. "I'd say calling you a bitch is a deal breaker."

Val laughed nervously. "You're not wrong. He and Mike are probably blasting me on the slam page right now."

We added some comments to Greg O.'s blog and logged on to Val and Jean's school's slam page. It was the longest, ugliest slam page I had ever seen. It was even more disturbing to read the comments in large font on Gordie's movie screen.

Has anyone noticed how ugly Carly looks with bangs?

Why would Miles date that fat pig?

She's not as fat as you, Kels. We know you're writing this.

Nikki D. was wearing long sleeves at the beach.
WTF?

She's a cutter. Like Swiss cheese.

Freak.

"Wow. I thought my school sucked," Alice said.

I didn't even want to see my school's slam page. It was bad enough reading and rereading the comments about me and the incident. I could only imagine what else the gadflies and the ruffians would say about me behind my back. *Sadie's always going to be a senior wannabe. Sadie wasn't good enough for Seth. Sadie's scar is disgusting.*

Gordie logged on as KINKY 3. He was a computer genius at school, the guy all the other guys called upon to encrypt their porn. He wrote:

I actually like Carly's bangs.

Then he wrote:

Nikki D. has always been really nice to me.

PIERRE wrote:

Wow. If she's fat, what does that make me?

"Good one," Alice said.

When we logged on to Alice's school's slam page, we found

threads and threads about Izzy and the heroin, and horrible things about how she's sleeping with guys for drugs.

Alice got quiet.

"What should we say, Alice?" Gordie said. "I'll say anything you want."

Alice stared at the velvet curtain wall. "Don't say anything. The trolls are right."

I felt sick to my stomach. I couldn't begin to imagine what Alice was going through.

We tried to agree on a movie. But that never happened. So we went back to troll-slamming.

It was addicting.

I learned a lot about Stewart "Stewy" Upton, ninety-seven, from his obituary. I read it to Dad on the way to the service. Sissy had chosen a photo of him dressed in a tuxedo and smiling through the same eyes but with a much younger face. I learned he was an avid collector of Civil War artifacts. (Alice was right. Old men did like Civil War stuff.) He loved music and travel and had been a lifelong Rotarian and supporter of various animal organizations. He was predeceased by his beloved mother, Ingrid; his sister, Tabitha; and a nephew named James. There was no mention of the lizard. Donations were to go to Rotary International or the Humane Society.

I had asked Dad to take me to the funeral. I felt like maybe I'd get a clue, some postmortem breadcrumb that would help me understand what Mr. Upton wanted me to do with the contents of the suitcase.

On the way to the service, Dad told me Mr. Upton had been a regular.

"Oh, yeah. Stewy was one of my old-timer customers. I'd drive the truck right up to his front door. He'd come out in his floppy sun hat and Bermuda shorts, always had exact change. And always got an ice cream sandwich." Dad smiled. "I'm gonna miss him."

A crowd of mourners filed into the Presbyterian church. We sat near the back and listened to Sissy get emotional as she tried to read a passage from the Bible. Her sister had to go up and help her finish. Sissy's whole family, decked out in all sorts of elaborate funeral hats, took up the first pews.

I kept thinking about how he said I was the *one for this job*. Of all these people in Mr. Upton's life, he chose me to do something noble with that bizarre old suitcase. It hit me that while I thought the contents of that suitcase were boring and creepy, it all meant something to Mr. Upton. And he chose *me* to do what he never could.

Dad dropped me off at work in my funeral dress and flip-flops, which made it a little tricky to sit on the crate directing Ramon and Papi and the other farm guys as they unloaded the trucks.

During my lunch break, I went onto Val's school's slam page after she texted, Check out the slam page. It's blowing up!

Other people were troll-slamming. Somebody named GANDHI-ISH wrote:

> Who cares about bangs, fatness, or other people's issues? Be kind, people!

Somebody named FLORAL ARRANGEMENT wrote:

> Go back to your caves, trolls. We're done here.

After work, Daniela drove me to Val's apartment complex, a cluster of three-story buildings surrounding a courtyard full of hanging laundry and a broken swing set. Daniela and Val's mom spoke Spanish while Val and I ate tamales and watched the six o'clock news. Unlike the previous summer, which had been a predictable four-point trek (work to home to pizza place to Shawn Flynn's, with occasional deviations to the beach), this summer was a wild card. Who knew I'd end up at an apartment near a strip mall, surrounded by statues of Jesus and the Virgin Mary?

"Five years of Spanish and I only know how to say, *Do you like to play tennis or football?*" I said to Daniela.

"Alice is downstairs," Val announced just after Daniela left to pick up her son.

Alice stormed in, red-faced and furious. She had found Izzy, temporarily at a psychiatrist turned drug lord's trap house in Westhampton. Izzy had run out of the house barefoot and jumped into the elusive dealer Hector's car. "Screw it. I'm done. I can't babysit her anymore. I guess she's going to have to hit rock bottom on her own. These are delicious, by the way," Alice said, in between wolfing down tamales.

We sat on the double bed Val shared with her ten-year-old sister and scrolled through the slam pages while I told them about Mr. Upton's funeral and Val told us how she was in a huge fight with Javi because he'd found pictures on her phone of the five of us from the night of the sand temple.

"He seems like a giant prick. I get he has lupus, but maybe this guy is not for you." Alice told it like it was.

"It's not like that. I'm...I'm just tired. I've been through it so many times with him. In the two years we've been together, I've lost a lot of my friends."

"So why are you with him?" Alice said.

She flashed a weak smile. "He has good qualities. He can be really affectionate. And he's funny, like when the two of us are alone together. And I love him. And yes, it's kind of hard to leave when he's sick. I feel bad."

Alice shot me a raised-eyebrow *What the hell?* glance when Val wasn't looking.

Val's mom brought us delicious coconut-flavored desserts. They reminded me of Grandma Hosseini's rice pudding.

"I feel like we should do some real-life troll-slamming," I said.

"Such as?" Alice licked her plastic spoon.

"Well, don't judge, but I'm kind of famous for my care packages."

"Wow. Okay, Grandma." Alice shook her head.

"Stop. I was thinking, what if we put together cute little care packages and hand-deliver them to the victims of trolls from Val's school? We'll do it anonymously."

Val tilted her head and thought for a minute. "Aw. I like it, Sadie. It's a really nice gesture."

"Maybe a little too nice," Alice said.

"Okay, but I'm feeling bummed about Mr. Upton and I want to do something in his memory. Will you humor me?"

Alice agreed. "We'll be little troll-fighting elves," she said, sticking her spoon in my dessert and shoveling the rest of it into her mouth.

We scraped up eleven dollars and left Val's building through the side entrance.

"Valeria!" A man's voice shot through the parking lot.

"Oh, God. It's my dad." A short, stocky guy in boots and a cowboy hat race-walked over to us looking very pissed off.

"What's he saying?" I whispered to Alice as we stood while Val's dad yelled at her and pointed at us.

"I don't know. I take French."

Val came back, eyes averted, while her dad stormed off.

"What's wrong?"

"I was supposed to work at my grandparents' store and I totally blew it off to do school-supply stuff. He'll get over it."

"Why was he pointing at us?"

"He said you white people are a bad influence on me." Val laughed.

"Hey. I'm half Iranian," I said.

"As far as my dad's concerned, you're white enough."

We drove to the pharmacy and wandered around, trying to figure out what we could buy with eleven dollars.

"Manicure kit?" Val said.

"No," Alice said.

"Journals?" I said.

"No," Alice said.

"Cheez-Its?" Val said.

"Come on, let's get serious," Alice said. "This." Alice held up a package of candy necklaces. "Who doesn't like candy necklaces?"

"You are so right." Val picked up another package. "Everybody loves candy necklaces."

We put the candy necklaces into tiny gift bags with cards that said *We're launching a troll-slamming revolution. We hope you'll join us. Have a great day!*

"A revolution, Alice?" I said, watching her write in script with a purple pen. "Isn't that a little dramatic?"

"I like revolutions," said Val.

The revolution started a few blocks from the pharmacy.

Alice's Subaru crawled up the street, and I jumped out wearing a rain poncho over my funeral dress and a baseball cap I found under the front seat. I sprinted to the porch of the saddest little beige house, with chipped paint and no landscaping. Mom would go out of her mind if she had to live in a flowerless house.

I dropped the tiny gift bag addressed to CARLY (trolled for "looking ugly with bangs") and ran to the car. Alice peeled out.

"Next," I said, out of breath.

We did the same thing for the girl referred to as *Swiss cheese* at a perky yellow house with impressive hydrangeas and a Volvo parked in the driveway. I almost chickened out when I saw the dim flicker of a TV through the porch window. But I dropped and ran.

It was exhilarating.

"What if they don't get the bags? Like what if their little brothers take them or something?" Val said.

"Then we're out three ninety-nine for nothing," Alice said. "Who cares?"

We texted pictures of me sprinting in my poncho and baseball hat to Gordie and Jean. Five minutes later, we got a cryptic message from Gordie: Meet me at the farm stand as soon as you can get there. I have something to show you all.

❧ NINE ❧

CURIOSITY DROVE US to the farm stand. On the way, Alice assaulted me with questions about Gordie, beginning with "Is he one of those people who raise their hands in class every five seconds?" and ending with "So why haven't you guys hooked up? It's so obvious he's into you." To which I had no choice but to out Gordie Harris.

"I was obsessed with him for two years until I found out the ruffians from my class saw him making out with some guy at the pizza place. They were the biggest homophobic assholes. They called him Gay Gordie for a long time on the slam pages. I have to say, he handled it all really well."

"Do you guys ever feel like the assholes are taking over the earth?" Val said.

"Not anymore," Alice said. "'Cause...revolution."

Jean parked next to the willow tree just as Gordie was pulling in. I had a feeling that it was going to be a long night.

Maybe even an epic night.

Gordie got out of his car looking really good in his dark jeans and gray fitted T-shirt. I, on the other hand, was in my dowdy funeral dress, with matted hair and a sweaty back from the poncho-and-hat disguise.

"Did your concierge arrange an excursion for us?" Jean said in his butler accent.

"Cut the shit, Jean. I don't make fun of your short refugee ass," Gordie shot back. Gordie Harris was very sensitive about his richness.

We piled into the Range Rover and headed down Montauk Highway with the windows down and the music blaring as night swallowed up the last of the sunset.

Alice tried to text Izzy, then threw her phone into her satchel and cranked vintage Red Hot Chili Peppers until Gordie turned down a narrow, unpaved road marked PRIVATE.

"Where are you taking us, Gordie?" I said.

"He's having us killed to sell off our organs. I knew there was something sketchy about this guy," Jean said.

We continued past the shadows of craggy trees bending away from the sweeping dunes. Gordie turned down a smaller dirt road. A stately mansion popped up out of nowhere. Voices echoed and music floated through the haphazardly parked sea of cars.

"Um. Where are we?" Val grabbed my sweaty hand.

Gordie turned off the car. "This, my friends, is Speakeasy, mythical haven for the socially advanced."

"What?" we all said.

"Come on. You're going to love it."

I smoothed down my wrinkled funeral dress and wished I had taken a few minutes to get myself together. Alice, Val, and I were dressed to buy care package supplies at the pharmacy, not attend a "mythical haven for the socially advanced."

I felt the vibration of the music as the people milling around the front gardens came into focus.

Gordie stopped before we got to the marble steps. "Just so you know, this place is invite-only. We don't want the poseurs and the wannabes showing up," he said, looking over his shoulder at me.

"Why are you looking at me?" I said, flicking the back of his neck.

He gave me his *Oh, come on, Sadie. You and I both know how much Shawn Flynn partygoers suck* expression and led us up the long stone staircase to the main house.

Inside, we stopped to listen to two guys playing "Blackbird" by the Beatles on guitars on a landing overlooking a crowded foyer. It was awe-inspiring.

Gordie motioned for us to follow him through a bar area to a kitchen, where a blond guy with jagged bangs and pink cheeks was pouring champagne into glasses and arranging them on a tray.

"Gordie, I was looking for you. You playing tonight?"

"Later. These are my friends." Gordie draped his arms around Jean and Val.

Blondie was apparently a twenty-seven-year-old trust fund kid named Jack who had turned his inherited estate into a haven for musicians and social justice world-changers.

"Champagne?" He held out the tray.

Gordie shook his head. "Nah. I'm driving."

"Where's Keith?" Jack looked around.

"Home. He'll be here next week."

We sipped the champagne, which tasted cold and crisp and delicious. Jean burped loudly and grabbed another glass.

We wove through the hallway and emerged in a massive ballroom, the size of my school gym, where a stage stretched all the way across the back wall. The ceilings were painted a coppery gold, and cavernous chandeliers hung above us.

"People are going to be playing soon." Gordie reached into his jeans pocket, pulled out a harmonica, and played a few bars.

"I didn't know you played the harmonica," I said, surprised.

"You don't know a lot of things about me." He raised his eyebrows and smiled.

"I play the viola," Val said.

"Yeah? I've never seen a viola jam, but I saw an incredible fiddle thing here once."

"Who's Keith?" Alice said to me after another girl ran up asking for him.

I shrugged. "No clue."

"Come on." Gordie gestured to us. We walked up a back staircase and Gordie opened one of the doors on the second floor. I expected to find couples making out on piles of coats. But ten or twelve people were sprawled out on couches drinking from red Solo cups and laughing raucously.

"These are the chat rooms," Gordie said. "Let's see if there's a free one."

Gordie led us through a maze of corridors and up a flight of narrow steps to a rectangular alcove. "Score," Gordie said, opening a closet and grabbing a bottle of champagne from a mini fridge. He popped the cork and filled our glasses as we settled onto two side-by-side leather sofas facing Long Island Sound.

"You should see the stellar view during the day," Gordie said, leaning back.

I felt the buzz of the champagne and slung my legs over Val's lap.

"You guys," Val said in her quiet voice, "I really like hanging out with you."

"Val's shitfaced," Jean said.

"No, really, Jean. I just do."

"Sadie, can you believe Gordie from your class was hiding this whole double life?" Alice said.

"No. I mean we all know Gordie Harris will be Most Likely to Succeed in the yearbook and probably invent something genius, but I didn't know he was actually cool." I looked over at Gordie.

"I don't want to be Most Likely to Succeed in the yearbook. It's too much pressure," Gordie said.

"Val's going to be Most Likely to Be Married with Kids by Twenty," Jean said, laughing.

"That is so messed up, Jean." Val slapped him hard. "Like, seriously, do you not know how freaked out I am about college and getting in and paying for it? And then you say something like that. You're Most Likely to Hide in the Art Room Forever."

"Okay, this is stupid," Alice said. "Who cares anyway? I don't want to be Most Likely anything. Gordie's totally right. Even if I'm Most Likely to Save Scores of Dogs, which is probably what my unoriginal class would come up with for me, I'd feel like I never saved enough dogs. It is too much pressure."

We were quiet, thinking about the overrated tradition. "I wonder if any of those Most Likelies in the yearbook ever live up to their label," I said.

"If you forgive me, I'll let you kiss my cheek?" Jean leaned over and smiled in Val's face.

She rolled her eyes. "Fine." He leaned closer and she pecked him on his beard.

"God, I just realized. I'm not Most Likely to do anything," I said. "I don't have a thing. You guys all have things."

"What does that mean?" Alice said, slurping the last of her champagne.

"You people are lightweights," Gordie said.

"You have things, Sadie," Val said, leaning down to hug my legs.

"Like what?"

"You're good at making care packages," she announced proudly.

"I think it's better to be a Most *Un*likely," Alice said. "Then when you do something awesome, everyone will be surprised, like when you saved that baby, Sadie. Right? If you went around saving babies every day, nobody would have given a damn. Except maybe the baby."

"Good point, Alice," Jean said. "We should aspire to be unlikelies."

"Who put weed in the champagne?" Gordie said, getting up. He played a couple of chords on his harmonica. "Let's go down. I'm about to get my groove on."

"No. No. No," Val said, pulling Gordie by the arm. "Let's stay here."

"Come on. I promise you'll love it."

"He keeps saying that," Jean said.

We made our way down to the ballroom just in time for the two guitar guys to call a bunch of other people up to the stage. The lights dimmed and we moved to the middle of the floor. A pretty woman jumped onto the stage and took a mic from one of the guitar guys. She looked like she belonged on a boogie board. "Sylvie, Sylvie," the crowd chanted. She smiled and tossed her wild blond curls. She reminded me of Shay.

"I'm taking requests," she said, so obviously comfortable performing in front of a packed room. I looked around at the people gathering. It was the most random crowd of revelers I had ever seen, a swarm of bobbing heads.

Sylvie sang an old jazz song, "Summertime," with a voice so smooth, so perfectly elegant, I got chills. She captivated the entire room.

Gordie looked over at us and smiled.

It stayed good. Every song, every singer, every instrumental made me want to cry, or hug someone, or jump up and down. The music filled me up. It serenaded my soul.

We danced in the middle of the crowd until sweat poured from our bodies and our feet ached.

"We need you, Gordie," one of the guitar guys said into the mic.

Gordie nodded and left us for the stage, where he belonged. He stood there in his dark jeans and fitted shirt and messy brown hair and smiled before he put the harmonica to his mouth and played the hell out of Stevie Wonder's "Isn't She Lovely?"

The crowd sang together, *"Isn't she lovely? Isn't she wonderful?"*

I knew all the songs from years of listening to Dad's music. I didn't even need to read the words projected across the wall above the stage.

We sang "Don't Stop Believin'."

And then we sang too many Beatles songs to count. The lyrics swam above the band and we followed karaoke-style.

"I'll never dance with another. Woo!"

I wanted to stay at Speakeasy forever.

It was well after two a.m. when the adrenaline retreated and the crowd, groggy and sweaty and eating the hot fries in waxed paper bags that had appeared from the kitchen, reluctantly disbanded.

"Are you okay to drive?" Val asked Gordie as we waited for the long line of cars to exit the makeshift parking lot.

"I'm good," Gordie said. His voice was hoarse. "So . . . was I right? Did you like it?"

"Hands down, best night of my life," Jean said. "The energy was like nothing I've ever experienced."

"Good people, good energy," Gordie said.

"The Beatles are my new favorite band," Val said. "I don't want this night to be over."

"Not yet! Not yet!" Val, Alice, and I chanted from the backseat.

"I'm starving. Is there any place to get food around here?" Alice said, stretching her long legs between Val and me.

"We have no money," I said.

"We can go to my house," Jean said.

"I doubt your mom will appreciate us foraging in the middle of the night," Gordie said. He drove over a stretch of lawn and inched into the long line of cars.

"My mom's a nurse. She's on the overnight shift. We're good."

We rode with all the windows down, singing at the tops of our lungs, until we got to Jean's ranch-style house at the end of a tree-lined street.

"Here we are, White Castle," Jean said. He fished a key out of a planter and opened the door. Paintings of palm trees and tropical flowers and bright-faced Haitian girls hung on deep red walls above the turquoise sofas.

Jean riffled through the refrigerator and brought out a glass container of rice and beans and another of fried plantains. He stuck the containers in the microwave while we studied an oversize portrait of Jean's family.

"Your dad looks exactly like you," Alice said, pointing to a gap-toothed, smiling man holding a baby Jean.

"That's what everybody says. He's gone. I mean, he passed away in the big earthquake we had in Haiti."

"Oh my God, Jean. I never knew that." Val's face turned red.

"It's not like I want to dredge it up all the time."

The microwave beeped. Jean took out the food and we devoured the soggy plantains.

"You all can stop being awkward. I'm fine." Jean licked grease off his fingers.

"We're not being awkward," Alice said. "If you want to talk about your dad, you can."

"There's not much to say. He was an awesome guy with a huge personality, and he died and left my mom to take care of me, my three sisters, and half the neighborhood because she was the only nurse around. It pretty much blew."

We hovered over the counter, shoveling spoonfuls of rice and beans into our mouths while Jean told us about how his family had searched for nearly a week before they discovered his dad was dead, and how his mom bribed a government official to get their family out of Haiti, and how they were homeless and lived in a church in Brooklyn until his mom found work as a night nanny to pay her way through nursing school and certification here.

"Does anyone at school know any of this?" Val said.

"No. And let's keep it that way," Jean said.

Jean went quiet. I couldn't tell if he felt like he had overshared or if he had something else he wanted to tell us.

"I'm going to show you guys something," he finally said. "But don't judge."

We followed Jean down a narrow hallway decorated with fancy wide-brimmed hats on hooks to a door marked JEAN-PIERRE. Jean stopped and turned to us.

"So I kind of have this weird hobby. It started a long time ago. I have no idea why I do this, but it's my thing."

"You're making me nervous," Val said. "It better not be that hobby where they stuff dead animals."

"You mean taxidermy?" Gordie said.

"No. It's not taxidermy." Jean opened the door and flipped on the light, and a hundred faces smiled at us.

We were speechless at first, taking in the full effect of the rows and rows of masks that hung on Jean's walls. They looked like they came from all over the world. There were tribal masks, Japanese masks, wooden masks, masks bursting with color, some disturbing, some charming. The only thing that unified the masks was that they were all smiling.

"Okay, I need a minute," I said. I felt like I was in a global bazaar fun house.

"I take it your thing is mask collecting," Gordie said.

"Actually, I made all these."

"Shut up," Alice said. "You did not make these."

"Yep. I kinda did. I studied indigenous mask making and started coming up with my own variations."

We sat on Jean's fluffy teal rug, gnawing on the extra candy necklaces and learning about the art of mask making. Our friend Jean-Pierre was a genius.

"I want to make a mask," Val said.

"Yeah. We'll get on that," Jean said, patting her on the back.

Gordie let out a long yawn. "Damn, it's late."

"Oh my God. It's almost five," I said, checking my phone. "I have to be at work in a few hours. I'm supposed to be sleeping at your house." I looked at Val.

"I'm supposed to be at Alice's."

Alice stood up and tossed her soggy candy necklace string in Jean's trash can. She swiveled, put her hands on her hips, and said, "Let's go to the beach."

We flung open the Range Rover doors, just as the sun crept up over the horizon. It was high tide and the waves were whitecapped and feisty. Gordie dug around the back for a blanket and a bunch of towels, and we went as close to the water as we could. We sat, five in a row, and watched the sunrise.

"Do you know I've lived out here since third grade and I've never made it to sunrise?" I said.

Gordie was the only one who had. I pictured him leaving Speak-easy with the elusive and mysterious Keith, who may or may not have been Gordie's boyfriend.

The colors of early morning layered the sky. Yellow sat on the horizon. Red faded to pink, and orange faded into deep purple. Jean ran to the car to get his sketch pad. Val and Alice lay back on the sand and snuggled under the blanket. Gordie wrapped a beach towel around my shoulders. For a long stretch of time, nobody said a word.

"Do you still have your Geiger counter in the trunk?" Alice said.

"It's not a Geiger counter, Einstein," Gordie said, laughing. "It's a metal detector."

"You really that hard up that you need lost coins?" Jean said.

"No. But who doesn't like treasure hunting?"

"Have you ever found anything good?" I said, resting my head on Gordie's shoulder, drawing body heat from his leg pressed against mine under the beach towel.

"Lots of things. I keep them in my treasure chest."

I never knew when Gordie Harris was joking.

I arrived at the farm stand in my grungy funeral dress with my hair sticking up and my teeth coated in bacteria. We had stopped at the convenience store to pick up breakfast when I realized I didn't have time to go home and change.

"I cannot believe you have to work. You poor thing," Val said.

"Hey, I have to teach art to toddlers in an hour," Jean said.

"Get out, people," Alice said. "Let's sit with Sadie until her boss gets here."

I told them they didn't have to, but in an act of solidarity, they joined me under the willow tree. We ate egg sandwiches and drank strong coffee and made fun of Gordie.

"Is that a harmonica in your pocket or are you happy to see me?" Alice said.

"Is that a Geiger counter in your trunk or are you happy to see me?" Jean said.

"Hey, pull up Greg O.'s blog," Val said.

"Has anybody seen it lately?" Gordie said, taking out his phone. He pulled up Greg O.'s page. It had exploded with comments and posts about Mayans and photos of Mayan temples made out of toothpicks, recycled strips of paper, reclaimed wood.

Thanks to our collective social media campaign and Gordie's magical abilities to boost website visibility, Greg O.'s site was going viral. Who knew so many people were into the Mayans?

This one looks real! Greg O. had posted about a mini temple made of clay.

"I think our work here is done," Gordie said. "I dare those asshats to screw with our man Greg now."

"Can we make more candy necklace care packages?" Val said. "That was really fun."

"Candy necklace revolution!" Alice said.

"We need a badass revolutionary name," Gordie said.

"How about the Troll Slammers?" Val said.

"Lame," Jean said.

"The Troll Assassins," Alice said.

"Too violent," Val said.

I stared at the shuttered farm stand. I could barely keep my eyes open. But then it came to me.

"I've got it."

They all looked at me.

"The Unlikelies."

"Yes!" Alice said, punching me in the arm.

"That is us," Jean said.

"Yup," Gordie said. "See? You can't tell us you don't have a *thing*. You're a natural-born revolutionary namer, Sullivan."

"The Unlikelies," Val said.

"Never speak of this to anyone," Alice said.

"That's a given," Jean said.

We all agreed.

When Farmer Brian pulled up, I was saying good-bye through the window of the Range Rover.

"Hey, do you want the suitcase? I can drop it off later," Gordie said.

"Yeah. I'll get it at some point."

"Maybe Jean would like the creepy Raggedy Andy doll, huh, Jean?" Alice said.

"Wait, what's Raggedy Andy?" I said. My heart quickened.

"You don't know what Raggedy Andy is, Sadie?" Alice said. "That's what the doll is called. Raggedy Andy. Duh. Who doesn't know Raggedy Andy?"

You need to rip off Andy's legs. Don't forget. Rip off Andy's legs.

And suddenly it all made sense.

❧ TEN ❧

MOM NUDGED MY leg with her pink slipper. "Sadie, Gordie Harris is outside."

I sat up, disoriented, in the darkened room and looked at my phone. "How is it after nine?"

Farmer Brian had shown mercy on me and let me leave work at lunchtime. I'd been sleeping ever since.

"You know sleep deprivation is not good for you, Sadie. How about you stay in and relax for once?"

"I am staying in. Can you tell him I'll be right down?"

My parents were used to my comings and goings. I didn't have a curfew or any annoying parental restrictions. But every few days they delivered their mantra, which always came out as more threatening than assuring: "We trust you implicitly, Sadie."

I rubbed my eyes, guzzled warm Gatorade, and smoothed down my bed head.

Gordie was on the porch with Dad and Mr. Ng. All day, since Alice had clued me in that Raggedy Andy was the name of the doll in the garment bag, I had been obsessed with getting my hands on that suitcase. I had texted Gordie no fewer than ten times before my eight-hour nap. Can you bring it tonight? Is tonight going to work? I suddenly really want that suitcase in my possession.

Chill, Sadie. I'll bring you your suitcase.

"So Mr. Upton wanted me to have a suitcase full of random belongings," I announced to my parents. "Which is very strange, but it was nice of him to think of me."

"You really left an impression on ol' Stewy," Dad said. "You need some help?"

"No, we're good."

I motioned to Gordie, who walked toward the Range Rover.

"Sadie tells me you're a shoo-in for valedictorian," Dad called after him.

I cringed a little.

Gordie's muscles flexed as I tried to help him with the bulky suitcase. "I got it," he said. "Where do you want it?"

I wanted it in my room.

Mom hovered awkwardly in the dining room, watching us drag the suitcase up the narrow staircase. "We're good, Mom," I said, closing my door.

"Holy origami cranes," Gordie said, looking up at the flock of cranes I had fastened to a string and hung in rows across my ceiling. He picked up the twin bobbleheads of Shay and me and shook aggressively until the heads nearly came off. "Can I help you with anything else, Sadie Cakes?" Gordie said, wiping his hands on his shorts and looking at my bulletin board, still scattered with pictures of Seth.

"Please don't ever call me that again."

"What happened with you and Seth anyway?"

"I don't know. I mean, I don't want to talk about Seth right now." The entire forty-five seconds up the stairs, I had contemplated sharing my promise to Mr. Upton with Gordie. I didn't want to rip Andy's legs off alone.

He sat on my bed. "Can I have some of this Gatorade?"

I nodded and knelt in front of the suitcase.

Then I caved.

I told Gordie everything, from the moment I retrieved the key from Mr. Upton's wallet to the things he said about me being *the one for this job* and *Do something noble* to the cryptic *You need to rip off Andy's legs.*

He sat and listened, nodding occasionally, until he finally said, "I'm thinking it's time to rip off those legs."

We opened the suitcase with the key and carefully removed the lizard's belongings, layer by layer, until we got to the garment bag with the leather buckles.

"There you are, Andy, you creepy bastard," Gordie said, lifting him by his red yarn hair.

I grabbed one of the legs and squeezed. It was stuffed with

something hard and bumpy. Gordie grabbed a pair of scissors from my desk.

"Be careful," I said, laying Andy down on the floor and spreading his blue-and-white-striped legs like he was a filleted fish. Gordie snipped the first leg off Andy's body and then carefully cut along the seam, beginning at his slippered foot. We pulled open the fabric and stared down at the rolled cheesecloth bags, the kind Grandma Hosseini used for making yogurt.

I opened the first rolled bag and felt a rush of adrenaline.

We stared down at the loose bright yellow gemstones.

"Holy shit, Sadie." Gordie picked up the next bag. More stones. And more. Each bag held dozens of gemstones the size of pencil erasers, some even bigger.

"These can't be real," I said, rolling a single stone between my fingers.

"I think they might be real," my well-to-do friend said, holding one close to his eye. "These are too light to be topaz. I think they might be yellow diamonds."

"We need to Google it." I reached over and pulled my laptop off the bed.

We Googled *yellow diamonds*. They looked a lot like yellow diamonds. Then we Googled *How to tell if a diamond is real* and did all the tests. We fogged one up with our breath. The fog disappeared immediately. We dropped one in a glass of water. It sank straight to the bottom. We lit a match in front of one. The flame did nothing to the stone. We tested the next stone and the next. We ripped open Raggedy Andy's other leg and found more cheesecloth bags of stones.

Tucked up in Andy's genderless crotch was one last cheesecloth bag. Inside was a piece of mint-colored stationery, rolled like a scroll.

I carefully unrolled the letter, dated 1992. We sat against my bed and read.

> *My love,*
>
> *If you are receiving this letter, I am dead. I implored my sister to deliver Father's suitcase to you, and despite her "feelings" about us, I believe she will honor my wishes. She most certainly has no use for Father's suitcase.*
>
> *I'm giving this to you because you are the kindest, most generous person I know. You will find a way to make good use of these, something I just couldn't do.*
>
> *I only wish I had been man enough to avenge the hell that man brought to my sister, my loving mother, and me, a little boy with no defenses.*
>
> *Please, darling, find a way to make the world a bit better. I hope you have forgiven my abrupt departure. You, dearest Bruce, were the love of my life.*
>
> *I often wonder if I was ever worthy of love.*
>
> > *Until we meet again,*
> > *Stewy*

"Finished?" I looked at Gordie.

He nodded.

I stared at the letter.

"That's some heavy shit," Gordie said.

I turned over the paper. On the back, Mr. Upton had written BRUCE LEONISI, JANE ST., NEW YORK CITY.

"This is bullshit," I blurted. "I'm Mr. Upton's ex-lover's backup do-gooder? First I'm plan B after the Hamptons Hoodlum gets caught, and now this."

"That's what you took from this, Sadie? Seriously?"

Gordie opened my laptop and Googled *Bruce Leonisi*. It didn't take long to figure out he had been dead for sixteen years.

"Now what?" I slowly poured the cheesecloth bags full of alleged yellow diamonds into a pile on my floor.

"If you want, I can take a few stones over to my grandmother's appraiser. She's always sending me over there," Gordie said.

"Yes. Please do that. I mean, if the lizard was so shady, we can't assume these are real, even if they did pass the tests."

"True."

"But, Gordie, can you even imagine what we could do with these if they're real?"

"I'd invest. Like in aggressive, high-risk, high-yield shit."

I looked at him. "No. As in saving-the-world shit."

He laughed. "I think you'd need a bigger pile to actually save the world."

We sifted through the stones, pulled out a few of the bigger ones, and restuffed Andy's shredded legs before we shoved Andy back into his garment bag. "Are we going to tell the Unlikelies?" Gordie said.

"Not yet. Let's make this one a Sadie-and-Gordie secret."

"You got it."

Gordie and I shared a frozen pizza on the porch with Mr. Ng and Dad before he left, still exhausted from the night before.

I lay on my bed, flushed and nervous. I didn't even want to think about what I would do if the diamonds were real. I thought instead about our night at Speakeasy and how much fun it had been.

I dialed Shay's number.

"Hey, Sadie."

"Guess what random person I just ate a frozen pizza with on the porch with Dad and Mr. Ng?"

"I don't know. Pooch? Gordie Harris?"

"Actually, yes. Gordie Harris."

"I saw the pictures. Looks like fun." Shay was using her fake voice.

"Are you okay, Shay?" I knew she hated it when I asked her if she was okay.

"Yeah. I'm fine. I'm just working a lot. I'm tired." Her tone was giving me anxiety.

"Do you just want to talk later?"

"Yeah. I still have to do a bunk check."

"Night, Shay-Shay."

"Night, Sadie."

I stared up at Shay's origami cranes and wondered what I had done to piss off my best friend.

❧ ELEVEN ❧

THE UNLIKELIES DELIVERED care packages to troll mill victims three nights in a row. My heart ached a little every time I read through the list of recipients:

Jackson R. (tortured for bad hygiene and weirdness)

Mary Michele (harassed for being overweight and sneaking food during class)

Erik (bullied for being from Sweden)

Annabella F. (slut-shamed after she slept with two guys on the same team)

Jamie (tormented for being thin and pretty)

We stuck handmade cards into tiny gift bags with candy necklaces and tied the bags with curly ribbon. Val had the best handwriting, so she was the message-writer. *We're bringing down the trolls. You're one of us now. —The Unlikelies.*

Val got a text from Javi just as we were finishing the care packages. They were back to being in love.

"Javi's friend Mike likes you, Sadie."

"The guy you were with when you stopped for strawberries?"

"Yeah. He thought you were cute."

"Why didn't he get out of the car?" I said.

"He's shy."

"Tell him I'm not over Seth."

"You are so over Seth."

"I'm not into guys with longer bangs than mine."

"One date. Mike will pay for your dinner. He's a gentleman that way."

"I can get free food at home."

"So do it for me."

Pause. Sigh. "Okay, Val. I'll do it for you."

We loaded the care packages in the cars and fanned out across the East End with lists of addresses and revolutionary music playlists. The Beatles. Dylan. Taylor Swift.

"*Haters gonna hate, hate, hate, hate, hate,*" Val belted out.

I delivered the candy necklaces in my poncho and baseball hat.

I darted up to front porches, ran to mailboxes, dodged stressed-out dogs and a couple of dads peering through the curtains. But every mission was successful.

At the end of the third night, we sat with our feet in Gordie's pool while Gordie blasted the slam pages with anti-troll GIFs. He found a picture of a troll and superimposed candy necklaces dangling all over it. Under it, he just wrote:

Choose kindness. —The Unlikelies.

"We need a mascot," Jean said.

"Oh my God, we so need a mascot," Alice said.

We spent the next hour arguing over the mascot. Alice wanted us to pick our favorite animals and then somehow merge all five animals into one. Val wanted to stick with the happy-faced troll wearing candy necklaces. Jean wanted something badass. I didn't care. I just wanted us to agree on something.

"We'll table this," Gordie said. "A good mascot doesn't happen in a day."

We ended up sitting in a circle on the pool deck, playing Val's "first and last" game.

Alice: "First time your heart broke."

Jean: "When my dad died."

Gordie: "Last time you kissed someone."

Me: "I've never kissed anyone."

Gordie: "Very funny."

Me: "It was Seth. But I have no idea the last time we kissed."

Val: "First pet."

Alice: "Twin kittens named Alice Jr. and Cattie."

Alice: "Last really good meal."

Gordie: "Sushi in New York on the last day of school."

Jean: "Last time you felt really happy."

Val: "Right now."

And then, because of the adrenaline and the extra gift bags burning a hole in the backseat, we went out again. We dropped off more bags, hitting Greg O.'s house last.

"See you tomorrow," Val said afterward with a big grin.

"Uh. Great. Yeah. Can't wait," I said sarcastically.

"Can't wait for what?" Gordie called out from the car.

"Javi's friend Mike likes Sadie. We're going on a double date."

"Have fun with that," Gordie said.

"Oh, I will," I said.

The next morning, the morning of the dreaded date, I was sifting through cherries out back at the farm stand when Daniela brought me my phone. "It's driving me crazy," she said.

I had a bunch of texts from Gordie. They all said the same thing.

Just left my grandmother's "friend." They're real.

An hour later Gordie and I were sitting hip to hip on my willow tree crate, brainstorming how to deal with the buttload of real diamonds that were stuffed in my closet behind my prom dress and my old field hockey sticks.

"If this one diamond was worth over seven thousand dollars, how the hell much are we talking here?" I said, holding the stone between my thumb and finger.

"A lot."

Maybe a normal person would have gotten excited about all those diamonds, about the possibility of poaching a few for a trip to California or a new phone or a cute outfit. But all I could think was, *Why me?*

"Let's just tell the others," I said. "I need help figuring this out."

We decided we'd tell them after my date.

I spent the entire day at work trying to process the fact that Mr. Upton was not deranged. He knew perfectly well that he had stashed a fortune in Raggedy Andy's legs. He knew he was dying. And for some reason, he believed I was the one who could redeem his father's evil deeds. The problem was I had no idea where to even begin.

Mom called just when I was leaving to go home and shower before Val picked me up for the date.

"Hey, Mom. I'm driving."

"Where are you?"

"Bridgehampton."

"I need you to come home. The victim advocate is calling in a half hour."

I pulled into a parking lot. "Does it have to be today?"

"Yes. And she wants me with you when she calls."

Even cutting through all the back roads, I got stuck in traffic. When I got home, Mom was on the porch frantically waving me toward the phone in her hand.

The victim advocate talked to me for forty-five minutes. She was nice enough, and I understood it was her job and she was trying to help me, to protect me, but the last thing I wanted to do was dredge up a play-by-play of the incident while my mother interrupted me every five seconds with "Don't forget the part about where he smashed your head" and "Don't forget the way he behaved when the cops arrived." I told her everything as I remembered it, but I wasn't sure if I truly remembered any of it, or if I was just rehashing what I saw on the video.

The worst part wasn't on the video. It was a five-second mental video, running on repeat. I took a deep breath and described the terror on baby Ella's rosy, tearstained face.

Mom chimed in to talk about my scars and which ones would probably be permanent. I had no idea the permanence of my scars would be a factor in determining *his* punishment.

"What about emotionally, Sadie?" Mom had put the phone on speaker and the woman was addressing the whole kitchen. "Any nightmares? Flashbacks?" Her voice was sweet but her questions were jarring.

"No."

Mom leaned toward the phone.

"Sadie's been coming down to our room a lot, sleeping on the floor. That never happened before the incident." Mom was skilled at the art of embarrassment.

"Well, that was fun," I said after we hung up.

Mom hugged me gently. And I let her.

After my shower, I waited for Val while my parents balanced plates of chicken and lemon rice on their laps in the Adirondack chairs.

Mom stopped eating and stared at me. "Daddy and I would like to talk about things, Sadie."

That was my least favorite sentence.

"Okay."

Mom began with "I had said all along we should have gotten you therapy after the incident, but your father and grandmothers pooh-poohed me. You do know there's no shame in therapy."

I had asked for this talk. I was the seventeen-year-old migrating down to the nook in my parents' bedroom with my stuffed harp seal.

"Sadie," Mom continued, reading the utter misery on my face. "You went through a trauma. And sometimes it takes a while for the mind to process that. There's only so much running around with your new friends you can do before you crash. I'd like you to see Willie Ng's therapist in Sag Harbor. The Ngs swear by him."

Mr. Ng's son Willie was addicted to Internet porn.

"How about I just don't sleep in your room anymore?" I smiled and batted my eyelashes.

"How about just one visit, hon?" Dad said with his mouth full.

"Fine. I'll go to Willie Ng's friggin' therapist."

"Shh," Mom hissed, looking over at the Ngs' house.

Val drove up then, just in time to save me.

"Have a good friggin' time," Dad said, smiling.

Val's car was stuffed to the brim with school supplies. I could barely find space for my silver-sandal-clad feet.

"What's wrong?" she said. "You look upset."

"Oh, my parents think I need therapy to deal with the incident."

"Do you? I feel like we never talk about it."

"I hardly ever think about it during the day. And then sometimes I get a flash of the scene, which was pretty horrific. And then I'll have some freaky dream and wake up all clammy and frozen in fear, at which point I go down and sleep on my parents' floor."

"Aww. Sadie, I'm sorry. Any time you feel like talking about it, I'm here."

"Thanks, Val. That's really sweet of you."

I ran my finger over the monster tail scar. It was still tender and slightly swollen. I understood my parents' concern, but I had a feeling rehashing the incident to Willie Ng's therapist would force me to relive something I was better off putting out of my mind. Forever.

The date was at a little seafood restaurant on the bay where people wore plastic bibs to catch lobster butter dribble. Mike had drenched himself in cologne. He wore a crisp button-down shirt with too much exposed patchy chest hair. He kept looking at me, but he didn't say a word.

"Does he speak English?" I whispered to Val on our way to the bathroom.

"Seriously, Sadie?" Val laughed. "He's American."

I hated myself for agreeing to go to dinner with Mute Mike. Val and I talked too much, to make up for Mike's mutism and Javi's lackluster personality. Val bragged about how my mom was Persian, which was very cool, and my dad was Woody the ice cream man. I told a story about the time a little kid crawled into the back of the truck and rode around for fifteen minutes gorging himself on ice cream before my dad found him.

I had no idea what sweet, smart, overachieving Val saw in Javi, who was a bump on a log with permanent resting bitch face. And his logmate wasn't much better.

At least the shrimp scampi was pretty good.

Val and I got a text from Alice just as the waiter was delivering dessert menus.

At the hospital. Izzy might be dead. Please come.

Mute Mike and I sucked on peppermints and stared at each other while Val and Javi fought in the parking lot until Val finally stormed away and we were off to the hospital. We were terrified for Alice and had no idea what to expect when we got there.

I almost didn't recognize Alice biting her fingernail on a bench next to Gordie in front of the hospital. Her red face was bloated and full of anguish. She twisted her long white braids in her hands and gave us a weak smile.

"What happened, Alice?" I slid next to her and wrapped my arm around her shoulders.

She shrugged. "Izzy's my best friend." She could barely get the words out. Her body bent forward.

"We know, sweetie, we know," I said, rubbing her shoulder.

"It's okay. Take a breath," Val said, sitting on the other side of Gordie.

"She OD'd. Who overdoses on a Tuesday afternoon?"

Groups of nurses and people carrying coffee cups and tote bags walked past our bench. A little girl with butter-colored hair and a teal dress bounced through the parking lot carrying a BABY BOY balloon. All the while, Alice's best friend, her Shay, clung to life in the ICU.

"I just let her go. I let her go away with that hideous dealer." All the pain and guilt, grief and regret poured out in rapid, quivering breaths.

Jean ran through the parking lot and stopped short in front of us.

"Alice's friend OD'd," Gordie said. "She's in the ICU."

"Let's just pray," Jean said.

We sat on the bench, holding on to Alice and praying for Izzy.

Please, please, please, please, please, I said to myself over and over again. I couldn't imagine Izzy, the bubbly horse lover from Girl Scouts, dying. I couldn't even begin to think about the grief that would come of it. I blocked out the thoughts with *please*s.

Alice's mom came outside. She was tall and blond and wearing a strapless black pantsuit, wedge heels, and lots of diamonds. She didn't look like she belonged to Alice.

"Come, Alice, let's go up." She eyed us suspiciously, the way a woman like her might eye a Middle Eastern–looking girl, a bearded black guy, a pigtailed Hispanic girl, and a disheveled white guy fawning all over her distraught daughter.

"Please wait," Alice said to us as she walked away.

We waited on the bench for three hours, talking about anything *but* what might be going on in the ICU. Gordie made fun of my date with Mute Mike. Val recruited us to help her with her growing school-supply empire. Gordie invited us to his Turtle Trail camping trip. Jean sketched out mascots, which were well done but still not quite right. We talked about how many people we knew who were doing Oxy and how Oxy was easier to get than weed. A doctor stood behind us eavesdropping and smoking cigarettes. It got dark and the lights around the parking lot popped on and made annoying buzzing sounds.

"Oh my gosh, Sadie. Is everything okay?" Hannah S. appeared out of nowhere. She was carrying a vase of carnations tied with an obnoxious shimmery pink ribbon.

"Hey, Hannah. I'm waiting for a friend." I wasn't about to give Hannah S. any more information than that.

"I hope he or she is okay," she pried, eyeing Gordie. "Oh, hi, Gordie."

"Hi, Hannah."

"My aunt had gallbladder surgery." She looked at me and then Val and Jean and Gordie. Confusion spread over her sunburned face.

"Oh. That sucks. I hope she's better soon," I said, hoping she'd get the hint.

"Thanks. Your friend, too." She walked away, clearly dazed by the rush of hypotheses that must have been flooding her gadfly brain.

"She's going to be sticking her head into every room in that hospital to see what friend Sadie Sullivan and Gordie Harris have in common," I said.

"It's a good activity for her. Keeps the mind sharp," Gordie said.

I remembered Andy's canaries, as Gordie and I were now referring to the stones. It still didn't feel real. But then again, having a friend who had a friend who had just overdosed on heroin didn't feel real either.

Alice seemed surprised to see us when she finally shuffled through the automatic doors, draped in a man's burnt-orange cardigan. The night was hot and sticky and loud with insect sounds and streetlight buzzing and constant ambulance sirens.

"I can't believe you stayed," she said with a wisp of a voice.

Nobody said a word. We were all so afraid Izzy was dead.

"I think she's okay." Alice sat on the edge of the bench. Val handed her a half-drunk iced coffee and she sipped it through the straw.

"I only saw her from the doorway. She looked like a corpse. In addition to nearly dying from the overdose, she got some rare blood fungus from the needles. So she's really sick."

"How are her parents reacting?" Val said.

"Her parents had no idea she was doing heroin. No clue. Like what planet are they on?" Jean took Alice's bony hand. She rested her head on his shoulder, then picked it up again.

"My parents grilled me. They demanded to know when *we* started doing drugs. When *we* started hanging out with dealers. When *we* turned bad." She lowered her head to her knees and wrapped her arms around her legs. "I lost it. I told them I tried everything to stop *her*, but *she* wouldn't stop. I should have stabbed that fucking dealer, Hector, in the face with his own needles."

A man came through the hospital doors. I saw him out of the corner of my eye looming like a stalker. "Alice."

We all turned.

"Daddy." She crumbled. "These are my friends from the home-grown hero lunch."

The tall, straight-backed, sandy-haired man walked quickly around the bench and held out his hand. Alice took it, and he pulled her up. They embraced as we watched from our bench, feeling like Alice's voyeur friends.

TWELVE

GORDIE DROVE ME home from the hospital. We parked in my driveway and I asked him what he would do with the diamonds. He said he'd have to think about it.

"I need a better hiding place," I said. "And then we need to call a meeting of the Unlikelies, when Alice is feeling better. And then I'll take suggestions."

He smiled. "You're being very businesslike right now."

"Yes. This is serious, Gordie."

I wanted to kiss him. I couldn't tell if it was a Pavlovian reaction to being in a dark car with a very attractive male, or some way to distract myself from the horribleness of Izzy, or if my old flame was rekindling against my wishes and common sense.

Gordie humored me. "Didn't old Stewy give you any clues about what to do?"

I tried to relay everything Mr. Upton had said on his deathbed, about the shady stealing from widows and the bootlegging and prostitution. I told Gordie Mr. Upton didn't have any heirs except Sissy, who had happily relinquished the suitcase and who Mr. Upton didn't think was up to this task. But other than that, I had no clue what to do with a shitload of diamonds.

The porch light went on and Dad opened the door.

"To be continued," I said and jumped out.

I texted Alice before I went to sleep. It's going to be okay.

She texted back, This is hell. Some guy she's sleeping with called 911 when she turned gray and her lips went blue and she choked on her own vomit.

I had seen my share of the dark side. Shawn Flynn's parties were notorious. There were the stomach pumpings and the paranoid freakouts. There were fights and that time a kid from the city had wandered into Shawn's parents' room and tried to hang himself. But Izzy's world was darker than the dark side. She was lodged in a blacked-out corner of that place where even hope had turned gray and blue-lipped.

Again, I woke in a panic. Again, I froze in my bed. And again, as much as I didn't want to, I made my way down to the nook in my parents' bedroom, where I slept like a baby in a seventeen-year-old body.

The next day, Alice and I waited for Val on the rusty swing set outside her apartment building. At some point that morning, Alice had chopped off most of her hair and colored it violet. She looked younger with cropped hair, like a pale, rosy-cheeked child.

Alice told me about her mom's conversation with a lady from the golf club.

"'This is what happens when immigrants infiltrate our communities. They shove drugs down our children's throats and leave them for dead.' She's assuming Hector is an immigrant. Which he is not. He's a blond kid from Nassau County."

"They're going to bring her back, Alice. That's what they do at these rehabs. They figure out how to fill people up again."

"They're not taking her to rehab. They're taking her home. I'm sure that will turn out just fine." Alice shook her head. "So she texted back."

Val bounced across the browning lawn in her white Converse high-tops, faded jean shorts, and blue-sparkle tank top.

"Any word from Izzy?" Val ran her hand gently over Alice's spiky hair.

"Oh, yes. She texted me to tell me to leave her alone because she is fine and I am a bad friend. And then she somehow blamed me for her getting caught. Because in her twisted mind, almost dying is getting caught." She paused. "I just texted her to hang in there and that I loved her," Alice said. "I told her to get better because we have a senior year to look forward to." She stood up. "I can't deal with this right now. Let's just go to Gordie's."

When we got to Gordie's, his mom greeted us with strawberry shortcake and a very long story about how Gordie's brother missed his plane from Vienna to London.

"Does she know anything about our night at the hospital?" I asked Gordie, nodding toward his mom, who was raving about Alice's newly cropped purple hair.

"No. It's better that way." He gave me a look that said *My mother lives in strawberry-shortcake land.*

We waited for Jean in the basement theater seats.

"Go to the slam pages," Val said.

"No. Not tonight," I said. "Alice doesn't need more stress."

But Alice wanted us to open up her school's page. She needed to see what was out there about Izzy.

It was all there, how Izzy OD'd and what a whore she had become and how she used to be sort of cute but now she's disgusting.

Gordie replied to every slam with:

> Cyber trolls, bullies, and miscreants—
> come to the light. Join us. It's beautiful
> over here! —The Unlikelies.

"Nobody knows what a miscreant is, Gordie," I said, shaking my head.

"It's an SAT word. They should know it."

Jean banged on the glass doors and Val jumped to open them. "What?" Jean said. "You're all staring at me."

Gordie and I looked at each other. I stood up, smoothed down my shorts, cleared my throat, and asked everyone to sit on the couch near the popcorn machine because I had to tell them something. After much grumbling and speculation, we stood in front of Val, Jean, and Alice and told them the entire long, convoluted Andy's canaries story.

At first they just sat there, looking baffled. Then came the barrage of obvious questions. I answered every one, grateful that no one seemed irritated I had kept the secret.

"I have no idea what to do with this," I said. "I need help."

"You can't just give out diamonds," Jean said. "People will trade them in to buy useless crap. Have you ever seen what the people who win the lottery spend that money on?"

"We also can't show up at a jeweler and cash them in," said Gordie.

"Why not?" I said. I had assumed we'd cash them in.

"It doesn't work that way. That would get flagged as suspicious activity, and then the IRS and parents and other irritating entities would get involved. You just can't."

We focused on what Mr. Upton had said, about his lizard father dabbling in bootlegging, prostitution, and stealing from widows, and tried to focus on modern-day things that would somehow redeem his shady dealings.

"So boozers, hookers, and rich old ladies," Jean said. "That narrows it down."

"Or old-lady boozer-hookers," Gordie said. "We'll buy a retirement island for drunk, old hookers."

Jean typed something into his phone. "We could easily buy our own Speakeasy, you know. There's a property on the water for sale at auction for four hundred thousand."

"Seriously, Jean?" Val said, glancing at me. "Can you stop? This is not helpful."

Alice stayed quiet. She chewed on her chipped green nails and stared into space.

"Hey, can we finally figure out our mascot?" Gordie said.

"What does this have to do with the diamonds?" I said, frustrated. Our brainstorming session was getting us nowhere.

"Maybe Andy should *be* the mascot," Val said. "Or not." She looked at Jean. "You're afraid of birds *and* dolls. Any other bizarre fears?"

"Just pirates. But the real ones. Not like from the movies," Jean clarified.

We loaded into the Range Rover, on a new mission to find a mascot.

"There's still a bunch of care packages back here," Val said. "Let's drop them on the way."

We had delivered care packages to every victim of trollery we could think of. But I had an idea.

"What if we give the rest of the care packages to the trolls themselves?" They looked at me like I was an idiot, but I explained. "We're going to kill them with kindness. Trust me. Trolls hate being called out. It's their worst fear."

"I defer to the queen of care packages," Gordie said.

"Okay, nerd boy. Let's do it," I said.

We scribbled notes and stuffed them in the bags. *If you choose kindness, we'll let you in. —The Unlikelies*. First stop was this kid A.J.'s house, the one who had started all the shit with Greg O. in the cafeteria. I sprinted across the street and stuck the bag in his mailbox. After that, we tossed a bag onto queen gadfly Meghan Rose Sharp's fancy front deck.

"You run like a gopher or a groundhog. I can't put my finger on it," Gordie said when I jumped back in the car.

"Gopher," Jean said.

"Thanks for making me self-conscious."

I modified my gait at the next three houses, then made Val do a few. All in all, we hit four ruffians, two gadflies, and three Izzy-bad-mouthers before we ended up parked in Mr. Upton's gravel driveway. There were no cars, no signs of life. Still, it was unsettling. But an idea had sprouted in Jean's genius mind as we were trolling for trolls and he absolutely had to get something from Mr. Upton's shed.

Jean grabbed an empty laundry bag from the trunk and instructed us to wait. He had a vision and wanted to use something from the shed to make a surprise mascot.

"You're going in there all by yourself?" Val said.

"Yes I am."

Jean returned with a full bag of shed stuff. He was very excited to start his mascot project. We went back to canary brainstorming on the way home, but once again, the conversation quickly degenerated. Alice didn't say much the whole night. I wished I could have done something to take the heavy weight off her shoulders.

The next morning, I woke up on my parents' floor with no sign of Flopper or a blanket or pillow, and snuck back upstairs before either member of the snoring section discovered me.

THIRTEEN

I DROVE THE Prius up the perfectly landscaped circular driveway of Alice's perfect white house with perfect hillside views. I was hoping Alice would emerge from her funk and help us sort school supplies with Val.

"Hey, Sadie," Alice said flatly after I rang the doorbell a dozen times and she finally shuffled to the door.

She led me through the immaculate rooms, each more nautical and sea-foam than the next. From the second-landing window, I could almost make out a square of ocean past the tree line.

Alice's room was as different from the rest of the house as Alice was. Tie-dyed tapestries covered with black-and-white photos of dogs covered the walls, and dream catchers hung from the ceiling.

The room smelled of essential oils. It smelled like Alice and a little bit like Shay.

We stretched out on the bed.

"Okay, tell me what I can do to help you feel better," I said.

"I don't think anybody can help me. I have this constant bad anxiety feeling. Izzy's parents are still planning to go to Croatia for their vacation. She convinced them it was the first time she tried drugs and she promised never to do heroin again." She threw up her hands. "Like, seriously, how are they letting her out of the hospital so soon?"

"It sucks so bad that you're going through this. It's too much."

"I can't even tell you what it has been like to deal with my best friend nodding off, trying to score smack all day, stealing money from my car, lying, smelling like shit because she never showers. It's hell."

"I'm so, so sorry." I reached out and touched her arm.

She turned on her side and faced me. Her mouth twisted from side to side.

"If I show you something, do you promise not to judge or tell anyone?" she whispered.

"Of course."

"It's weird, Sadie."

"Perfect, Alice. It's the summer of weird."

I followed her up a back staircase to a dark, creaky attic with high ceilings and swathes of cobwebs. We went through a smaller room and Alice moved an old hutch.

She pushed a handleless door inward and we inched sideways

through the narrow opening. The room, not much bigger than a closet, was empty except for a long folding table pushed up against the back wall. On the table, different-colored half-burnt candles were lined up in front of a row of handmade dolls.

"What the hell is this?" A chill ran all the way through me.

"You said you weren't going to judge."

"I'm not judging."

"You sound judgy."

"Oh my God. I'm not judging." I took a breath. "What is this, oh, friend who shall not be judged?"

"It's a voodoo altar. I made a voodoo doll of Hector, the dealer, and I am in the process of trying to eliminate him." She said it in a matter-of-fact way, as if eliminating drug dealers using voodoo was a thing.

I tried really hard not to be judgy. "Wow."

"I've spent a lot of time on message board support groups for addicts' loved ones, and at some point voodoo altars popped up. Sadie, I know it sounds crazy, but who knows? It could work." She picked up a doll made of black cloth with sewn-on button eyes and pins sticking out of its body.

"This is my attempt at a Hector poppet. I'm supposed to burn a black candle for seventeen minutes each day for nine days and drip the wax on the poppet. I'm only on day three. You guys have been distracting me."

I bent down to get a better look at the Hector poppet.

"Then what do you do?"

"I wrap him up and bury him in the cemetery with nine pennies and a bottle of rum, and that should do it."

She looked at me, trying to gauge my expression. I nodded. "I get it. I'd be making poppets, too, if my friend was a heroin addict."

"I just want Hector out. And I want my Neigh back." She wiped shavings of candle wax from the table and set little Hector down in his spot.

"Jean would not like this room," I said, walking out of the voodoo-altar-poppet closet.

"No. He would not," Alice said, pulling the door shut. "But we're not telling Jean. Or anyone else."

We went down to the hammock under a big oak tree in Alice's backyard.

"Will you come help Val tonight, Alice? Work can be a good distraction."

"I guess. I'm not going to be fun, though."

We lay side by side staring up at the thick overgrowth above us.

"Hey, I never asked you how the date with Javi's friend went."

I laughed. "Not good. He told Val he thought I was stuck-up."

"You're, like, the friendliest person I know. Was Javi an asshole?"

"Pretty much."

"Damn, I wish Val would get rid of that guy," Alice said. "She's too nice."

"Do you want to hear something awkward?" I said, turning toward Alice. "I kind of, sort of have feelings for Gordie Harris and I can't help it and I get he's gay, but, like, I get fluttery when he's close to me."

"Fluttery."

"Yes, Alice. Fluttery. I have to just put it out of my head, which I can do. It's my body that keeps doing the fluttery nonsense."

She stared at me blankly.

"What, Alice? Is that just too cheesy? God, I'm a loser."

She shook her head and stared down at the hunter-green hammock fabric. "Like that wasn't totally obvious."

"It's that obvious?"

"Yeah. It's pretty obvious. Maybe you're just missing sex and projecting it onto Gordie since he's around all the time."

"I've never actually had sex, so I'm not technically missing it."

"You didn't with Seth?"

"Everything but."

"Oh, yes, the good old everything but," Alice said. "This whole thing with Izzy has distracted me so much I don't remember the last time I thought about hooking up."

"Absent fluttery might be better than unrequited fluttery," I said, awkwardly swinging my legs over the side of the hammock.

"Okay, Sadie. I'll only go tonight if you promise never to use the word *fluttery* again."

"Fine. I'll never say FLUTTERY again." I leaned down and kissed Alice's forehead.

"Where are you going?"

"I have to run home before we help Val. You'd better be there. Otherwise, I *will* torment you with the *F* word forever."

On top of doing shifts at her grandparents' store and working on dozens of college scholarship applications, our petite, pigtailed Valeria was running a school-supply-collection empire.

Gordie, Alice, and I met Val at the farm stand, where Mute Mike hovered by his car waiting for Javi and Val to finish fighting.

"I'll see you there," Val said to Gordie and me as she loaded the last of the empty cardboard boxes into the back of her car en route to sort school supplies. A sullen Alice sat in Val's passenger seat. Izzy was refusing to acknowledge her texts.

Some guy near Amagansett had let Val use his barn to store the supplies she collected at the end of the school year, after she had the brilliant idea of asking kids from all the area schools to dump their unused supplies into bins during locker clean-out day. Then she hit up civic groups and churches, synagogues and summer camps.

"Man, Val's in a shitty situation," Gordie said.

"I know. She feels like she can't break up with him because he's sick. But I'd dump him because of the jealousy. It's annoying."

"How's *your* boyfriend over there?" Gordie said, raising his eyebrows and looking at Mute Mike across the parking lot.

"You're one to talk," I shot back. "Your boyfriend must be worse than Javi if you won't even talk about him. Or are *we* too lowbrow to meet *him*? Is it that guy Keith everybody was talking about at Speakeasy?"

He shook his head and stared forward. "You know what? I need to make a quick stop before we meet up with those guys."

"Wait, where? Val thinks we're right behind her."

"It'll be quick."

Gordie turned off the car on the edge of the farm stand parking lot and ran back inside. He came out with Farmer Brian, who was locking up, and a bag of sweet corn. He cut in front of a truck and turned right toward Southampton. A few more turns, and we pulled down a long driveway flanked by tall hedgerows.

"Come on."

"What are we doing?"

"Just come."

The house, which had yellow shingles and a white gazebo to the right of the garage, was landscaped immaculately. Dozens of blown-glass figurines and wind chimes dangled from a grove of birch trees to the left of the house. I stood on the front lawn while Gordie rang the bell.

"Mom! Mom! Gordie's here," a man shouted from behind the open windows on the first floor. The front door flew open, and a tall, gangly guy stepped out. He high-fived Gordie.

"What's up, Gordie?" the guy said, pressing his hands flat against Gordie's cheeks.

"I wanted you to meet my friend Sadie."

He turned and followed Gordie down the steps.

"Sadie, this is Keith. Keith, this is Sadie."

Keith extended his hand. "Nice to meet you, Sadie. I have a birth-day coming up."

He shook my hand and dropped it abruptly.

"Really, when?" I said, trying to figure out the connection between Keith and Gordie.

"Next week, on Tuesday. I'll be twenty-seven years young."

"That's great," I said.

"Gordie's taking me and David and my girlfriend, Zoe, to Speak-easy after ice cream cake at Turtle Trail."

Gordie took the bag of corn out of the backseat. "We can only stay five minutes, okay, bud? We brought you some sweet corn."

A lady with fluffy white hair and a powder-blue housedress stepped onto the front porch.

"Frances, this is my friend Sadie. She works at the farm stand," Gordie said. "We brought you some fruits of her labor."

"Lovely to meet you."

"How do you guys know each other?" I said as Frances gave me a warm hug.

Gordie draped his arm around the lady's shoulders. "Frances is my nanny. Keith and I have been buddies since I was a baby, huh, Keith?"

"Gordie and Sadie have to leave in two minutes," Keith said.

"That's okay, love," said Frances.

"Gordie can't shuck with me this time, huh?"

"He'll be back."

"I'll see you tomorrow at eleven thirty at Turtle Trail, right?" Keith said.

"Eleven thirty sharp," Gordie said. Keith set down the bag of corn and hugged Gordie.

"Bye, Sadie. You look like Princess Jasmine."

When we were in the car, Gordie said, "Keith has a bit of a Disney princess fetish."

"I've been called worse," I said. "He's sweet."

"Yeah. When I saw how well he was doing at Turtle Trail, I decided I needed to work there. And according to half our school, Keith and I have been dating for years."

It took a minute to register. The whole *Gordie Harris is gay* rumor started when the ruffians saw Gordie "hooking up" with some guy. The "some guy" was Keith. And the hookup...wasn't.

He stared at the road as we drove through the maze of hedgerows.

"So are you or aren't you gay?" I said it. I had to lay it out there.

"No. I'm not gay."

"Oh."

Silence.

"Aren't you a little old to have a nanny?"

Gordie laughed. "I'll never be too old to have a nanny."

"Where were you guys? I'm so overwhelmed right now." Val was drenched in sweat and trying to prop open a heavy barn door. "It's miserably hot in there. Jean's late and Alice is just sitting on a bucket."

We followed Val into the barn turned school-supply-stockpile warehouse.

"We need to sort the stuff into piles and box it up before the mice start getting at it," Val said. "A guy from the Rotary is donating backpacks, but I want to get it all sorted first."

The barn smelled like hay and tractor fuel. It was cluttered with rusty tools and stacks of old billboards. "*Biscuits and honey, five cents,*" Gordie read. "I could go for a biscuit with honey right about now."

"Can we focus?" Val was in worker-bee mode. She scurried around barking orders. Gordie and I were the only ones working. Jean was stuck at his job and Alice didn't move from her perch on an upside-down bucket. She held a stick in her right hand and her phone in her left. She drew *suck it* with her stick in the sawdust. She cleared that *suck it* and wrote a larger, neater *suck it*.

"Alice, get up. We need your muscles," I said. She wouldn't get up.

"Gordie, do you have any latex gloves in the back of your junkyard car?" Val called from the front of the barn. "I keep thinking a spider's going to eat my hand."

"No. But I have condoms. You could fashion a glove," Gordie called back.

Gordie Harris wasn't gay. Gordie Harris kept condoms in his car. It was getting more intriguing by the minute.

Jean arrived in cargo shorts and a fedora. "It's sweltering and I'm only helping if you scare those pigeons away." He lingered outside the barn door.

"We have a lot of neuroses to deal with here, don't we?" Gordie said.

"Oh, so you're not afraid of anything?" Val said, shoving a three-ring binder into an already full box.

"Being obsolete, maybe," Gordie said. He tossed a stack of notebooks into a clear plastic bin and lifted his gray ARMY T-shirt to wipe his face. I tried really hard not to notice his stomach and thought of how Alice had banned the word *fluttery* from our lexicon.

Alice dug the stick into the thick wood floor so violently it left a shallow gash; she still refused to move from her perch or join in our sorting. Even without her, we got a lot done. By the time we had sorted the mountain of supplies and boxed up the notebooks and binders, colored pencils, rulers, and other glaring reminders that yet another back-to-school was around the corner, it was dusk. And we were hot and filthy.

"Let's go find some biscuits with honey," Gordie said, lifting a plastic bin.

"Where are we going to find biscuits with honey?" I said. "This isn't Georgia."

Jean tried to push Alice to Val's car while she was still seated on the bucket, but she toppled face-first onto her impressive string of *suck it*s.

"Ahh. Cut the shit, Jean," she yelled, scrambling to get up from the barn floor.

"Ha. Now you're as gross as the rest of us," Val said. "We need to swim." Val put her hands on her hips and raised her eyebrows at Gordie.

"Nope. My parents are having a party."

We stood around drinking water and trying to decide whether we should drive all the way to the beach or just go home and shower like normal people.

"Wait, I know where we can go," Jean said.

"Where?" Val said. "I'm not going to the town pool."

"My girlfriend's house. She has a great swimming pond."

"Good one," Val said.

"Not kidding," Jean said.

"How have you not mentioned you have a girlfriend?" I said, wondering if he was serious.

"Or that you know people with 'swimming ponds'?" Val added.

Jean just smiled and jumped in the car.

We navigated the back roads in near darkness and tried to keep up with Jean's crazy driving.

Alice didn't say much from Val's backseat. She checked her phone and bit her nails and sighed a lot. But at least we got her out of her house and away from her dark arts and dark thoughts.

We finally pulled behind Jean on the side of a back road and walked single file down a path in a heavily wooded area. The path led to an unkempt lawn that stretched up a steep hill.

"I don't feel like swimming. I just want to go home," Alice said. She lagged behind the rest of us and held her long white-and-navy-striped skirt in a bunch near her knees.

"Fine, Alice. I'll take you home. Let's go." Val turned down the path.

"Forget it," Alice said, marching forward.

I fell back and walked alongside her.

"Can you try to put Izzy out of your mind, just for a little while?" I said softly. "You've been a really good friend. You've done everything you could, Alice."

She nodded and smacked at the growing swarm of mosquitoes.

Jean ran around the back of the house, which was covered in flat, hand-painted butterflies, hummingbirds, irises. The house had tattoos.

We grilled Jean about his supposed girlfriend and found out she was an eighteen-year-old Japanese girl named Umi who he'd met the summer before when he asked her to model for one of his masks. It turned out she lived in France and her sculptor mother owned the house and let Jean use the art studio over the garage.

"How do you communicate?" Alice said.

"In French, obviously," Jean said. He laughed. "I hooked up with Umi last summer, which her mom sort of doesn't know about. She certainly doesn't know the full extent of it." He raised his eyebrows and flashed a smile. "She made Umi stay in Paris for a stupid internship this summer, but we talk pretty much every day and she's coming here for Christmas break."

Jean pointed out the studio but wouldn't let us in because of his half-finished top secret mascot project.

"Alice, what's wrong?" Val bent over Alice, who had sat down in the grass, cradling her phone. She ran her hand through her hair and tossed her phone on the ground. I reached for it and looked at the text. It was from Izzy.

Pooch. Please help me. I'm at the shrink's. I'm so cold.

Alice jumped up. "I have to go get Izzy."

Gordie put his arm around Alice. "*We* have to go get Izzy."

❧ FOURTEEN ❧

WE LEFT JEAN'S and Val's cars at the farm stand and loaded into the Range Rover, bound for Westhampton.

"A guy from the city rents a summer house in the middle of nowhere," Alice said. "He's a friggin' psychiatrist and he got his license suspended after they caught him prescribing Oxy to anyone with cash. Now he's dealing heroin. He's, like, forty years old and hooking up with girls half his age in exchange for drugs."

"That is sickening," Val said.

"Oh, you don't know the half of it," Alice said. She wrapped her arms around the front of her and stared out the window. "The shrink is even worse than Hector. I can't believe her parents let her go out. She just got out of the hospital."

For a while nobody said anything. We were anxious about what we would find at the trap house. Val sat between Alice and me furiously texting Javi, who had been looking for her.

"Is anyone else a little nervous about this?" Jean said as we turned onto a narrow road. It was so dark we could barely see in front of us.

"Pull up over there, Gordie," Alice said. "Cut the lights. You guys stay here. I'll be back in a minute."

"Wait, you're not going in there alone. Let me go with you," Gordie said.

"Hell no. You look like a narc." Alice threw her wallet and keys on the dashboard.

"I'm going," I said.

"No, you're not."

I followed her anyway, leaving the others fighting in the Range Rover about who looked the least like a narc and should be going with us.

We held on to each other and followed the beam from Alice's phone light up the long driveway. Three cars were parked near the garage. According to Alice, none of them was Hector's.

"Maybe your spell worked," I whispered.

Alice tried the door. It was open. The hot, dank house smelled like rotten garbage. We walked down a narrow hallway toward a back kitchen connected to an open great room. The room was hazy with cigarette smoke, and eerily quiet except for a low moaning and the sound of running water. It took a few seconds for my eyes to adjust to the smoky dimness.

There were mattresses laid out in the middle of the floor, and people lying on the mattresses. I noticed the arm of a man flung out, covered in scabs, and a woman in white shorts and a Snoopy T-shirt lying next to him, her eyes half open. And there was a girl perched inside an open fireplace, with soot covering her feet.

"Where's Izzy?" Alice said to an old guy lying on the couch staring at the muted TV screen. The light from the screen danced across the faces of the mattress people. A discarded pizza box on a glass-topped coffee table housed a pile of needles and a square of charred foil. The man on the mattress dragged his filthy fingernails across his stomach. I took a few steps closer to the fireplace. The girl turned her face and smiled at me.

"Ward, focus, I'm trying to find Izzy," Alice said to the old guy on the couch. Her voice was strong and fearless. She was superhero Alice, and I was her awkward sidekick.

"I think she's in the shower," the guy said, his eyes still staring straight ahead.

Alice turned toward me and rolled her eyes. "Dirtbag," she said. "Let's check upstairs."

I grabbed Alice's hand. It was cold and clammy. She squeezed my hand back and pulled me toward the stairs. At the top, a stained-glass sailboat night-light lit a small bathroom that stank of urine. Brown stains splattered the tiled wall. Water ran from the sink faucet.

"Should I turn it off?" I whispered.

"No. Don't touch anything. Stay here." Alice put her hand flat on my chest. "I mean it, Sadie."

I stood there while Alice stormed down the hall and flung open a door.

"Get the fuck away from my friend," she yelled. A few seconds later Alice came out of the bedroom with Izzy, who was wrapped in a crumpled sheet.

"I decided to stay," Izzy said. Her stringy hair was stuck to her face.

Alice held Izzy's hand and yanked her along. "Come on, Sadie."

I followed them down the stairs and helped half carry the barefoot Izzy through the maze of trees. We pushed her into the backseat next to Val and squeezed in.

"Oh, thank God," Val said. "We were freaking out."

"Who's this?" Izzy said, touching my face with ice-cold fingertips.

"Remember Sadie from Girl Scouts?" Alice said.

"Hi, Neigh!"

"Hi, Sadie. You're still doing Girl Scouts?" Izzy said, smiling. She turned toward Alice. "You're my best friend, Pooch."

"Yes, sweetie, I am." Alice's expression softened. Her eyes filled with tears.

Gordie drove straight to the hospital.

Jean turned on the playlist and we serenaded Izzy with "Blackbird" by the Beatles all the way to the emergency room.

Alice's dad met us at Gordie's car. Her mom was on the phone, pacing near our bench, trying to figure out how to find Izzy's parents, who were out at a charity gala. Alice and her dad rushed Izzy inside. I imagined the people from the golf club were already playing a mean game of telephone starting with *Isn't that a shame? Another one of our girls on heroin* and ending with *Damn immigrants holding our kids hostage.*

We lingered on our bench in dazed silence until Alice told us that Izzy had been admitted and she was going to stay with her. As the rest of us sat in the farm stand parking lot talking about the trap house, Alice texted a picture of herself eating Izzy's roommate's hospital food while Izzy slept. She captioned it Yummy.

Gordie dropped me off last. The whole way home he told me how pissed he was with himself for letting me and Alice go into that house alone.

"We're not delicate little violets, Gordie. We don't need a body-guard to protect us."

"I didn't say you were. It just felt really wrong sitting in the car while you and Alice went into that house."

We talked in my driveway. I didn't want to leave.

"Gordie, do you think I could get a hug?" I said, my voice cracking.

He smiled. "Yeah. You can get a hug."

He got out and met me on the passenger side. He scooped me into his broad chest and hugged me for a long time. "Some fucked-up shit, huh?" he whispered.

"Ya think?"

"Can you do me a favor, Sadie?" He stepped back, held my shoulders, and looked down into my eyes. "Can you never go into a trap house again?"

"I have no desire to ever go into a trap house again, Gordie. Trust me."

"Good. Glad that's settled." He squeezed my shoulders. "Good night, Sullivan."

It was too much. All of it. The smells and sounds and spattered blood of the heroin house. Izzy's vacant eyes. The diamonds. The ridiculously unclear expectations of an old dead man.

I bypassed my parents' floor and crawled between them in their queen-size bed. I lay facing the ceiling, playing with Flopper's tail and thinking wild thoughts amid the weirdly comforting snores and nose whistles of my mother and father.

"Look who decided to grace us with her presence," Dad said the next night, only half joking.

Grandma Sullivan banged around in the kitchen while Mom set the table and Grandma Hosseini carefully removed teacups from the china cabinet.

"Hey, Grandma, do you know how to make homemade biscuits?" I asked Grandma Sullivan as she salted the boiled potatoes.

"I do."

"Can you teach me how to make them?"

She eyed me suspiciously. I had never shown interest in doing anything in the kitchen.

"I suppose."

"Tonight?"

"No. I'm going for lotto tickets after supper."

"I'll take you and we can get biscuit supplies."

"I'll be too tired."

"Please?" I gave Grandma Sullivan a pouty lip.

She eyed me again. "I guess we could whip up some biscuits."

Later, after we'd eaten half the biscuits with vanilla custard and fresh, sliced strawberries, I left a glass container of biscuits with a tiny tub of farm stand honey and a note addressed to Gordie Harris on Gordie's front step. The note said: *Kinky 3, Thanks for introducing me to Keith and Frances. It was really nice to meet them. Hope you're still craving biscuits with honey. I'll collect my five cents later. —Cakes*

I flipped through my *Guide to Northeast Colleges* in the dim light of my sweltering room. It was after midnight, still too early for Shay to be back in her bunk, but I tried her anyway. When she didn't answer, I texted, Should I put Pepperdine on my list? I wondered if Shay even wanted me near her, after her string of avoidance texts, all of which had to do with how *busy* she was.

I'll let you know if I ever make it to Pepperdine, she texted back. These campers are driving me crazy. I'm never having kids.

I wrote, Remember when we babysat that kid who wiped his ass with a bath towel and put it back on the rack and you used the towel to dry your hair?

She didn't write back.

I didn't want to go to sleep. I was getting anxious at the thought of waking with that deep ache in the pit of my stomach. I considered starting the report Mom had been hounding me to write, but rehashing the incident didn't seem like a good late-night activity. I logged on to baby Ella's grandmother's Facebook page. She hadn't updated it in weeks. I clicked on the NeighborCare link. The sum collected hadn't changed. Still $120.

Still not enough.

The only thing I could think about doing in the middle of the night was to remove the fortress of junk I had stacked in front of the suitcase in my already overcrowded closet and dislodge Andy from his garment bag. I extracted the cheesecloth bags from Andy's dismembered legs and loins and set them on the middle of my bed. One by one, I dumped the contents into the pink plastic barf tub.

Counting diamonds was strangely therapeutic.

❧ FIFTEEN ❧

"YOU'RE WEARING THAT?" Mom said when she arrived at the farm stand to get me for my appointment with Willie Ng's therapist in Sag Harbor.

"Did you want me to wear my prom dress?"

"How about something that doesn't have stains all over the front?"

"This is residue from blueberries, because I work at a farm stand. It'll be a good thing to start with in the therapy session. It's a metaphor for the stain the incident has left on my psyche, at least according to you."

"Sadie, why do you have to be like that? I just want to help you process what happened."

"Mom. I barely even think about what happened. I have no idea why I've been so freaked out at night."

"We're here to figure out why. Let's just go into this with an open mind, honey. Can you try not to be so irritable? I just want you to have what I didn't have." What Mom didn't have was any kind of emotional support when all hell broke loose in Iran and her family was forced to flee, which meant no chance of college for Mom.

I crossed my arms in front of me and stared out the window as she sped down the back roads.

"Don't mention anything about Willie Ng," she said under her breath before we went into the white clapboard house turned psychiatric wellness center.

Mom stayed the whole session, which went better than I thought it would. I cried, mostly because he got me to talk about the baby and how terrible it was that she had to go through that ordeal. Mom cried talking about how scary it was to see me in the hospital and how anxious she got every time the phone rang. I was beginning to think she needed therapy more than I did. The therapist, an old white guy with thick white hair and a Mickey Mouse T-shirt that had more stains than mine, talked about the effects of traumatic events, and that my bad nights were normal and, basically, that everything was going to be okay.

After we blew our noses, I told Mom I would be willing to see the guy alone next time and that I was sorry I had been cranky. She smiled and rubbed my back.

"Can you imagine Willie Ng in here talking about his porn?" I joked.

"Not funny, Sadie. The Ngs are going through a hard time right now."

We went for manicures and Chinese food and talked about Mom's life in Iran before all hell broke loose.

"I wish my mother believed in therapists," Mom said, her mouth full of noodles.

"You can't *not* believe in therapists," I said. "They're not fairies."

"They might as well be to Grandma Hosseini." Mom cracked open a fortune cookie and read, "*Your shoes will make you happy today.*"

We looked down at Mom's cream-colored high-heeled sandals and my once-white Converse, caked with grime, and laughed. "Profound, Mom," I said. "Really deep."

The Unlikelies came over to "watch a movie on my laptop." Dad and Mom were already settled on the porch drinking decaf and eating peach pie out of the pie pan.

"Why don't you just watch it on the television?" Dad said. "Why are you all going to crowd around a laptop?"

"It's not really a movie. It's a new YouTube thing," I said, turning up Dad's Springsteen music ever so slightly, just to make sure they couldn't eavesdrop, before ushering Alice, Val, and Gordie into the front hallway and letting the door slam behind me.

"That wasn't suspicious at all," Gordie said, lying down on my bed after we made our way up to my room.

Alice was distracted with her phone. She looked up and smiled weirdly at Val and me. "Izzy's parents want you guys to visit Izzy with me," Alice said.

"Why us?" I said, glancing at Val.

"They think some good, clean, homegrown hero fun will be good for Izzy." Izzy's parents truly believed they could nurse her back to health with chicken soup and gossip magazines like she had a nasty case of bronchitis.

Val and I agreed to go, but I could tell by the look on Val's face that she was as uncomfortable with the idea as I was.

"Nice bobblehead," Alice said, shaking Shay and me. "Hey, let's text Shay."

Alice took a close-up of her silver nose ring with my phone and sent it to Shay, captioned with the classic Girl Scout mantra Make new friends, but keep the old. One is silver and the other's gold.

Shay didn't reply.

We waited for Jean, who was late because he was *creating* and later because he decided to take Dad up on his invite to *sit and hang out for a few*. By the time he got upstairs with his mysterious bag, the rest of us were over hearing about how Val and Javi were in a great place and he took her to dinner at Red Lobster and they had crazy great sex in Javi's car.

"Okay, vomit," Alice said, taking down a photo of Seth from my bulletin board and holding it up. "He's really hairy, huh?"

Gordie laughed, turned over on his side, and hugged my Flopper.

As Jean fumbled around his duffel bag preparing his big reveal, Alice texted, How does it feel having Gordie Harris lying on your bed?

OMG. Stop, I texted back.

Let me guess . . . it rhymes with buttery. Or sluttery?

I texted back, Fluttery fluttery fluttery fluttery.

"I'm going to be royally pissed if you don't like this. I've been working my ass off in the studio trying to get it right," Jean said.

"Show us. Show us," we all chanted. I jumped up and locked my door.

Jean reached into his duffel bag and brought out our new mascot.

At first, we didn't know what to think. It was beautiful and bizarre at the same time.

"I took the Civil War dolls from Mr. Upton's shed and made miniature custom masks," Jean said as we examined the five smiling masked Union soldiers joined together at the hands.

There was the bearded Ulysses S. Grant Haitian carnival mask with curved horns, the wooden Salvadoran goddess mask in pigtails, the metal Persian warrior mask interwoven with intricate Celtic symbols.

"This is a perfect Sadie mask," I said, moving in to look more closely.

Gordie's Scottish mask was made of wood and painted bright blue and white. Jean had fastened a tiny kilt around the soldier's waist. And Alice got her many-colored smiling dog carved from a coconut shell.

"This is brilliant. Not only did you capture the essence of the Unlikelies, the masks somehow look like *us*," Gordie said. He got up and half hugged Jean, who nodded and broke into a huge smile.

"Phew, I was nervous."

We positioned the line of tiny-masked soldiers in all different kinds of light, making sure there was nothing near them identifying my bedroom. Alice got her camera from the car and shot until we caught the right angle.

And our mascot avatar was born.

Gordie promptly uploaded it and blasted every single site we had ever anti-trolled.

Kinky 3, Cakes, Hermanita, Pierre, and Cecil were gone forever, replaced by smiling, hand-holding masked soldiers standing five in a row.

It was the perfect blend of mysterious, powerful, and weirdly inspiring.

"Everybody get comfortable," I said. "We have a lot to discuss."

Things got real when I unearthed the pink barf bucket of yellow diamonds.

Alice, Val, and Jean stared at the polished stones layered at the bottom of the bucket while Gordie arranged the masked soldiers, Flopper, and my bobbleheads on the window seat.

I Googled *yellow diamonds*. "They do call them canary diamonds," I said, surprised.

"Why do you think I've been calling them that?" Gordie said, laughing.

I studied the screen. "They were so rare in the nineteen twenties there were well-known smuggling networks going from Africa to Canada to major US cities."

Gordie let out a howl. Jean was staging a bobblehead and masked Civil War doll orgy.

"Is anyone listening to me?"

"I am," Val said.

"I'm playing with diamonds," Alice said.

"Shh," I hissed. "My mother has bionic hearing. Call them *canaries*. Now we know why the lizard spent his time in Nova Scotia. He was smuggling," I said, closing the laptop. "Come on, can we focus?"

I had to threaten to kick everybody out before they agreed to help me brainstorm legitimate ways to redeem the lizard's evil deeds. I passed out green index cards and we sat in a circle on the floor, hunched over with pensive expressions.

Five minutes later, we each dropped a stack of folded cards into the middle of our circle. I gathered them up and drew the first folded card: *Start a homeless shelter for vulnerable youth.*

"That's Val's handwriting," Jean said, grabbing the card. I slapped his hand and drew again.

Hotel for old, drunk hookers. I threw Jean's card at him.

Bed-and-breakfast for old, drunk hookers. I threw Gordie's card and punched him.

Humane Society. (They need a new facility.) "Nice, Alice, but Mr. Upton already gave a lot to the Humane Society."

They wrote another batch of cards, but we found a reason to veto each idea.

"In all seriousness, I'd buy land," Gordie said. "Just stretches of open land that developers could never get their hands on. I'd be like the modern-day Teddy Roosevelt."

"That's not a bad idea," Alice said.

"Although we wouldn't be able to get much. Maybe in Siberia," Gordie said. "But that'll be prime real estate when global warming ramps up."

Frustrated and exhausted, I got up and ripped the green index cards into bits. We stuffed the diamonds back into the cheesecloth bags and into Andy's legs and groin, prompting more annoying jokes from Jean and Gordie.

"Love you guys. Bye, now," I said, pushing the Unlikelies out the door.

I flung my exhausted body facedown onto my bed.

My pillow smelled like Gordie Harris.

❧ SIXTEEN ❧

VAL'S CRAPPY CAR was immaculate on the inside since she'd gotten rid of the school supplies. "You're so orderly," I said, moving the
dried-out Palm Sunday palm leaf so I could check myself in the mirror. There it was, the monster tail, curled tight under my brow line. In
the early afternoon light, it looked like a slightly lighter tongue color.

"Are you dreading this, too?" Val said as we set out for Izzy's
house.

"I don't want any part of this. But Alice would do it for us."

We merged with the endless procession of impatient cars.

Val sighed. "Can I just tell you, Sadie, I'm reaching the end of my
Javi rope."

"I thought you just had a great night. What happened now?"

"It's not one thing. It's all the stuff I've told you. He doesn't talk about anything interesting. He's pissed at me half the time we're together. He takes too many naps. He doesn't want to go to the beach or to concerts or do any of the activities I like. He wants to binge-watch his shows and play video games and take hookup breaks. That's it."

"Is it possible he takes naps because of the lupus?"

"You're not helping, Sadie. At all."

"What does Mute Mike do during the hookup breaks?"

"He makes us something to eat."

"Okay, that's weird."

"There's a new lupus medication that's supposed to help a lot, which means Javi might have more energy to do things with me. But it's not covered by his insurance *and* it's a thousand dollars a month."

"How is that even possible?" We passed the farm stand. "I wish I could be like all those rich people buying twelve-dollar hunks of cheese," I said.

"People pay twelve dollars for cheese?"

"Yes, cidiots do. And then they throw eleven dollars' worth of the cheese in the trash can and take off in their BMWs while your boyfriend suffers on the couch," I said. "He's not too sick to hook up, though, huh?"

"Is any guy too sick to hook up?"

I thought about the diamonds, lying there in the back of my closet. I almost said something about slipping a couple to Javi. But I didn't have time to process that thought.

Throngs of hydrangeas greeted us in front of Izzy's gray-shingled house.

"What is with these mega houses?" Val said. We got out of her dwarf car, parked next to twin SUVs. "Can you imagine trying to clean this place?"

"These people have staff."

A lady wearing a white tennis skirt and a lavender V-neck top waved from the open front door. "Girls, we're so glad you came. Alice told me all about your homegrown hero projects."

"Thanks," we said in unison.

"Thank you for being there to help Izzy," she said, pouring iced lemon water from a pitcher on a tray. "It's been quite an ordeal," she said, handing us glasses.

She didn't seem to realize that the *ordeal* had been a year in the making.

We found Alice sitting on the floor at the top of the spiral staircase. "Look what I brought Izzy," Alice said with a baby voice. Three puppies ran between Alice and Izzy's brother, Tanner.

"They're fresh off the streets of Jersey City. I'm giving their foster mom a break."

"Ew. It pooped, Pooch." Izzy's brother pointed to a load of puppy poop on the hardwood floor.

"Tanner, go get paper towels."

"That's nothing compared to Izzy's massive diarrhea situation. She's been going for days," Alice whispered when Tanner was downstairs.

"Can you poop out heroin?" Val said.

Alice laughed. "Only if you swallow it in bags and smuggle it across the border."

"Hey, guys," Izzy said as we entered her room. "Come here, puppies."

Izzy looked nothing like the scraggly-haired girl wrapped in the filthy sheet. She was clean and dressed in sweatpants and a black-and-white-striped shirt. Her long strawberry-blond hair hung in waves down her back.

We hung out on Izzy's bed, making fun of Alice, telling Gordie and Jean stories. We didn't talk about that night or heroin or the way Izzy's legs twitched or the way her face glazed over every so often, in between sweet smiles.

We showed Izzy Instagram pictures we had taken of Gordie's basement movie theater. "He's hot," Izzy said.

Alice looked at me and smiled. "He is hot. He's also gay."

"Or not," I said before I could catch myself. I felt the heat rise up through my face.

Alice and Val pressed me until I told them the Keith story.

"Well, this is an interesting turn of events," Alice said.

"Speak of him again and I'll say the *F* word a thousand times," I said.

"*Fuck?*" Izzy said.

"No. It's a way more irritating word than *that*." Alice flipped through an old photo album and showed us pictures of her and Izzy on horses, on sailboats, rolling down grassy Hamptons hills, smiling toothless smiles.

"Here's the one I was looking for," Alice said, pulling out a faded photo of two little girls standing in front of Dad's truck. "It's us with Woody the ice cream man." Dad grinned in the background, giving a thumbless thumbs-up through the window.

"That might just be the coolest dad job in the universe," Izzy said.

"I like to think so," I said, studying the picture.

There were moments of awkward silence, moments we might have filled with words of encouragement or support. But we chose to avoid the real reason we were there: to try to keep Izzy out of trap houses.

"I want to be a homegrown hero," Izzy said after we told her about the Rotary luncheon. "I don't know if I have it in me."

"Everyone has it in them, Iz," Alice said firmly.

"I got my hero status by doing something really stupid," I said. "But then again, my great-grandmother, also named Sadie, lost both her feet saving children from a burning building."

"Do you think she was ever sorry she did that?" Val said. "It must have been tough getting around."

"My grandma Sullivan, her daughter-in-law, calls her the family fool."

"My grandma drinks a fifth of vodka every day before lunch," Izzy said with a strange smile. "It doesn't seem to affect her golf game, though." She got under the covers. "God, I'm exhausted."

Izzy gave me the photo of them in front of Dad's truck. She hugged Val and me and told us to come back and hang out again. We left her surrounded by sleeping puppies and Alice.

"That went well," Val said, right before a text came in from Alice.

Maybe someday you'll meet Izzy when she isn't using. I guess she had a secret stash. I can't do this anymore.

"What?" Val said.

Neither of us had a clue.

"Why have we not called the cops on the trap house?" Val said as we sat in my driveway trying to figure out how to help Alice.

Why have we not called the cops on the shrink's house? I texted Alice.

Because I didn't want Izzy to get arrested.

I wrote back, We need to try SOMETHING.

Later that night, the five of us met in front of Jean's work for a five-minute powwow. Val and I had typed a letter wearing latex gloves, because paranoid Val didn't want the cops to find fingerprints. We wrote down the dealers' names, and the psychiatrist's address, and a detailed description of the trap house and what was going on there. We signed the note *The Unlikelies* under a photo of our avatar and dropped it in a Bridgehampton mailbox.

We would have to wait. Hope. And wait.

❧ SEVENTEEN ❧

I THREW THE last few heads of romaine out back and husked the butter-and-sugar corn for the people who were too lazy or busy or entitled to do it themselves. A black Mercedes pulled into the lot. I wiped my hands on my shorts and squinted in the bright sun.

"Well, if it isn't Sadie Sullivan," Gordie said, getting out of the passenger side. His mom jumped out and propped her designer sunglasses on top of her sassy bob. She opened the back door and pulled out reusable shopping bags.

"Hi, Sadie. Nice to see you. We are on a quest for peaches. Gordie makes a mean cobbler."

"Oh, yeah? Gordie, when were you going to make me some cobbler?"

"You want cobbler? I'll make you cobbler," Gordie said, examining the peaches as if he were old Mr. Upton himself.

"My whole side of the family is heading down from Maine this week," Gordie's mom said, shaking her head. "They're assuming I'll have a big Hamptons meal ready upon arrival." She was one of those moms who talked to everybody like they were her best friends. She was fresh-faced and very perky.

Gordie packed containers of cheese curds and strawberry jam into a reusable bag. His mom asked me to help her choose flowers for her basket.

"Steven and I are beyond thrilled Gordie's been hanging out with you and the other kids. Reid ditched him last summer for that nutty Claire. And it's taken Gordie a long time to get over Sylvie. He was a mess for a while."

Sylvie. Sylvie. Who was Sylvie?

I knew Gordie would be mortified by his mom's oversharing. But I wanted more Gordie Harris dirt.

"Yeah, I've been there," I said.

"She strung him along for a year. I told him not to get involved with an older woman. Anyway, good riddance. She was a flake. You kids are welcome at the house anytime. I mean that."

"Thank you, Mrs. Harris."

"Call me Bonnie."

"Mom, you all set?" Gordie called from the register.

They piled two hundred dollars' worth of stuff on the counter. I wouldn't mention the multiple bricks of twelve-dollar cheese to Val.

"How's Izzy?" Gordie said as his mom chatted with Daniela about her impending company and how she still needed to get all the guest rooms ready and buy the steamers and God forbid they didn't have wine from a local winery.

"I thought she was okay when we went to see her, but then Alice said she was strung out the whole time we were there. I feel so bad for Alice. She just sat there looking through photo albums of her and Izzy from when they were little."

"The whole thing sucks," Gordie said.

"Those dealers are lizards," I said.

"Evil lizards. Hey, I'm taking Keith and his friends from Turtle Trail to Speakeasy tomorrow night for Keith's birthday. You want to go?"

"What about your relatives from Maine?"

"I'll ply them with cobbler and make a quiet exit."

"I want cobbler."

He smiled. "I owe you for those damn good biscuits."

I waved to Gordie and his mom as the Mercedes drove off. *Sylvie. Sylvie.* I remembered the beautiful blond Shay clone singing onstage that night at Speakeasy.

You'll never guess who Gordie used to date, I texted Val and Alice right away. I couldn't resist.

I asked everybody to meet at the duck pond before we went to Keith's birthday night at Speakeasy.

We sat on the faded lawn, dried out from days of cloudless sun, and picked at the brown blades of grass and our mosquito-bite scabs. I had been thinking a lot about Mr. Upton's words, about his wishes.

I scooted back and faced the others, took a sip of warm seltzer water, and cleared my throat. "Let me just get this out." They looked up. "I was thinking I would like to send a diamond to the baby from the incident. Her name is Ella. Her father, clearly also a lizard, is in jail and hopefully will be for a while. Her grandmother started a NeighborCare page, which is not doing well. I want them to have a diamond."

They all thought it was a great idea, and I felt relieved, until things got complicated.

We argued over logistics, the details of the operation. We agreed it would be pretty obvious if we sent only Ella's family a diamond. So we would choose a few families from around the country on NeighborCare. We would wrap the canaries in simple packages, with a personalized note, and send the packages from various spots on Long Island.

"Nobody sends loose diamonds in the mail," Alice said.

"Do you have a better idea?" Gordie said.

She didn't. Besides, even if a couple of diamonds got lost along the way, there were more. Plenty more. It wasn't a grand plan, but it was a beginning. And most important, it felt right.

We sealed the deal with ten hands piled in the middle of our circle.

"I can't believe I'm missing tonight. I'm literally sick to my stomach," Val said. She had given in to Javi's guilt trip and promised she'd hang out with him. She got in her car, and the rest of us left to pick up Keith and his friend David and Keith's girlfriend, Zoe.

I jumped out of Alice's Subaru when we pulled behind Gordie and Jean in Keith's driveway. "Happy birthday, Keith," I said, rummaging around my bag for a wrapped gift.

"We were supposed to bring gifts?" Alice said.

Gordie made the introductions.

"Twenty-seven years young," Keith said.

"Impressive, dude," Jean said.

"Can I open it?"

"Of course," I said as Keith took the gift and ripped off the tissue paper.

"I have to show my mom. Thank you. This is awesome." Keith put the Woody's Ice Cream hat on and ran into the house.

"Can I get one of those?" Zoe said.

"On your birthday, Zo," Gordie said. "Sadie's a good gift giver, huh?" He smiled down at Zoe, who was under five feet tall, and seemed like half of Keith's size. Keith's friend David stood next to the car with his hands in his dress pants pockets. He looked older than Keith, with the slightest hint of gray dusting the ends of his shaggy black hair.

"Can we go?" Alice shouted out the window. "It's hot as balls out and I refuse to let my car idle."

"She has purple hair," Keith announced, running down the steps.

"Yes, yes she does," I said.

Speakeasy didn't feel right without Val. Gordie was busy introducing Jean to the throngs of girls fawning all over him. Keith had a minor freak-out when we couldn't find his headphones, but we recovered them from deep in Gordie's cluttered trunk.

"He's really sensitive to sounds. He wears the headphones and then he's good to dance," Gordie said as we followed Keith, Zoe, and David into the ballroom. The infamous Sylvie practically attacked Keith.

Alice and I went out to the back hill, where a few people sat around a bonfire.

Val texted, I feel like I'm in prison. Send pics. What am I missing?

I texted her a picture of Alice lying in the grass. The boys ditched us to flirt with women. You're missing nothing.

"I stopped by Izzy's this morning," Alice said. "She was outside playing badminton with Tanner."

"That's great," I said.

"Maybe, except I've known Izzy her whole life. She's never played badminton and she's never hung out with Tanner. It's almost like she was putting on a show. And she was abnormally nice. Another red flag."

"People change. Maybe she's trying to get a new lease on life." I didn't even believe what I was saying.

"Maybe." Alice rummaged around her vegan leather satchel for gum. "Izzy's mom cried when she saw me. She's really unhinged, that one. I've never seen an ounce of emotion on her Botoxed face. Now she can't stop blubbering."

"Can you blame the woman?" I said. "Her daughter is being stalked by lizards."

"There are lizards everywhere, Sadie. Swarms of lizards."

"I know."

"I just know in my heart if Hector's out of the picture, it'll be so much harder for Izzy to get the shit."

"Keep stabbing the poppet."

"I will."

When we went back inside, Jean was dancing with a group of girls. Keith and David were jumping up and down in the middle of the dance floor, and Zoe was swaying near the stage. Gordie played harmonica next to Sylvie, who was singing a song in Spanish. Of course perfect Sylvie spoke Spanish.

I sent a recording of the beautiful moment to Val with the caption Mucho barfo.

Val texted back immediately: Jealous?

Maybe I was a little jealous of Sylvie. The night wasn't nearly as magical as our first night at Speakeasy. But the energy of the room crept up through my soul and pulled me into the swarm of thumping, moving, gyrating bodies. It was only when Gordie called Keith up so the whole room could sing "Happy Birthday" that I noticed the smile on Sylvie's face droop ever so slightly. Part of me wondered if it was because Keith had grabbed the mic and was telling everyone about the Woody's Ice Cream hat Sadie had bought him.

When we were all standing around Gordie's car, waiting for David to find Keith and Zoe, who, according to David, were definitely making out, Gordie whispered something to Jean.

"Why are you whispering?" Alice said. "That's rude."

"Can't we have any guy things?" Gordie said. "You're like my mom."

"If you must know, he asked me if I got any chicks' numbers. And I did not, because I'm into Umi."

"Wow. This chick must be pretty special," Gordie said.

"Can you stop saying *chick*? You sound ridiculous," I said.

"Oh, okay, Political Correction Officer."

"Umi gets me to the core," Jean randomly announced.

"Dreamy," Alice said as David, Keith, and Zoe came from behind Speakeasy.

"Were you right, David?" Alice winked. He nodded and rolled his eyes.

When I got home, I collapsed onto my bed fully dressed and still damp with sweat. I played with Flopper's whiskers, fell into a deep sleep, and didn't wake until Mom flicked me with her clawlike nails and threatened a ten o'clock curfew if I couldn't get myself up for work.

❧ EIGHTEEN ❧

JEAN'S CAR FLEW into the farm stand parking lot so quickly adrenaline shot through me. It ushered in a flood of images: the sedan, the baby's cries, my head crashing down on the toolbox.

"What the hell, Jean? You can't drive like that," I yelled when he flung open his dented car door.

He ignored me. "Why do you never check your damn phone?"

I motioned toward the truck of crates I was helping unload behind the farm stand. "Uh. I'm working."

"Sadie, the cops busted the trap house."

"Wait. What?"

"Yeah, I got a news alert and I rushed over there. They have the whole property taped off. There are, like, twenty patrol cars—unmarked cars, DEA, I think."

I was shocked.

"I can't believe they took our note seriously. Do you even know how amazing this is?" I shoved Jean.

"Who knows if it was the note? Maybe the cops were watching that house for a while."

"Whatever. It's done. They busted that awful place," I said, grabbing Jean's hand.

I had missed dozens of texts.

Take that, you soulless lizards, Val texted.

Did they nab Hector? Alice texted.

We had no idea.

That night, Mom and Dad had the news on in the background. They didn't even notice the news lady standing in front of the Westhampton rental house, her back to the yellow police tape. Hers was the headline story about how the East End task force and multiple other agencies had worked in tandem to take down the psychiatrist turned drug lord. The news liked that angle.

I hummed with adrenaline, attached to the newsfeed on my phone, as I spent the night on the porch with my parents and the neighbors.

"Oh, Dad, I have a cute picture to show you." I grabbed my bag from the front hall table and riffled around for the Izzy picture. "Look, it's Alice when she was little. She's with her friend Izzy. And look who's smiling in the background."

Dad studied the photo. "Well, I'll be damned. I had a lot more hair back then."

"You're not balding, Woody," Mom said, looking at the picture.

"No, but it's thinning. Look how thick it was. That was before the new truck."

I almost told them Alice's best friend was mixed up in drugs and that she was supposedly healing in her perfectly appointed house. I would have told them the light version of the story and left out the part about me risking my life to go into a trap house. But even the light version was too heavy for my parents. I didn't want them to think I was going to get mixed up in drugs, or that Alice was, in some way, a bad influence.

Alice texted us, Almost time for eleven o'clock news. Somebody watch channel seven. Want to see if they give Hector's name.

I went inside and sat in front of the TV, mindlessly overeating salted almonds while the newspeople reported on a massive fire in an abandoned lot. How is this nonsense news? Jean texted.

The headline popped up before they showed the video of the heroin house. FORMER NEW YORK PSYCHIATRIST ARRESTED IN MASSIVE EAST END DRUG BUST. There was nothing about the drug dealer known as Hector. There was nothing about the people rotting away in that house, or their festering scabs.

Fuck the news, Alice texted. Hector slipped away like the slimy piece-of-shit worm that he is.

I'm thinking of signing onto all our anti-trolling sites with our avatar, like streamlining, taking it to the next level, Gordie texted.

Well, get on it, nerd boy, I texted. I had no idea what he was talking about.

Alice disappeared from our thread. I imagined her stomping around in her attic, stabbing the little Hector poppet with pins as the candles cast creepy shadows on the walls.

I signed on to Ella's NeighborCare page. Nobody had donated.

Still awake, huh? Gordie texted. I had moved on to Ella's grandma's Facebook page.

How did you know?

I can see you on FB. Why are you on FB?

I've developed this weird obsession with the baby from the incident. Her grandma posts pictures sometimes.

You are sweet, Sadie Cakes.

Don't fucking call me that.

Okay. Okay. I'll stop.

Thank you.

Come over.

Why?

Just come over and hang out.

My stomach dropped. Gordie was obviously bored and nerding out with his Unlikelies avatar project and wanting a friend to keep him company. But I couldn't help that fluttering, that stupid fluttering. I'd spent two full years of middle school running away from that feeling. I would stand behind him in the cafeteria line or unexpectedly turn the corner and run into him, and my face would get hot and he would look away and I would, too.

Can't (obviously). Go to sleep.

It happened again that night. I woke with such a rush of terror I thought I was screaming. But I wasn't. At least not out loud. Flopper and I made our way down to the nook in my parents' room. Within seconds, I was back to sleep.

"Sadie. Sadie, your phone is buzzing," Dad yelled. "Why the hell did you bring your phone down here?" My heart raced. I hadn't even heard the phone.

"Sorry." I jumped up, went into the living room, and read a long, drawn-out drunken text from Seth. First he rambled about how he was hanging out with a group of Australians and one of them reminded him of D-Bag. Then he cut to the chase. I miss you so much. I'm thinking we should try. North Carolina isn't that far, Sadie Cakes. Can we talk?

I stood on the tufted wool rug, a relic pulled from an uncle's warehouse stash. I noticed Mom had changed out the pillows. She had a pillow obsession. That and trays. She loved serving trays. And teacups. I blinked a few times and reread the text.

Seth hardly ever entered my mind. Still, it would be so easy to be pulled in, even if it was obvious he was drunk and lonely and having a moment of weakness.

I miss you, too, Seth. But I think it's better if we just don't do this right now.

We could try, Sadie.

My stomach turned. There was only one way out.

I'm sort of seeing someone.

He wrote back immediately. Who?

A friend's boyfriend's friend. You don't know him.

I omitted the fact that Mike was mute, odd, and the only thing resembling a date that I could muster since Seth left.

Good luck with that, Sadie.

I almost texted Shay. But I didn't want to get another *Sorry, Sadie. Dealing with camper stuff.*

So I curled up on the couch with my Flopper, pulled up NeighborCare.com on my laptop, and scrolled through dozens of fund-raising pages. There was too much need. I could see how Mr. Upton had become paralyzed. As many lizards as there were in the world, there were even more people, animals, communities in need. We were meeting at Gordie's the next night to select our "recipients," but it seemed impossible to choose which ones were worthy of our found diamonds. The family with the house fire? The dog with the congenital eye condition? The badly beaten horse? The funeral costs for a man who was murdered?

I rolled over on my side and closed my eyes.

I slept half the day and spent the other half watching movies on my phone.

"My head hurts bad, Mom," I called down the hall. "Can you get me something to take?"

"Maybe we should mention this to the victim advocate," she said, handing me Advil and water.

"Mom, we don't need to mention every single thing to the victim advocate."

"Sadie, every little thing may add time to his sentence. Remember that." It struck me that the entire time I was running around with the Unlikelies, *he* was in jail waiting for a trial. Or at least I imagined he was. I didn't really want to know.

My phone buzzed. I ignored it. It buzzed again. And again.

It was Alice.

At the hospital. Izzy OD'd. Tanner found her in his bathroom. Can you guys please come?

I stared down at the text, trying to figure out how Izzy OD'd in her own house.

I went into the kitchen, where Mom was back to cooking chickpeas in front of the small TV. She jumped when I walked up behind her.

"Can I take the Prius after dinner?"

"Not tonight, Sadie. I have to take Grandma Sullivan for lotto tickets."

"She can't miss one night of lotto?"

Mom tapped the wooden spoon on the side of the pot and drizzled olive oil over a plate of sliced tomatoes. "Oh, sure! And then the one night she misses, her numbers come up. I'm not having that on my head."

The news guy with the heavy, shellacked hair was reporting from in front of the trap house. I barely recognized the wooded lot in the daylight. "And now more on that bizarre psychiatrist-drug-dealer case out on the East End. Investigators found a massive stockpile of heroin, cash, purportedly stolen merchandise, and drug-related paraphernalia at the Westhampton home rented by Dr. Ward O. Nelson. According to officials, the public was instrumental in cracking this case."

" 'If you see something, say something' works," an officer said, looking into the camera. "Together we're working for a drug-free community."

I laughed out loud.

"What's so funny?" Mom said, licking salty oil off her fingers.

"Nothing."

I texted Gordie, Pick me up.

"I'm at the hospital more than my grandmothers," I said, climbing into the Range Rover. Gordie was freshly showered, and I could smell his spearmint gum from the passenger seat.

We passed the big blue H sign and parked near Alice's car. I remembered lying on the stretcher in the ambulance while a guy with coffee breath applied pressure to my head, and the blood from my knees stuck to the thin blanket.

Alice looked up at us from the bench with rage in her puffy red eyes. "They blamed me."

"What? Blamed you for what?" I said, eyeing the mean-faced nurse smoking nearby.

"They said we were the only ones who visited her, that we must have smuggled in the heroin."

"That's bullshit," Gordie said.

"Do you want us to talk to them?" I put my arm around her trembling shoulders.

She shook her head and rested her face in her hands.

"Tanner kept trying to get their attention and, as usual, they blew him off. He was finally able to tell them about some guy who pulled up while they were playing badminton. Remember I was like, why the hell is Izzy playing badminton with Tanner?"

"Yeah."

"Well, now we know."

"Was it Hector?"

"No. Apparently this time it was a dark-skinned guy in an Audi. Hector is white with friggin' floppy blond bangs and blue eyes. And he drives a BMW."

"Hector's blond?" Gordie said. "Hector doesn't sound like a blond-dude name."

"Yes. He's blond. I have no idea who stopped by in an Audi."

"So did her dad apologize for blaming you?" I said.

"No. He just shook Tanner and asked him why he hadn't said anything earlier."

The hospital wanted to let Izzy out after she was "stabilized." Izzy's parents convinced them she was a danger to herself and if anything happened to her, they'd sue the hell out of every doctor, nurse, and roll of toilet paper in the building. Then Izzy's mom called all the residential rehab places on Long Island, trying to bribe them to open up a bed for her daughter.

"It's easier to find a friggin' trap house on Long Island than a rehab bed," Alice said.

She was probably right.

Jean brought brownies to Gordie's basement, where Alice sat in a movie theater chair with a washcloth on her head. Val had laid it there, insisting her mother cured everything with a damp washcloth.

"I cannot deal with the lying and bullshitting anymore," Alice said. She took off the washcloth and bit into the brownie Val was holding up to her mouth. "It makes me sick. It's so obvious that the more normal she acts, the more full of shit she is."

"She's going to be okay now, Alice," Val said. "They just need to get her into a rehab place. They're gonna know how to help her."

Alice laughed. "Hector checked Izzy's drug buddy out of rehab and escorted her right back to the trap house. He's quite the gentleman, that Hector."

Val repositioned the cool washcloth on Alice's forehead and covered her with a Princeton blanket, one of the many Ivy League fleece throws Gordie's family had collected from the older Harris brothers.

We settled into our designated chairs with the brownies, lattes from the latte machine, and a list of potential NeighborCare candidates.

Gordie pulled up NeighborCare.com. We started with Ella. Her fund-raising had stalled permanently. Even with the local Alabama news story, they hadn't reached $200.

"She's so cute I want to cry," Val said. "Look at her two bottom teeth sticking out." Alice lifted the washcloth to check out baby Ella.

"I don't get how people always say 'pray for us,' like prayers are going to help," mumbled Alice.

I leaned over and whispered, "Okay, voodoo priestess." Alice glared.

"What?" Val said, looking back and forth between Alice and me in confusion. We pretended not to notice.

"Prayers help, I promise you that," Jean said.

"Okay, guys, can we figure this out? I feel like we've been dragging our asses so much *we're* going to be ninety-seven when we decide what to do with the canaries," I said.

First on the list: Ella, baby, Alabama, child of lizard. Next was Jean's suggestion, a Haitian mother of six from Boynton Beach, Florida, who found space in her heart and home for special-needs foster children. Then came Marigold, a five-year-old with a rare form of bone cancer. And Mrs. K, a teacher from Alaska who was trying to raise $20,000 to start a safe home for teen prostitutes.

It was hard to explain how we landed on the pages and unanimously voted yes, over and over again. When I was home, searching through hundreds of NeighborCare.com profiles, trying to find the people Mr. Upton would have approved of, it was nearly impossible. But with Jean and Gordie and Val and Alice—as out of sorts as she was—it was swift and harmonious. It was as if Mr. Upton was there to guide us from beyond the grave.

We decided four was enough for our pilot run.

"Okay, we have our list. Gordie, work your magic," I said, dusting crumbs off my cramped legs.

We sat for hours, vetting each person by stalking them, their friends, their families on Facebook, Twitter, LinkedIn, and other websites. Gordie did his computer genius investigating, dug out valid addresses, made sure all the candidates were airtight, or as airtight as anyone could be through the murky portals of cyberspace.

We ate our weight in brownies, popcorn, and leftover three-bean salad from the main kitchen. We drank volumes of lattes.

And then we were done, and I felt at peace with our plan.

We sat for a minute, wondering what to do with ourselves now that the burden had been lifted.

"I think we should dump the lizard's suitcase," Gordie said.

"Why?" I said, surprised.

"I don't know. It's sitting there in your closet for what? Why are we keeping the creepy silk bathrobe and shit?"

I felt unsettled. I hadn't thought about throwing away any of it. It seemed sacred in some strange, twisted way. But maybe Gordie was right. Maybe Mr. Upton should have dumped the suitcase a long time ago. Maybe it would have given him closure.

"We should bury it somewhere. Or burn it. That would be fun," Jean said.

"Why are we wasting our time on this?" Gordie said, marching over to the basement kitchen. He rummaged around under the sink and pulled out a box of heavy-duty trash bags. "Come on. Let's do this."

We caravanned to my house and parked out front. Val and I tiptoed up to my room, took out the contents of the suitcase, piece by piece, feeling the seams and the pockets to make sure we hadn't missed any stray canaries. Then we dumped it all into trash bags. His expensive dapper suits. His robe. His collection of women's hairpins.

"Are you sure we shouldn't smoke one of the cigarettes? Just to see what an antique cigarette tastes like?" Jean said as we loaded the garbage bags and the empty suitcase into the backseat of the Range Rover. Val made a face, grabbed the cigarettes out of his hand, and dumped them in the bag.

I secured Andy and his canaries in the garment bag, then rode with Gordie to the dumpster behind the supermarket, where he hurled in the empty suitcase with the Nova Scotia stickers and the two heaping trash bags, and we drove away. I thought about my original plan, to donate the suitcase to the Smithsonian, but Gordie was right. That suitcase and all the memories it carried felt creepy. It belonged in a dumpster.

That night I hid the letter to Mr. Upton's lover in a Spanish folder under my window seat and lay in bed staring at the origami garlands hanging from the ceiling. The moon cast filtered light on the mismatched paper cranes.

Let's make Izzy an origami crane chain, I texted everybody.

I don't like birds, Jean texted back.

It's not about you, Jean, I wrote. The other Unlikelies must have already been asleep.

❧ NINETEEN ❧

ALICE FACETIMED IN the morning to tell me that the police called her mom out of the blue, and her mom collapsed into a howling heap, fearing Alice was dead from drugs. But it turned out they were just calling because they were in possession of some stolen property they believed belonged to Alice's family: a ring forged out of rare white gold and embedded with rubies, a diamond tennis bracelet, and a strand of priceless pearls.

Alice's mom had fired their cleaning lady, Olga, a lovely Polish woman with five kids, when her jewelry went missing. That started a chain reaction, and Olga lost all of her East End clients.

Alice recounted her parents' conversation with the cops.

"No, ma'am," the cops had said. "Your jewelry was found at a drug dealer's house."

"I had no idea Olga was a drug dealer," Alice's mom had said.

"Mom, it wasn't Olga. Izzy stole your jewelry," Alice had said. "Now excuse me while I puke."

And she did. Alice puked her guts out.

"Why did she need to steal? Izzy has tons of money," I said.

"Dealers don't take AmEx Platinum, Sadie."

To get the canary packages delivered before Gordie's upcoming camping trip with the Turtle Trail Recreation people, I had to call in sick to work.

"How'd you get out of work?" Gordie set the bag of care packages on the backseat.

"I told Farmer Brian I had a migraine. I feel really bad. Let's hope my mother doesn't need cucumbers or something."

It was just the two of us, headed west toward the wealthy towns of Long Island's North Shore. I thought it made sense to play things safe by mailing the packages from Roslyn, Great Neck, and Manhasset, where we figured people probably had loose diamonds lying around.

We had typed the message, printed it out on bright yellow card-stock, and stuck it on top of the tissue paper that covered the tiny sealed baggies, each containing two stones. *These are real yellow diamonds worth many thousands of dollars. We are sending them on behalf of a wealthy benefactor who wanted to help others. We saw your NeighborCare page and were touched by your story. Best of luck to you.*

We didn't get the Unlikelies involved in Mr. Upton's promise. It wasn't about the Unlikelies. It was about righting the lizard's wrongs.

Gordie confided in me that his parents contributed generously to the Turtle Trail Recreation Center and always had, and that his father had a form of autism.

"What are you talking about? Your dad is a gazillionaire." I glanced back at the packages on the seat behind Gordie.

"Yes, and he's also on the spectrum, as they say. He couldn't talk until he was almost seven."

"Wow. And he built a software empire."

"He and my mom are about as mismatched as two people could be. And yet they work."

I laughed. "I get it. My mother fled the Iranian Revolution only to meet my father, an ex–New York City cop, after his stand-up comedy routine offended her and she hit him."

"No way."

"Yeah. He made a joke about Muslims having four wives, and she chased him down after the show, hit him, and told him he had no idea what he was talking about. It was love at first sight."

"Woody was a cop, huh?"

"Yeah. He lost his thumb on the job and quit. My uncles kind of pressured him into the family ice cream business. But he loves it."

"Does he still do comedy?"

"He thinks he's doing comedy. Every night. On our porch."

We talked about colleges and our dysfunctional class and Alice's terrible predicament.

I turned up the music, and we car-danced until we got to the first post office. Before I handed Ella's package to the guy, I kissed it three times for good luck. At each post office, when the person asked, "Is there anything fragile, liquid, perishable" or whatever, we said no. We tried not to look at each other, because even though there were no questions about cut or clarity, we felt like we were doing something very, very shady.

When it was all done and we had stopped for Mexican food at a strip mall somewhere between the fancy towns of the North Shore and the fancy towns of the East End, I asked Gordie a question.

"Are you glad you went to the homegrown hero luncheon? Like, are you glad you got involved in all this?"

He crinkled his eyes and chewed his burrito and wiped his mouth and said, "It's better than watching Reid feel up Claire all summer."

I nodded. "That must be how Mute Mike feels."

"And David. Keith and Zoe are getting hot and heavy."

So Gordie preferred the Unlikelies to being a third wheel.

That was something.

"Sadie? Uh. Can you come here, please?" Mom got that high-pitched tone only when there was an issue.

I had been napping on the couch, waiting for Alice to pick me up. Mom took off her gardening gloves. "I just got a call from Farmer Brian asking me how your head is," Mom said.

I froze.

"Sadie?"

"Yeah, Mom?"

"Have you been keeping your headaches from me so I don't bug you?"
She didn't know I missed work. I had dodged a massive bullet.

I resumed my nap position. "Not really. My head hurts sometimes, but it's not a big deal. I think this one is menstrual."

Mom sat on the edge of the couch and rested her hand on my
ankles. "Do you think maybe you should take it easy with all the late
nights and running around?"

I turned and stared at her. "The late nights and running around
are exactly what I need right now, Mom."

She sighed heavily. "Suit yourself."

I did actually have a headache, and I was exhausted from getting
up early to mail the packages. But I had promised Alice I'd do errands
with her because she said she really needed moral support. Of course,
the "errands," like everything else we did, were not normal.

Our first stop was Izzy's house to pick up things for Izzy, who
was still in the hospital. Izzy's mom had refused to leave the hospital
waiting room until a rehab bed opened up and the hospital agreed to
transport Izzy directly to the rehab center. She was afraid Izzy would
jump out of the car if her parents tried to drive her. She was finally
realizing Izzy's heroin problem was more than a passing phase.

Alice sped up Izzy's sloped driveway and slammed on the brakes.

An elderly woman with a distressed expression let us in. "Thanks,
Beverly," Alice said. "We're going to get some stuff for the hospital."

Izzy's room felt haunted, like the specter of happy, horseback-riding Izzy was smudged on the walls, sobbing into the pink floral fabrics. It was stuffy and smelled slightly of sour vomit. Somebody had gone through the drawers and closet, probably in a desperate search for hidden heroin. Izzy had lined up her nail polish bottles from brights to pastels. I picked up a silver-framed picture of Izzy and Alice when they were all smiles and freckles and Alice didn't have any of the hardware or paint obscuring her face. I noticed a quote Izzy had written in pencil and pinned to her headboard on pink lined paper. *No one saves us but ourselves. No one can and no one may. We ourselves must walk the path. —Buddha*. It made me want to cry.

Alice went into the closet. Most of the contents had been piled on the bed, pockets picked through, shoe boxes vetted. She crawled to the back and used a ruler to pry out the tight corner of the carpet. Underneath, stuck into a groove in the plywood, was a green felt bag. Alice pulled it out.

"And bingo," Alice said. "She told me she threw this out, but I knew she was full of shit." Alice pulled a phone out of the bag and handed it to me. "This is her secret drug phone, compliments of Hector." She slid the phone into her bag and pushed down the carpet corner. I imagined Izzy sitting in her white desk chair using the ruler to make a school project or do a math assignment. I wanted to get out of her sad, sad room.

Alice grabbed Izzy's stuffed pig—her version of Flopper—and a notebook and some toiletries from the bathroom. We eased into the slow crawl toward the hospital.

"You can't bring those things in," a snotty receptionist said, snatching the plastic bag full of toiletries.

"Why not?" Alice said. "It's just perfume and mouthwash and stuff." She held up the list Izzy had dictated.

The snotty receptionist made an *Are you an idiot?* face and said, "Because our patients drink perfume and mouthwash to get high."

Alice looked at me and shook her head.

When we walked into the family waiting room, we found Izzy's mom asleep on the grubby loveseat. She opened her eyes and smiled up at us.

"Hi, girls." She looked years older than the day she had greeted us at their house. She wasn't wearing makeup on her pale, blotchy face, and deep silver roots sprouted from the top of her head.

She stood and embraced Alice. "She's so mean to me. She's cursing and telling me I ruined her life." Her whole body trembled and she bent down to rest her head on Alice's shoulder. She sobbed and sobbed; her muffled cries rang out like strange bird sounds.

Izzy's mom apologized for "falling apart like that" and went on and on about how Izzy was a good kid and where did she go wrong as a mother?

"You didn't do anything wrong," Alice said. After, as Alice and I walked through security toward Izzy's room, Alice whispered, "She did a lot of things wrong. But nobody deserves this shit."

Izzy sat with her feet tucked under her on a scratchy-looking lounge chair facing a pretty, dark-haired, fair-skinned girl.

"Pooch and Sadie, this is Lexie. She's my new bud," Izzy said.

"Hi," Lexie said meekly. "I'll see you soon, Iz." She walked down the hall toward the patient rooms.

Izzy's hair was pulled back. Her face was white as rice and her eyeballs were almost orange. "Lex has issues, but she's really sweet. She got in trouble for stealing from the elderly to buy shoes, and people were so cruel to her. They have no idea what this girl has been through. Everybody sucks."

I glanced at Alice, who mouthed *Holy shit* as Izzy clutched her stuffed pig and stood up to move her chair over.

She's the Hamptons Hoodlum, I mouthed back.

The conversation quickly shifted to Izzy's mother.

"She's an overreacting bitch. I can't look at her ugly face. I can honestly say I don't even feel like using, but she's forcing me to stay here." Izzy shifted in her seat. "Do you know that woman is telling the doctors I'm suicidal?"

"Why?" I asked.

"They'll let me out of here if I'm not a danger to myself or others, so my mother is telling them I've sworn I'll kill myself. Which I will. Because I'm in this hellhole." She stopped. "Actually, you know what? I'd rather be here with these freaks than with her. I hate that bitch. She's the biggest psycho of all."

I nodded and let her continue with her mom-hating diatribe while Alice sat there playing with her nose ring. She didn't look at Izzy. Not once.

"Where's Hector?" Alice finally said.

Izzy acted like she didn't know what Alice was talking about. She made a face. "What? I don't know. I thought we were talking about my mother."

"C'mon. You know where he is. You know they busted the shrink's house. Where the hell is Hector?"

"Why do you care where Hector is? You're obsessed with him. I think you're just pissed that I was hooking up with him and blowing you off."

Alice's pasty complexion flushed pink. She balled her fists and glared at Izzy. "I fucking stood there and watched Hector stick that needle into your groin. Remember? When the blood sprayed all over me? He just keeps coming back to stick needles into you and you keep letting him do it, Izzy. He has ruined your life, your parents' lives"—-Alice pointed toward the waiting room—"and Tanner. That kid worships you."

Izzy stood up and padded away in her rubber-bottomed blue socks and mint-green bathrobe. She didn't turn back.

I linked my arm through Alice's and we walked out to the waiting room. Izzy's mom's expression was hopeful, as if the home-grown heroes would somehow infuse her daughter with sunny, sober thoughts.

"She looks good," Alice said, leaning down to kiss her cheek.

As we passed our bench yet again, Alice took Izzy's drug phone out of her bag and held it up. "Well, I guess *you'll* have to tell us where Hector is," she said. Then she looked at me with a weird smile. "Are you ready for the next errand?"

❧ TWENTY ❧

ALICE TOOK ME to the animal shelter where she worked and intro-duced me to a kennel full of rowdy dogs, clamoring in their cages to give us kisses. She showed me the most recent batch of photos she'd taken of the big, broad, brindled pit bull wearing the pink bandanna around her neck. Alice had a gift for photographing unwanted dogs and making them wanted by forever families.

After I helped her with her kennel chores, she wiped her hands on her jean shorts, took a sip from her water bottle, and hesitated.

"Tonight's the night we bury the poppet. He's waiting patiently in my bag."

"We?"

"Will you go with me? I can't go to a cemetery alone."

"Fine. I'll go with you. How does it work again?"

"We need to bury the poppet in the cemetery with nine pennies and a bottle of rum, except I have no idea where I'm going to get rum. My parents drink wine and Scotch." We walked away from the cacophony of barking and howling sounds.

"My parents drink tea and beer," I said. "Does it have to be rum?"

She stopped and put her hands on her hips. "Yes, Sadie. These spells are very specific. And I know you think it's friggin' idiotic, but it has to work."

I still didn't think getting rid of Hector was the answer to all of Izzy's problems. But I knew Alice wouldn't quit until she finished the Hector poppet spell.

"The only place we ever get served in my town is the Japanese restaurant," Alice said. "And they're not going to give me a bottle of rum. Sake maybe."

"I think I know where we can get some rum," I said.

We went back to my house for dinner with Mom, the grandmas, and Dad, who pulled up late after a long day serving happy memories on cones. After dessert, Alice and I pulled out our weak supply of camping gear from the garage.

"I have to say, I don't know if I'm up for this camping trip tomorrow," Alice said, shaking out my butterfly sleeping bag. "I hate camping. It's disgusting."

"Come on. It could be fun. Don't you think we all need a little break?"

"I don't even know if it will be all of us. Do you really think Val will leave Javi? And Jean is still trying to get somebody to take his weekend lawn-mowing gig. Besides, I don't know if babysitting a bunch of developmentally disabled people is a break."

"We're not babysitting, Alice. They're adults. We're just keeping Gordie company. God, stop being so negative all the time." I riffled through a plastic bin for flashlight batteries.

"Okay, Mom." She sat on the step and watched me collect the batteries and stack the flashlights, bug spray, and waterproof mat before we told my parents we needed to buy snacks for the camping trip.

❦

We pulled up in front of Shawn Flynn's hedgerows a little after nine. I was sure we would be early and I would be able to make small talk with Shawn and D-Bag, grab a bottle of rum, and leave. But it must have been one of Shawn's happy-hour-starts-at-four parties, because people were already stumbling all over the place.

"You can totally stay in the car," I said to Alice, whose violet hair, piercings, and camo skirt didn't exactly fit in with the bikini chic.

"No, I'm dying to see what one of these parties is like. I've heard they're exponentially more obnoxious than anything we have in my town."

"I'm sure." We bypassed the inflatable bounce house, probably left over from one of Shawn's little sister's over-the-top kid parties (a vomit disaster waiting to happen), and went around back.

"Oh my God, Sadie, where have you been? I've texted you, like, five times." Parker was drunk.

"Hey, Parker." I hugged her and reintroduced Alice. Parker had also been in troop 186. "Sorry. I've been recovering still. My spleen is really acting up."

"Oh, you poor thing." Parker made a pouty lip. "I feel terrible. I have a bunch of cranes I've been meaning to drop off."

"That's so nice of you to keep making them," I said, pulling Alice into the crowd.

Music blasted from the Flynn mega-speakers and people were actually dancing. Shay and I always tried to get people to dance at last year's parties, and nobody would.

"Sadie, where's D-Bag?" Seth's friend Alec said, dripping water all over my sandaled feet.

"I think he's up in Shawn's room," I lied, glancing over at Alice, who was taking it all in. I grabbed Alice's hand and pulled her toward the laundry room entrance. Lucky for us, the door opened. I checked the cabinets above the washing machine. "Voilà," I said. A row of small bottles was shoved behind the detergent and fabric softener.

"Do I even ask?"

"Shawn's housekeeper has a bit of a drinking problem. And I was the friend who washed the puke towels the morning after parties."

"Of course you were."

I grabbed one of the small bottles of rum, tucked a ten-dollar bill under one of the other bottles, and led Alice out the front door. It was both a relief and a disappointment that nobody noticed I had been missing from the parties for weeks.

"Yeah, pretty much what I expected," Alice said when we were safely in the car and en route to the old cemetery. "Was there any part of you that wanted to stay?"

I considered the question, thought about the times I would get a little nervous if I had to miss a party, worried I would be out of the loop, afraid I wouldn't get the latest round of inside jokes. "No. Actually, I'd much prefer to be burying a drug dealer poppet in a cemetery with nine pennies and a bottle of rum." I laughed. Alice laughed so hard she snorted.

"When you put it that way, it does sound kind of weird."

We parked at the edge of the cemetery.

Alice whispered, "Come on. Let's do this."

With the light of our phones, we waded through brush that was probably full of ticks and thick, overgrown woods to the cemetery, a mismatched plot of seven or eight stones. Alice reached into her bag and pulled out the Hector doll, which she had wrapped in black cloth, tied with twine, and knotted precisely nine times.

"Here, start digging." She gave me a serving spoon.

After several minutes of digging furiously, tossing rocks, and burrowing around stubborn roots, I looked up. "I think we're good."

"Remember, we're supposed to walk away without looking back," she said, kneeling down. I nodded. She placed the wrapped poppet in the hole, along with the bottle of rum and the nine pennies, supposedly gifts to the spirits, and we quickly covered the hole with dirt.

"Let's go," Alice said. We walked back through the creepy wooded lot and sped away in the Subaru.

"Feel better?" I asked before I got out.

"I think so," she said.

I hoped, for Alice's sake, her spell would work.

Usually, the only thing my parents ever fought over was yard work. Mom was abnormally protective of her garden and she went ballistic if Dad accidentally mowed one of her plants. She might be less upset if he mowed me.

But that night, my parents had a huge fight. They fought so hard I was sure Willie Ng could hear them over the sound of his porn. They fought about how to best help me get over the night wanderings. Dad said to let me be and allow me the freedom to hang out with my friends and get over it in my own time. Mom accused Dad of still not being over what happened to him when he lost his thumb. Dad accused Mom of taking away his stand-up comedy, the only thing that helped him stay sane. She told him not to go there.

I stayed in my bed, still as the summer air, overhearing the whole ugly interaction. I woke terrified in the middle of the night, sticky with sweat. But Flopper and I stayed right where we were.

I didn't want to cause any more trouble.

By breakfast, the storm had blown over, and my parents were annoyingly affectionate.

"You must be pretty comfortable with this crew to introduce them to your Flopper," Dad said as I tucked Flopper inside my sleeping bag and rolled it up.

"Hey, there's no shame in having a Flopper, Woody," I said. My parents loved that I was hanging out with the homegrown heroes, that I was going camping with the Turtle Trail folks, that I had found my do-gooder people. "And guys, please stop worrying about me. I'm good. I'm really good."

I kissed them and got into Gordie's car before *Are you sure? Let's talk about it* could escape from either of their mouths.

TWENTY-ONE

SOMEHOW WE ALL managed to get out of our tangled interpersonal and work situations to meet at the farm stand at nine a.m. By the time we loaded our gear into the Range Rover, there was barely any room for us. Alice called shotgun and gained full control of the music, which would normally have involved a lot of nineties grunge. But Alice was now a Beatles convert. It was a beautiful day, clear and not too hot. The clouds were faint brushstrokes high in the sky. The air rushed in the open windows as we zigzagged through the back roads to the state park.

Val was pretty down. She smiled, because she always smiled, but her eyes were full of worry and guilt. Javi had picked a fight, told her she was a pain in the ass, ordered her to get out of his room. But she still felt bad for leaving him. And nothing we said could ease that burden.

The Turtle Trail bus had just pulled into the campground when we arrived. Twenty people, ranging in age from early twenties to late thirties, made their way down the steep bus steps. They lit up when they saw Gordie.

"Look what I'm wearing, Sadie." Keith waved his Woody's Ice Cream hat in my face. It smelled like dirty couch, which meant Keith was getting a lot of use out of it.

A woman with thick glasses and short red hair leaped into Gordie's arms. He picked her up and swung her around. Her Wonder Woman backpack went flying.

"Come on, Anna Banana," he said. "Let's set up camp."

It took us two hours. I gave up trying to help with the tents and focused on food storage. Gordie and Jean built a massive fire pit above the high tide line and we set out a circle of folding chairs. An older guy with salt-and-pepper hair and seersucker shorts followed Alice back and forth to the bus. They chatted about sand fleas and bug spray and how Alice liked to sprinkle cinnamon on her s'mores.

When Alice genuinely smiled, the worry creases in her forehead disappeared.

When the campsite was finally set up, we tied sneakers and rubbed sunscreen on noses and lined everyone up for a beach hike. The sun was still high in the sky when we set off down the beach. Seabirds swooped down over the calm water and cut back up in groups of two.

Jean waved a stick in the air. "Get away from me, you nasty bitches," he yelled, prompting widespread teasing.

We walked slowly, meandering up to the dunes and back down to the water, collecting shells and sculpted wood, worn smooth by the unrelenting waves.

"What's that on your face?" Anna Banana said, pointing to the monster tail.

"I had an accident."

"What kind of accident?"

"I banged my head on a toolbox."

"Ouch," she said. "Does it hurt?"

I touched it with the tip of my finger. "No. Not anymore."

We were all hungry by the time we got back to camp. Gordie and the Turtle Trail director handed out sandwiches and bags of chips while Alice and Val and I pulled soda cans out of a tub of ice and sat down on a blanket.

One of the women jumped up and whispered something in Gordie's ear, then erupted in giggles.

"Does anyone not flirt with Gordie Harris?" I whispered.

"Jealous?" Alice said.

"No, Alice. I'm not."

We, the Unlikelies and the Turtle Trailers, stuffed ourselves with s'mores and played tug-of-war and beach volleyball, and Gordie led the campfire songs with his harmonica.

Bedtime took a while. We helped some of the women in the bath-house with their teeth brushing while Gordie helped the director organize the medications. When everybody was tucked around the fire with their blankets and their ghost story ideas, we retreated down the beach and built our own campfire.

Gordie passed around a bottle of wine from his parents' wine cellar that didn't taste any different than Grandma Sullivan's boxed wine. We tore open bags of potato and tortilla chips and chased the chips down with the outlandishly expensive cabernet.

"I just swallowed, like, eighty bucks," Jean said.

"For that price we should really be enjoying it. Put down the chips," Alice said.

"I can't. I need the chips," Val said. "It's burning my throat."

Gordie held up the bottle. "Cheers to the Unlikelies. May this be only the beginning of our renegade adventures."

"Cheers," we said, touching our chips together.

"Stop backwashing, you pig," Alice said, hitting Jean.

"By now the canaries should have reached their destinations," Gordie said.

"You sent them overnight?" Val said.

"Yup."

We sipped the wine and stared at the fire. I tried to picture Ella's mom opening the package, staring at the diamond, feeling relief. She would be able to buy Ella toys and baby sneakers and hair bows and a baby swimming pool and floaties and bunny crackers and milk and books. Lots of baby books. It made me so happy to think about what we had done.

"How will we even know if the mission's successful?" Val said.

"The same way we vetted the recipients," Gordie said. "Facebook stalking."

Alice stood up, stretched, and sank back down in her chair with her animal shelter fleece blanket.

"The first time I drank wine it was from an old man's glass at the country club when I was twelve," Alice said. "Izzy dared me."

"Oooh. We should play truth or dare," Val said.

"No," Alice said.

"How about just truth?" Val said.

"Okay, Val. When was your first sexual experience?" Alice said.

The fire crackled. The Turtle Trailers' voices rose and fell.

"I guess it was a year and a half ago. With Javi."

"Was Mute Mike in the other room preparing ants on a log?" I said.

"Probably." Val laughed.

"Well, well, well, straight-A, school-supply maven Valeria *is* a closet freak," Jean said. "There was talk of it in the locker room."

"You mean the art room, I'm sure," Val said.

I couldn't look at Gordie, or the way his face flushed from the fire. I didn't want him to talk about his conquests, or gorgeous Sylvie. The wine traveled through me and warmed me inside. I took another drink, then changed the subject. "Did you guys know Jean and Umi are applying to all the same colleges?"

"Damn, you really are into this girl," Gordie said.

"God, college is stressing me out. I've applied for seventy-four scholarships and counting," Val said. "It's torture."

"What if we just skip college and hang out here forever?" Gordie said.

We toasted to that.

A trace of sunlight peeked through the clouds to the west of us as night dropped over the choppy Atlantic.

We dug our bare feet into the cool sand and sat back in our chairs.

It was nice to be in the moment, not checking phones for hospital updates, or stalking Hector, or arguing over what the hell to do with my promise to Mr. Upton. It was nice to just be friends on the beach with a fire and the waves and wine and chips on a perfect summer night.

The Turtle Trail campsite grew quiet. I pulled at my hoodie strings and stared at the bonfire embers. I could feel Gordie next to me, silent, staring like I was. Our knees brushed together. The fluttering started deep, in that place where the body meets the soul. He was my secret.

"Gordie, we have a problem, Houston!" a voice came from behind the tents and scared the hell out of us.

"What's wrong, David?"

"Keith won't flip a coin for the spot near the door. So now what?"

Gordie got up. "Come on. I'll get him to flip a coin."

"I call heads."

Alice stood and wrapped herself in her blanket. "I'm tired." She disappeared into our tent. Val and I followed.

"You guys okay?" I said.

"Yeah," they both said.

We talked about our families. We talked about our friends.

We decided it was serendipity that we found one another when we did.

We agreed that choosing the perfect college was almost as much pressure as finding the perfect relationship. And sometimes it was impossible to have either. Ever. And the thought of that was seriously depressing.

Alice told us she was in no mood for relationship drama and really just wanted a puppy. She also admitted she was finally able to sleep soundly now that Izzy was in the hospital because she didn't have to worry about waking up to an *Izzy's dead* phone call.

Eventually, Alice and Val crashed and I lay on my side, holding Flopper and listening to Alice grind her teeth and Val mouth-breathe. I thought about that breathless, tingling ache I used to feel when I was under Seth's blanket in the dark, pulling at his T-shirt, taking in his smell. It was pretty obvious why I'd stayed with him. But I felt so much more than I ever did with Seth just touching knees with Gordie. I wondered if he felt it, too, and what it would be like to be under Gordie's blanket.

I needed air.

I lifted the tent flap and tried to unzip it quietly.

"What happened?" Val whispered, half asleep.

"Nothing. Going to the bathroom."

I wandered toward the cluster of Turtle Trail tents surrounding the last of the sizzling bonfire cinders. The breeze felt great on my itchy legs. I pulled on my hoodie and shined the flashlight down on the sand, afraid a crab might pop up and bite my bare toes.

"What are you doing, Sadie?" Gordie half whispered from behind me.

I jumped. "Gordie! Why are you lurking around?"

"I can't sleep. Jean is all sprawled out and there's literally no room. Come on. Walk with me."

We walked toward the open beach and the nearly full moon.

"Thanks for coming, by the way. It's nice having non–Turtle Trail people here for one of these outings. The director isn't exactly friend material, and Keith and those guys are always trying to get rid of me."

"They're probably sick of all the women flirting with you."

"Yeah, right."

"Seriously. You're Mr. Popular at Speakeasy. The girls were flocking the other night."

He laughed. "It's the harmonica."

We climbed up a mini sand dune and sat between tufts of sea grass. I pulled my knees up to my chest and rubbed coarse sand on my ankle bites. Gordie shined his flashlight in my face.

"Stop. You're blinding me." He turned it off and stretched out his legs. They were lean but strong and perfectly hairy, so different from Seth's mass of fur.

"I can't imagine what people from school would think if they discovered Gordie Harris and Sadie Sullivan on a deserted beach, huh?" Gordie said.

"They might not be that surprised. You know, I had a huge crush on you in middle school." I felt strangely at ease confessing the secret that had once consumed middle-school me.

He smiled and flicked a bug off my leg. "I heard rumblings about that."

"You did?"

"People told me you had a crush on me. I didn't actually believe them. I assumed it was another asshole conspiracy to aggravate me, so I ignored them."

"Wait."

"What?" He leaned closer, trying to gauge my expression.

"Nothing. I don't even know why I brought up middle school." He knew I liked him and didn't do anything about it. Clearly he wasn't interested.

"So do you want to talk about that fireproof box you thought we should get for the diamonds?" I said, turning away from him.

He reached over and pulled my ponytail. "I liked you, too, dumbass."

Middle-school Sadie would have died right there. She would have exploded, releasing giant balls of pent-up longing into the sea. Almost-senior, Shawn-Flynn-party-veteran, incident-survivor, recent-visitor-to-a-trap-house Sadie remained calm.

"Oh, really? Nice of you to let me know."

He laughed. "Uh. I wanted to. Shay was *not* having it."

"What do you mean?" My stomach flipped.

"It's stupid now, but I saw Shay in CVS one night, a long time ago."

"Okay. And?"

"I asked her if I should invite you to that ridiculous Valentine's Day party at Parker's house where you weren't allowed to show up without a date. She literally turned around and ran away. So I took that as a no and said screw it."

I squinted up at the moon, thinking hard about that party and whether I had gone and who with. It came back to me, how Shay and I were scrambling for dates. How Shay made me go with her neighbor's dud friend because we were not going to miss that party. And the party sucked, because everybody felt beholden to the dates they had scraped up. And I only had eyes for Gordie Harris.

Why would Shay have done that to me?

"Well, this is awkward," Gordie said.

I wanted to text her, to ask her what kind of friend did that? She never mentioned CVS.

I turned to face Gordie and took a breath. "I still feel it, you know?" I said quietly. I did. I still felt all the middle-school feelings. And I felt bigger, deeper, high-school-and-beyond feelings.

"You do?"

"I do."

And then his lips were there, against my cheek, pressed on my neck. His lips were on my mouth. His tongue was in my mouth. His hand was on the back of my head. My hand was under his T-shirt, feeling the ripples of his back muscles, his chest muscles, pulling his shirt over his head.

Every hair on my body stood on end. Every skin cell woke up. We were practically naked before I could even remember where I was. It was that fast and that inevitable.

"Gordie! Gordie!" a voice called from down the beach.

"Oh, for fuck's sake." Gordie shot up and pulled on his clothes.

"Gordie, help me." The woman's frantic voice got louder. A dark figure hurried down the beach.

I yanked up my shorts and threw on my leprechaun T-shirt. I still felt a quiet buzzing inside.

"It's Zoe." Gordie grabbed my hand. I turned on the flashlight and tied my hoodie around my waist.

"We're here, Zoe," I called.

"What's wrong, Zoe?" Gordie said, rushing ahead of me.

"I'm scared. Mom usually tickles my back at night. I can't sleep without back tickles, and the ocean is too loud."

Gordie took Zoe's hand and led her toward the campsite.

"If I find you some milk, do you think you could sleep?" he said sweetly. "Come on, wipe your feet on the towel."

"Do you want to sleep in my tent?" I said. Gordie's head whipped around. I smiled and reached out to grab his arm. I pulled him close to me and whispered, "Oh. My. God. Gordie." I kissed his earlobe and left him standing there.

I spent half the night tickling Zoe's back while she held Flopper. I couldn't stop thinking about what had happened on the beach.

And I couldn't stop the fluttering.

❧ TWENTY-TWO ❧

IT TOOK A while for the photos, the posts, the cheering kitty GIFs to start appearing, but we eventually called phase one of the Upton Promise Project a huge success. The woman from Florida with all the foster children posted photos of her kids and praised God. The woman from Alaska posted a photo of herself in front of the FOR LEASE sign on the building she wanted to house escaped prostitutes in. She had made a giant LEASED sign and was holding it with a THANK YOU, BENEVOLENT ANGEL sign. The parents of Marigold, the five-year-old with the rare cancer, had posted pictures of her in her hospital bed holding up the care package with a sign that said THANK YOU, SPECIAL FRIENDS. I LOVE YOU.

Nothing yet from Ella's family. But I knew it would only be a matter of time.

The Gordie beach encounter had left permanent waves inside me. I thought about it all the time—in the shower, as I sat drinking lemonade with the farm stand guys, as I hung out on my willow crate fielding the-hunt-for-Hector texts from Alice.

It was a busy day at the farm stand with two tourist buses swallowing up all our good produce, and a bunch of locals and city people grumbling about the slim pickings the rest of the day. Daniela had to bring her son to work, and her son was a whiner. He wanted a lollipop. He wanted the iPad. He wanted to get on the tour bus. I was relieved when Dad showed up to take me to therapy.

Dad drove me to the appointment in the ice cream truck, which was embarrassing. He waited in the truck with his *Daily News* and his bag of pistachios while I went in to bare my soul to Willie Ng's therapist. Or half bare my soul.

"I know the victim advocate mentioned you may be entitled to weigh in on the ultimate sentencing decision. Are you comfortable writing the statement about how the incident has impacted you, both physically and emotionally?" He sat upright, his purple pad in his lap, his glasses propped on his white tangle of hair. "Because we can work together if it feels overwhelming."

I stared at the crack in the glass of the framed Monet's waterlilies print that hung over his head. "I haven't been thinking much about the incident lately. But I can definitely write something on my own."

He tapped his pen against his cheek. "How about the night wanderings? Have those subsided?"

"Not really. It's easier to calm myself down now, though."

"Had you ever had sleep issues like this before the incident?"

I thought about it.

"Actually, when I was little. When we first moved out to the East End, I slept with my parents almost every night for a long time."

He nodded. "Lots of transitions happening this summer, too, huh?"

He was right. There were lots of transitions happening. Maybe more than I wanted to confront during the waking hours.

More pen tapping. "How about when you're at the farm stand? Any feelings of dread? Physical reactions? Anxiety in general?"

I stared at the Monet crack again. I remembered the flood of fear I had felt when Jean tore into the parking lot, but didn't feel it worthy of reporting. And then I thought of the snapping. Every time I walked past the spot where I hit the gravel, I snapped my fingers twice. Every single time. It was just a thing I did. I wasn't going to tell the guy that either. That was just crazy.

"No. Things have been going really well."

"Good. Good. You're doing good, Sadie."

I felt like I was holding a balloon and releasing a tiny bit of air, just to get through the session, because if I released the balloon, if I let it fly around the room and blow the shit in my head all over this guy, he wouldn't know what hit him. And the truth was, most of the shit in my head had nothing to do with the incident.

"How'd it go?" Dad said when I finally got out of the stuffy office.

"Good. Good," I said. "Really good."

Dad dropped me at the barn, where Val was waiting with a carload of backpacks and her clipboard. It was the big night, the school-supply pickup picnic.

Gordie showed up late with Keith and Zoe after Alice, Val, Val's two uncles, and I had loaded box after box of sorted supplies into the Subaru, Uncle Juan's pickup truck, and Uncle Milky's Mustang. We stuffed the rest of the heavy bins into the back of the Range Rover and made our way to a church not far from Riverhead, where a group of men had gathered near the church steps.

"Limonada!" Papi from the farm stand shouted when I got out.

"No way! Hey, Papi!" I ran over and high-fived him.

"And how do you know Papi?" Gordie said.

"I know a lot of people, Gordie," I said.

He put his arm around my waist and leaned in close. "I need to see you," he whispered.

"You're seeing me right now," I whispered back, the waves rolling through me.

"You know what I mean," he said, walking away. "Limonada."

The men drank beer from cans and laughed raucously. We followed Val to the back of the church, where a group of kids played soccer in an overgrown lot.

"Valeria," somebody shouted. The kids swarmed.

"Come on, chickies," Val said.

The kids stood in two lines and waited patiently for us to lead them to the bins. Each chose a brand-new backpack stuffed with school supplies. I glanced over at Gordie, who was bent down and smiling at an adorable little girl in a floral sundress.

"*Gracias*," she said shyly.

"*De nada*," Gordie said.

"Have fun in school. Work hard," Keith said to each kid.

Val marched around with her clipboard, answering parents' questions and talking with grateful grandparents, many weathered from long years in the fields.

When we were finished, Val's mom invited everyone down to the cool, brightly lit church basement, where the crowd was greeted with salsa music and platters of tamales and plates of cakes and cookies. I grabbed a soda and some tamales and sat on a folding chair between Alice and Zoe.

"Do you have enough tamales, Alice?" I said, pointing my plastic knife at her obnoxious stack.

"Maybe," she said, chewing.

"You could make a Mayan temple out of those," Jean joked from across the table.

"Nice of you to show up after all the work is done," Alice said.

"Hey, I gotta earn a living," Jean said. "I'm setting up for the epic Tiny Art Show. You'd better be there."

"Of course I'll be there," Alice said. "I'll even take pictures."

Parents and grandparents danced on a stage above the crowded tables. Packs of kids ran around playing tag and popping cookies into their mouths. Every last kid, even the older ones, carried their backpacks.

"Limonada, *baile!*" Ramon, one of the other farm stand guys, came up behind me and grabbed my hand.

"Uh. No, *gracias.*"

"Go dance with the guy," Alice said.

I reluctantly climbed the steps to the stage turned dance floor and let Ramon attempt to teach me how to dance. My friends made fun of me from their table, until they were all dragged up there. I felt like I was finally getting the hang of it when the lights blinked on and off and a tiny lady with long braids asked everyone to be seated.

"Where is Javi?" Gordie said on the way to the table.

"Val said he's been really sick the past couple days," I said.

"I'm not saying he had to lug boxes into truck beds. The dude could have shown up to be nice." Gordie had a point.

A bowlegged man in jeans and work boots turned off the music and the crowd finally quieted down. The woman onstage was a social worker at the migrant center. She talked in Spanish and Gordie translated for us, because even though we were in the same Spanish classes, Gordie Harris was proficient and all I could say was *Do you like to play tennis or football?*

"*Gracias,*" the woman said.

"That means *thank you*," Gordie said slowly.

"Yeah, just wait until we're in a room full of Farsi speakers," I said.

Val was a different person than she had been in front of the homegrown heroes luncheon crowd. She thanked the community for supporting her grandparents and her parents through difficult circumstances and credited the true heroes in the room, the men and women who worked so hard to make a better life for their children.

"Now what is she saying?" I elbowed Gordie, who was smiling and saying, "Aww."

He stopped to listen. "And now she's thanking us for our help and support."

We all blew kisses up to the stage.

"Do you think her dad likes us yet?" I whispered to Alice when he shook our hands enthusiastically after the event.

"He should," she said. "We're a hell of a lot better than Javi and Mike."

As much as I wanted to take Gordie up on his invitation to hang out in his basement, I resisted a final Just come over already. I can't stop thinking about you text and stayed to help Val break down boxes and organize her clipboard for the next collection.

Alice left early to visit Izzy, and Jean had to finish getting ready for his Tiny Art Show. It was just Val and me on the steps of the church, sipping soda and resting our aching feet under the dim light of the cloud-obscured moon.

"You did it, Valeria, goddess of school supplies." I clapped my hands. "I'm so proud of you."

She bent down and played with her shoelace. "It wasn't enough. I could have done so much more," she said softly.

"Oh, Val, don't say that."

I tried to read her face. Her lips twitched back and forth like a rabbit's nose.

And then the tsunami came. She sobbed and sobbed and couldn't get words out. I put my arm around her petite frame and handed her clumps of receipts from a box to wipe her nose until the tears finally stopped.

"These families are my friends, my community, and they're struggling so bad."

I nodded.

"They get threatened, treated like garbage. They can't earn enough to get ahead, and they're constantly worried about their families back home."

"You know, Val, we could use some of the diamonds to help the community." I knew it was an impulsive thing to say. But I meant it.

She looked at me and smiled. "That's so nice of you, but let's wait, okay?" She took my hand and squeezed it. "I think we need an actual plan, not just to throw diamonds at random people here. But thank you so much for offering, Sadie. That means a lot to me." She stood and picked up her clipboard. "Sorry. Tonight was just really emotional for me."

"You're an amazing human being, Valeria."

"It takes one to know one, Sadie."

I stood up and took her hand and hugged her for a long time.

We were quiet on the way home, drained and ready for sleep. Right before she dropped me off, Val said, "Sooooo. When were you going to tell me you're sleeping with Gordie?"

"I'm *not* sleeping with Gordie."

"Yet."

"Okay, yet." I smiled and closed the door behind me.

I didn't know what possessed me to check Ella's mother's Facebook page at midnight after a very long day. I should have taken a shower, painted my scraggly nails, slathered vitamin E oil on the monster tail, and gone to sleep. But instead, I logged on to NeighborCare. The same sad little dollar amount sat there, stagnant, next to the picture of Ella and her weary grandma.

I logged on to Ella's mom's Facebook page. At first, it didn't register. Then I felt sick. And the sick feeling stayed with me deep into the night.

There was a picture of Ella's mom in a tight dress and heels holding shopping bags from a clothing store with the caption *Momma goin' out tonite!* And a picture of Ella's mom in front of the liquor store holding two bottles of expensive tequila with the caption *It's goin' down!* And a picture of a group of women, clones of Ella's mom, sticking their heads out of a cheesy white limo with the caption *In yur dreams!*

How could she? How could she spend that money on shitty clothes and liquor? How was she not saving it for Ella? I felt violated. And furious. And so, so sad.

The next morning I sulked around the farm stand mad at the world. I couldn't stomach the endless stream of city people throwing credit cards at me like I was invisible and then running off with their flowers and twelve-dollar hunks of cheese.

I couldn't believe how delusional I had been, thinking Ella's mom would shower her baby with baby things.

I probably shouldn't have called Shay when I was in a miserable mood.

"Hey, Sadie. What's up?"

"I have a random question and can you just answer it honestly, please?"

"Yeah. What is it? You're making me nervous."

"Why did you let Gordie Harris think I had a date for Parker's Valentine's Day party when you knew how much I liked him back then?"

Silence.

"Shay?"

"I'm trying to remember what you're even talking about. Where is this even coming from?"

I took a deep breath.

"Gordie Harris told me he saw you in CVS and asked you if he should ask me to Parker's party and you turned around and took off. But I wasn't going with anyone." My throat ached. "You knew how much I liked that kid." I couldn't hold back the tears.

Silence.

"Okay, I have no recollection of that whatsoever."

"I just want to know why you did it."

"I don't remember running into Gordie Harris. But you know what, Sadie? I don't have time to sit around and reflect on it. I am completely overwhelmed. And instead of asking me how I'm doing and helping me deal with the fact that I am not dealing well at all, you just want to tell me how great your new life is with Pooch and Gordie Harris and some random bearded guy."

She took a breath.

"I'm glad, Sadie. I'm glad you're having so much fun. But I'm not. I just really need to go right now."

And she was gone.

I sat there feeling like a horrible human being. Because Shay was right. I had been fixating on the idea that Shay was blowing me off without thinking about her at all.

Papi and Ramon passed by in the truck and honked repeatedly, cranking their music and waving out the window. I mustered a weak wave and plodded through the rest of the sweltering, fly-infested day.

I couldn't stop thinking about Shay. I needed to make it up to her. I texted Gordie, I could really use a friend right now.

"I have to be home in an hour," I said, swinging my feet off the bridge. Gordie rushed over, his hair messy. The duck pond was surprisingly empty for late afternoon.

"Sorry. Traffic." He was all out of breath.

"It's my grandma Hosseini's birthday. We're having a pancake dinner promptly at six thirty."

He sat down next to me. "Hi," he said, smiling.

"Hi." I smiled back.

He leaned in and it was all lips and salt and tongue and sweetness.

I had worried the days after the beach night would be awkward. But it was just the opposite. Everything with Gordie was easy.

A yellow Lab came up out of nowhere with three tennis balls stuffed in his mouth.

"Really, buddy?" Gordie said, pulling away from me. He nodded politely toward the elderly owner. Gordie held my hand and we stared at the stream moving slowly below the bridge.

"I have to talk to you about something. I wasn't going to tell any of you, but it's just bothering me so much," I said. I told him about Ella's mom. I pulled up the pictures on my phone. "I don't know why, but I'm embarrassed. And I feel like I let you guys and Mr. Upton down."

"You have got to be kidding me with this," he said as he scrolled through the photos. "What a lowlife."

"I know. Gordie, I think about Ella all the time. If you had seen her screaming in the car that day...Her little face was so scared."

He rubbed my back and I moved closer to him.

"And there's all this pressure to honor my stupid promise to Mr. Upton. It's too much."

"We'll figure it all out. I think the answer to the diamond thing is going to come to us. Like, we're seeking the answer, but I think we should let the answer come to us."

"Okay, you sound like a fortune cookie."

He ran his fingertips up and down my leg and looked over his shoulder. Three-ball Lab and the old guy refused to leave.

I told him about Shay and how I had thought she was blowing me off, when really she was struggling and I was the one not listening. I had assumed Shay would go off to California and be the center of the social scene and make dozens of friends and have the best summer ever while I sat on my porch and read magazines. But she was exhausted and overwhelmed and lonely and I wasn't there for her.

"Shay's cool," Gordie said. "She'll understand if you just talk to her."

"I know it'll be okay. It's really hard going from seeing each other all day every day to figuring out three hours' time difference and three thousand miles of separation."

We watched the dog chase and return the balls over and over again.

Gordie looked at me with an expression I hadn't seen before. He picked at the soft rotting wood on the bridge and looked up again. "So, Frances has lymphoma."

"Oh, no. That's terrible, Gordie. I can't believe you let me talk about my lame problems while you had Frances on your mind."

"Your problems aren't lame. Anyway, we don't know yet if it's bad or curable. But she's really worried about Keith, you know, about who's going to take care of him if something happens to her."

"Of course."

"I'm hopeful. I've gotta be. She's my nanny."

"I'm so sorry, Gordie."

We sat there quietly for a while, until it was time for me to leave for the birthday dinner. Gordie took my hand and led me through a maze of smaller paths in the shadowy forest until we got to a clearing. We stopped and he pulled me into him and we hugged under the tree canopy. I leaned up and kissed his cheek and his lips softly.

"That was exactly what I needed," he said, looking into my eyes.

"Me too."

I tried to FaceTime Shay after ten pounds of pancakes and Grandma Hosseini's heavily frosted chocolate birthday cake. When she didn't answer, I texted, I'm so very sorry, Shay Shay. Then, a few minutes later, I texted, And I'm here for you.

She texted back a smiling emoji and an I'm sorry, too, Sader. I promise I don't remember CVS.

The next day, on my lunch break, I made Shay a care package of Tate's cookies, which would be smashed by the time they reached California, but I knew they would remind her of home. I tucked a deep blue hydrangea between two pieces of waxed paper and stuck it inside the pages of our local newspaper. I sent it priority mail with a note that said *Roses are red, hydrangeas are blue. One hundred seven days 'til I see you.*

❧ TWENTY-THREE ❧

GORDIE AND I scrolled through random slam pages, throwing our avatar up all over the place and undermining the hard work of America's trolls while we waited for Val and Alice to show up before Jean's Tiny Art Show. Jean hadn't said much about what to expect from the show. We knew it was the culmination of weeks of little kids doing art with Jean every day. That was about it.

"I bet Stewy Upton's ghost is hovering over us right now saying, 'You kids are slackers. Honor my promise. Do something noble, you damn fools,'" Gordie said in his Mr. Upton voice.

"Poor Mr. Upton. He was very particular about his fruits. And his vegetables."

Val came through the sliding doors in a pale pink dress. She looked so pretty, but her eyes gave it all away.

"You broke up with Javi, didn't you?" I said.

Val's eyes widened. "How did you know?"

I gave her a big hug. "Friends know these things, Valeria."

We squeezed onto one of the theater chairs and Val told us that Javi backed out of Jean's Tiny Art Show, where he was finally supposed to get to know all of us, because he wanted to sit on the couch and play video games with Mute Mike. She confronted him about not showing up at the school-supply pickup night. He told her he was sick of her nagging. She told him she was sorry but it needed to be over and she hoped they could be friends. He told her if she wasn't spreading her legs for him, he didn't need another friend. She grabbed his phone, threw it in the toilet, and left.

"Where was Mike during all this?" I asked.

She started laughing. "Making a quiche from scratch."

"Of course he was."

I held her hand and Gordie brought her a milk shake from the upstairs kitchen. We told her we were proud of her for doing what she knew she needed to do.

"It's almost like he said that thing about spreading my legs because he wanted me to leave, but he didn't have the balls to let me go."

"Maybe. Or maybe he's just an asshole with lupus," Gordie said.

"At least he has Mute Mike," I said. "And homemade quiche."

Val rested while Gordie and I kept troll-busting. We found a site in Nebraska where guys scored girls on any number of degrading things. Gordie added:

Choose kindness, boys, and we'll let you in.
—The Unlikelies.

"Where the hell is Alice?" Gordie said.

"She said she might visit Izzy first. I'll text her to meet us there."

I had assumed the Tiny Art Show was named after the size of the participants, but as it turned out, the art was tiny, too. The children had painstakingly glued beans on canvases in the shapes of butterflies, trees, and fish. One child had even made a tiny bean portrait of Jean, beard and all.

Jean greeted people with smiles and warm hugs, dressed to the nines in a bright pink shirt and blue bow tie. We admired the tiny masterpieces and sipped club soda from fancy plastic cups with turquoise umbrellas.

"Kudos to you, Jean-Pierre," I said when Val and I finally pulled Jean aside.

"Why, thank you. My protégés did all the work." He took a sip of my club soda. "Is Alice here? She said she was going to take pictures."

"Not yet." I was getting nervous. Alice was always early.

The artists got rowdy as the party went on. A boy wearing a cape took down the tiered display of cupcakes, causing half the crowd to dissolve into a teary, snotty whine-fest until Gordie suggested I summon Dad to the rescue. Woody's truck showed up ten minutes later to deliver ice pops free of charge to the horde of cupcake-deprived little kids.

Val and I shared a chair while Gordie charmed Jean's mom and her friends.

Val checked her phone repeatedly.

"Anything from Alice?" I asked.

"Nope."

"Javi?"

"Nope. I threw his phone in the toilet, remember?" We laughed.

"You okay?"

"Nope."

We helped Jean take down the tables, fold up the chairs, and put away the decorations before we walked across the street to a pizza place. Gordie brought a pizza out to the curb where Jean, Val, and I sat inhaling helium from the Tiny Art Show balloons.

"I can't believe Alice blew me off," Jean said in helium voice.

"I'm single," Val said, also in helium voice.

"I'm hungry," I said in helium voice.

At that moment, all our phones went off at the same time.

Please come to hospital. Losing my shit.

We got to the hospital in record time.

Just before the elevator doors opened onto Izzy's floor, I noticed someone had stuck a yellow KICK CANCER'S ASS FOR GARY! sticker on the wall above the buttons. I wondered if Gary had kicked cancer's ass. When the door opened, we heard a low, grunty howl, like a walrus giving birth. It took only a minute to realize the sound was coming from Izzy's mom. She was writhing on the floor outside the visitors' lounge, nearly smacking her head on the edge of the doorway. Izzy's dad knelt awkwardly next to her. Alice stood stiffly, her eyes wide, her hands in her denim jacket pockets, her body pressed against the wall.

We walked boldly toward the scene. A distracted nurse passed us and snaked around the pathetic pile that was Izzy's parents. Alice turned and motioned for us to follow her into the tiny family room, where a vase of peach-colored fake flowers lay toppled in the middle of the floor.

I saw Tanner sitting in the corner, his ten-year-old face frozen in fear. Alice managed a weak smile and then shook her head. "It's not good."

Gordie moved in for a hug and Alice collapsed into him, shaking and sobbing.

I stood there paralyzed, convinced Izzy was dead.

"What happened?" Val said, resting her hand on Alice's back.

"She's gone. She disappeared. The hospital was discharging her because a bed opened at some rehab facility in Connecticut. She said she wanted to go down to the bathroom and freshen up while her parents sat here falling for her bullshit, yet again, and she disappeared."

She lifted her head from Gordie's chest. "We ran around the entire friggin' hospital searching for her. Security searched. The cops searched. She's gone." Alice wiped her nose on her jacket sleeve. "She has no phone, no wallet, nothing. Her mom had wanted to transport her to the rehab place by ambulance, and her dad was like, *No, let's stop at home and get her a few things and maybe have steamers and sweet potato fries at her favorite restaurant before we dump her at rehab.* Yeah. Nice work, Elliott."

The hallway commotion intensified.

"Do they need you to stay here?" Val said, holding Alice's hand.

"No. Let's go. I was just here to say good-bye to Izzy," Alice said. "But obviously she had other priorities than rehab in Connecticut. Those dumbass cops are never going to find her."

I thought of Izzy's sweet face, the way she lit up when Alice showed her childhood pictures.

"I have this sick feeling," Alice said in the elevator after she helped Izzy's dad get her mom off the floor and into a chair. "I'm so afraid she's going to die." Tears streamed down Alice's face. Val handed her tissues. I focused on the KICK CANCER'S ASS FOR GARY! sticker.

"How can we help?" Gordie said. We stood in the parking lot, watching cops search the perimeter for Izzy. "There have to be places we can look."

Alice played with the knot of silver rings on her right hand. "There are places. There's a place in the city. I went with Izzy once when Hector was in rehab. I have to go through Izzy's drug phone."

"Do you really think she'd go all the way to the city?" I said.

"Sadie, Izzy would go to the bowels of the earth for heroin."

Dad was on the porch when I got home.

"What a great event, huh, sunshine?" He motioned for me to sit.

I had already forgotten about Jean's Tiny Art Show. "Yeah, Jean did an awesome job." I took the can of honey-roasted peanuts from the table and shook nuts into my mouth. We sat there crunching,

233

Dad and me with the fireflies and Bruce Springsteen, until I hit Dad with a question.

"How did you lose your thumb, Dad?"

He must have known I'd ask again, though I'd stopped a long time ago, after his answers were always different, but equally ridiculous. *A bird was hungry and I let him have a nibble. A snapping turtle got mad at me for taking her bus seat. Grandma Hosseini lopped it off with garden shears when I married Mommy.*

He took a sip of beer. Then another. "I guess you're not going to buy *The tooth fairy needed it to poke people*, huh?"

"No, Dad."

He set the beer down and leaned forward a little. "I got bit by a strung-out prostitute because I was trying to pry her kid away and she wasn't having it. She fought and clawed and the kid wouldn't let go of her mother, and the woman clamped down on my thumb. She severed the tendon straight through."

"Oh my God, Dad." I saw it all in my head, the shock of toddler hair, the desperate mother, the teeth bearing down on my sweet father's hand.

"But I was Mr. Tough Guy and didn't go to the hospital until the damn thing was necrotic."

"What's that mean?"

"Dead. My thumb tissue was dead. So they hacked it off."

I pulled Dad's thumbless hand up to my mouth and kissed it. "I still love you, thumb or not."

"I love you, too, sunshine. I was never cut out for the force.

Sometimes it seems like I'm a sponge, like I absorb people's moods. There were too many rotten things on the job. I didn't have thick enough skin for all the bad scenes. It really messed me up for a while."

I knew exactly what Dad meant. I was trying to kick the anxiety I had absorbed from Val's guilt and sadness and Alice's fear and worry. I must have inherited Dad's skin, because mine wasn't thick enough either.

"That's why the ice cream business is perfect for me. I absorb all that happy, carefree energy. It's a blast."

I let go of Dad's hand to grab more peanuts. "So you lost a thumb and Great-Grandma Sullivan lost her feet. I guess it runs in the family."

Dad laughed. "And my old man was missing a nut."

I nearly choked. "That's way too much information."

"Didn't lose it saving anybody, though. He was just born with one nut. Your grandmother teased him mercilessly."

"Why am I not surprised?"

Later, after I had showered and dabbed vitamin E oil on the monster tail, I snuggled under clean sheets with my Flopper and my fans blowing. Jean texted just before I fell asleep.

We all need a night out.

❧ TWENTY-FOUR ❧

WE DECIDED WE were going to do something fun and light for once, like a carnival or mini golfing. Things were getting intense again, and Val really needed a distraction. Mute Mike had shown up at her house early in the morning with her old math notebooks, a framed photo of her and Javi, and the watch she had given Javi for his sixteenth birthday. She broke down and Mike actually talked to her. He told her he really didn't know whether Javi was deliberately pushing her away so she could live her life without feeling guilty about the lupus or if he was just an asshole. Val texted me a picture of Mike walking out of her building with the caption Mute Mike the snack man. Sent to do the dirty work.

I finally heard from Alice during my lunch break. Not up for going out tonight. Need to find Izzy.

I went to her house after work, smelling of hay and sweaty money. I marched straight upstairs to where I knew she'd be and found her kneeling at the altar, her hands clenched at her sides, her pale skin streaked with tears. I knelt beside her and rested my hand on her leg.

"Who's this?" I said softly, nodding toward a new poppet.

She smiled. "This is my poppet to find a missing friend." She picked up the doll and turned it over. "I made her out of Izzy's Abercrombie T-shirt. That's the only item of clothing I could find." She sniffled. "This is a picture of Izzy and a picture of Saint Muerte. I was supposed to stuff her with items from Izzy and all the people looking for her, so I folded three of their family Christmas cards and I put in this little tin of mints from her aunt's wedding and the business card of the cop supposedly leading the investigation. And I wrapped her in lace and tied it with one knot, and now I need to say the holy death prayer for nine nights until Izzy's found." Alice's voice was high-pitched, almost ethereal.

"That sounds good, Alice."

I sat on an unstable stool while she messed around with the candles and situated her Izzy doll.

"I think you should come out tonight. Val needs us right now. We need each other."

I figured she'd put up more resistance, but she rubbed her hands on her skirt and pushed herself up from the floor and said, "Yeah. I'll go for a little while."

We met at the duck pond just after six, when all the birds were at their most *fluttery*. Jean wouldn't get out of the car.

Alice was in a foul mood. Val barely talked. I almost told Gordie to take me home, where my grandmothers were in the backyard beating all the rugs in our house with wooden spoons.

"I have an idea," Gordie said. "But no judgment, okay?"

When Gordie Harris said *No judgment*, it usually meant he was going to expose yet another facet of his excessive family wealth. This time, it was the *Harmony*, a colossal yacht.

"Oh, shit. No. You're lying," Jean said when we pulled up to the marina where Dad used to park the ice cream truck so we could look at all the pretty boats.

"Stop. Don't make a big deal. It's embarrassing." Gordie held his phone to his ear. "Jay, we're coming down."

"Who's Jay?" I said.

"He's the captain."

We followed Gordie with his messy hair and his beat-up Converse and his ratty I LOVE NEW YORK T-shirt onto the gleaming yacht. Captain Jay and two other guys nodded hello and busied themselves preparing for our excursion. Gordie led us up to a deck in the front of the yacht and dove on top of a massive sectional sofa. We all piled on and quickly assumed the relaxed, pillowed posture of the very rich.

"Gordie, get me a cocktail, darling," Jean said. "I'm going to have a look around."

The boat glided slowly toward open sea.

"I could get used to this," Val said, sipping her lemon Pellegrino and sinking into a bed of ivory cushions.

Alice scrolled through her phone.

"Alice, we are on a yacht cruising the Atlantic on a beautiful summer night. Can you put your phone away for a little while?" I snatched the phone out of her hand.

"It's not my phone, Sadie. And it's a little hard to enjoy all this when my best friend is missing, you know?"

She had been searching Izzy's drug phone for signs of Hector, texting contacts, trying to find anyone linked to Izzy.

"I'm literally texting *Hey, have you seen Hector?* to every single contact in Izzy's phone."

"You're not abandoning Izzy if you take a little break. I promise." I tucked the phone into my jacket pocket.

"She's in the city. I know she is."

I looked at Val. Val looked at Gordie.

"Hey, Alice," Gordie said. "What if we went to the city with you to look for Izzy? Would that help?"

"I'll go," I said. "I have the next two days off. I'm in if we can go tomorrow."

"I'm in," Val said. "I'll totally go into the city."

Alice's face softened. She motioned for us to come closer. The boat lurched forward and I fell across her lap, and we lay there tangled and laughing. Gordie tossed a container of hummus and a bag of pita chips on the coffee table and sat on the chair next to Val.

"Jean's steering now. Brace yourselves," Gordie said. "He's like a five-year-old."

I wrapped my arms around Alice and held her like I used to hold Shay when she was upset.

"It's going to be okay," I whispered. "The poppets will fix it."

Jean's head emerged from the lower level. "I'm king of the world!" he shouted.

It was almost as if Gordie had paid somebody to erect the most glorious sunset in the history of sunsets.

We made fun of Jean's tongue sticking out while he sketched furiously, intent on capturing the layers of color as they appeared on the horizon.

"I think it's time to break out the big guns," Gordie announced, glancing at me. He went down to the cabin and came back up with a saxophone. He sat back and played, and we felt the notes bounce off the deck and fall into the sea. The music surrounded us. It found its way inside me. I held on to Alice and Val and closed my eyes as Gordie Harris's music turned me into pure air.

"Show-off," Alice said, wiping tears from her cheeks.

Gordie put the sax in its case and stretched. "You're just jealous the men have all the talent in this operation." He slid open a cabinet and grabbed a bunch more food. We lay around stuffing our faces and watching the lights zoom by. I couldn't stop looking at Gordie. I loved his smile. I loved the way his hands were strong and smooth. I loved how he didn't care how rich he was or how poor we were compared to him.

Unlike the rest of us, Val didn't eat a thing. She smiled and said things like *I really needed this* and *I'm so glad I have you guys*, but her head and her heart and her stomach were in breakup land.

"So how long have you two been banging, may I ask?" Jean said, pointing his fingers at Gordie and me.

"Oh my God, Jean. You're such an ass," I said, mortified.

"We might as well discuss, right?" Gordie looked at me.

"What do you want to discuss? That we have hooked up? Yes. We have hooked up. No. We haven't banged."

"I don't know if I'm cool with this," Jean said. He made a sweeping hand gesture. "I kind of like this Unlikelies dynamic we've created. Now you two are going to screw it up with inevitable couple drama. It will happen. You know it will."

He wasn't wrong. Our hooking up definitely complicated things.

"Nice, Jean. Way to be positive," I said. "I don't know if I'm comfortable with you judging my business."

"Sadie, can I have a word with you?" Gordie held out his hand and pulled me up.

"This is all so awkward," I said as I searched for my flip-flops and hurried down the stairs.

"Go ahead, abandon your friends," Alice called after us.

And then we were in the bedroom with the huge bed and the million-thread-count bedding, attached and struggling to get clothes off because our bodies didn't want to separate, not even for a second.

"Stop. Stop. Stop." I pressed the palm of my hand into his chest and looked up at his face in the dim light. His cheeks were flushed.

"Okay. I didn't plan to go there," he said, smiling. "I just wanted to talk about the situation. Shit, Sadie. What are you doing to me?"

I took a deep breath and put my T-shirt on. "Regroup, Gordie.

We're being rude. What did you want to say?" He kissed me two, three, four times.

"Basically that I can't stop thinking about you. Like all day and night. I just think you are incredible. I mean, I always did, but then you were with Seth, and whatever. I like you. A lot."

I buzzed like a hornet wedding.

"And I get what Jean is saying, but...sorry...don't care right now," Gordie said.

He stopped talking and looked at me.

All my body parts battled over first dibs at Gordie Harris.

"Are you saying you want me to be your girlfriend, strange boy?"

"Uh. Yes."

My lips found his and I wished we were alone on a boat heading for eternity. But I felt bad for ditching our friends and I knew if we stayed any longer we'd be proving Jean's point.

"Come on." I pushed him toward the door. "Let's not be assholes."

Gordie announced our couplehood and gave a little speech about how he loved *us* and didn't care about the future and he liked me and let's just all be cool with that. He got flustered and passionate like he did in civics debates at school. And, just like at the civics debates at school, he was met with bland acknowledgment.

"Gordie, relax, man," Jean said. "Congratulations. You like each other. Just keep the PDAs to a minimum. Nobody wants to see that shit."

We sailed back to reality early, even before the Hamptons cars had arrived at their fashionably late dinner reservations. We needed to get home and rest up and lie low, and then just plain lie to our parents about the upcoming, fabricated Turtle Trail Recreation Center overnight trip to New York City.

Alice texted us that night at three a.m., One of Izzy's junkie friends just responded. All he wrote was: Stop bothering me. Hector's dead.

❧ TWENTY-FIVE ❧

I CALLED ALICE right away and tried to gauge her reaction to the Hector news. "I'm beyond happy. This means Izzy has a chance."

"Don't you feel bad, a little, about the poppet?"

I was thoroughly creeped out thinking about the cemetery and burying the doll and the rum and the death curse. I had never met Hector, but I still felt guilty.

"No, Sadie. I wouldn't have made that doll if I didn't want it to work. Do you believe in the power of the voodoo now?"

When I asked my parents if I could go into the city to assist with another Turtle Trail field trip, they happily let me go because I was going to be with the gay class valedictorian and my other wholesome, do-gooder friends. I stooped as low as I had ever stooped and justified it by telling myself I was helping a friend save someone's life.

I remembered this girl from my school named Kelsey Rollins who played the cello. Kelsey Rollins cut school regularly to feed her gaming addiction by telling her teachers she had music lessons. They believed her because Kelsey Rollins was a music nerd and why would she lie to teachers?

I was Kelsey Rollins. Except instead of pretending to have music lessons so I could game in my basement, I was pretending to take developmentally disabled people on a field trip so I could hunt down a heroin addict.

I felt really, really bad.

Grandma Sullivan and Grandma Hosseini were the only ones at the house when Gordie arrived bright and early. He waved as I grabbed my stuff.

"That boy loves you," Grandma Hosseini said in Farsi.

"What did she say?" Grandma Sullivan called after me. I ignored her.

Gordie's dad called no fewer than five times between my house and Alice's to remind Gordie to turn on the AC in the brownstone, flush all the toilets once we got there, and check the sugar jar for ants.

"How many toilets do you have?" I said.

"Too many."

We had perfected the art of bullshitting. We stopped at Alice's and acted sad and despondent. Alice's parents thanked us for taking Alice out of the East End to get her mind off Izzy. We stopped at Val's and acted warm and loving. Gordie assured her mom (in Spanish) that a night away was just what Val needed to get her appetite back. We stopped at Jean's and raved about the Tiny Art Show to Jean's mom, who was resting on the couch with her feet in a bucket of ice. She told us how we had changed Jean, that he wasn't the loner he used to be, and how nice that was to see.

Trying to act perfect, fully functional, innocent, and wholesome all at the same time was exhausting. Gordie played music and we didn't talk until the Manhattan skyline popped up out of nowhere. Then we got serious about a game plan.

Alice told us the building Izzy took her to had an ornate gate with black leaves.

"You've got to give us more than that," Gordie said.

Alice stared out the window. The walls of the Midtown Tunnel whipped past us.

"I remember looking up at a cool building with a gargoyle. It was somewhere downtown, definitely south of Times Square because we walked through Times Square and I made Izzy stop at the M&M's store."

Gordie parked in front of an immaculate brownstone near Gramercy Park and we jumped out. Inside was all chocolate mahogany and expensive Persian rugs. The largest New York home I had seen prior to entering Gordie Harris's seven-bedroom, six-bathroom, four-floor brownstone was my uncle's two-bedroom, one-bath, second-floor apartment in Astoria, Queens.

And Grandma Hosseini called that uncle the family success story.

"I call the master bedroom," Jean yelled from the top of the staircase.

"I'm going to text this guy Ahmed," Alice said, studying Izzy's drug phone. "I met him once at the shrink's house but he has a New York number. He looks like a sumo wrestler."

I'm in the city. Where are you? Alice texted from the drug phone.

We waited awhile for Gordie to turn on the AC, flush all the toilets, and check the sugar jar. Ahmed didn't respond. So we hit the streets, a flock of beach-bred kids skating on adrenaline, fear, and the thrill of being on our own for the entire night.

"I'm nauseated," Val said, clutching her taut belly.

"You haven't eaten in days, Val," I said.

"Water," Val moaned.

We stopped for waters at a bodega and continued down the path Alice didn't remember. "It was snowy last time I was here" was her excuse.

We walked east to west, staring up, like the world's worst tourists, trying to find a gargoyle standing guard over an ornate gate.

"Puppy!" Alice stopped in front of a homeless guy sitting cross-legged with a puppy between his legs and a copy of Walt Whitman's *Leaves of Grass* in his hand.

"Can I pet her?" Alice leaned down.

"Sure. Her name is Annabelle." The guy had eyes the color of moss, bad acne, and a sign propped in front of his duffel bag that said HOMELESS. FOOD APPRECIATED.

Alice nuzzled the tiny puppy against her face.

"How'd you end up homeless, dude?" Jean said, reaching out to pet the puppy.

"Long story, man. It was one unfortunate series of events after another. It's so tragic it's almost comical."

"Any chance you know where we could score some smack?" Alice said.

I was mortified.

The guy stared at her, perplexed. "Nah, you guys don't use."

"We're looking for somebody who uses. Missing, of course. It's so cliché I could barf," Alice said.

"Yeah, I get the old *ask the homeless guy to help find your strung-out loved one* question all the time. Nah. My drug of choice is McDonald's. But there's a pack of asshole kids with asshole dogs that hang out down around St. Mark's. They'll give out dealer addresses for money."

"Thanks, dude. Very helpful tip," Jean said.

"I don't want to give Annabelle back," Alice said.

"You better give my baby back."

Gordie handed the guy a twenty-dollar bill. "Godspeed, bud."

"Same to you, man."

We passed countless ornate gates and a few gargoyle statues as we snaked around the streets of Manhattan, trying to fish the murky memory from Alice's brain.

We stopped in Union Square to watch old guys play chess next to an assembly of chanting Hare Krishnas and a pack of skateboarders veering dangerously close to all of them. I was hot and my feet ached already.

"This is ridiculous, Alice," I finally said. "There are millions of people and, apparently, thousands of ornate gates in this city. Can you try to remember something else?"

"I have been trying, Sadie. I was pissed off that day and I specifically remember I was freezing and cursing my life. That's it."

"Guys, you know we could be so far off. Izzy could be out in Montauk, like, a block away from where we were last night. Or Jersey, or Arizona," Val said. "We should have thought this through a little more carefully."

The Hare Krishnas didn't move. They sat in their saffron dresses with their bald heads and wisps of hair sticking out of their skulls like tails, and they chanted. Their faces showed no signs of distress or anger or fear. I almost got sucked into their cult, just to escape the drama.

"Let's go. These people are getting on my nerves," Alice said, turning. We argued over which way to go.

Alice refused to share her pretzel with Jean, who then insisted we go back so he could get his own. As they all waited in line for pretzels, I sat on a bench and held a water bottle against my aching feet. I watched a couple not much older than me as they wrestled with a baby who didn't want to sit in her stroller. They were as mismatched as we were, the pretty, fair-skinned, brunette, Ralph Lauren–model type with an NYU bookstore bag slung over her shoulder, the tattooed guy with piercings and a leather cuff, the dark-skinned baby girl in a peach-colored dress. A very hot guy in soccer cleats and a bright yellow jersey called out to them. The Ralph Lauren girl stood, picked up the crying baby, and kissed the very hot guy as the pierced guy grabbed the stroller and followed after them.

I would have loved to know *their* story.

We were almost at the High Line park when Alice stopped short and stared down at Izzy's drug phone. Her eyes got wide.

"It's Ahmed."

Yo. Izzy. I heard you were at the nest.

"I don't know what the hell the nest is. Ahhh. Let me think." Alice paced back and forth, and finally replied, I was. I went out and now I'm lost. What's the nest address again? So f'd up!

"That's perfect," Gordie said.

We stood in a circle, staring at the phone like it was an egg about to hatch. After an excruciating two minutes, Ahmed texted, Near Fourteenth Street.

Alice texted back, Thanks. What's the building number?

Trying to find molly on St. Mark's.

"The dipshit didn't answer my question."

"That's the street the Walt Whitman guy was talking about," I said.

"Let's go," Val and Jean said at the same time.

"Jinx," I said.

Jean made a face. "What the heck is jinx?"

St. Mark's Place was packed with tattoo parlors, noodle restaurants, and drug paraphernalia shops. We wandered into a bizarre store where some disturbed artsy person had packed glass cases with naked dolls.

A guy with a feather-shaped birthmark on his cheek sat on a blowup doll, smoking a joint.

"Dude, do you know where we can score some smack?" Jean was getting bold.

"Yeah, sure. Down at the precinct two blocks away, dickwad," the guy said.

"We are losers." I grabbed Jean's sleeve and yanked him out of the store. "We are totally incapable of being shady or discreet."

Gordie treated us to Chinese food with his American Express card because we had spent all our cash on pretzels and water.

"If I had that card, I'd so be at Bloomingdale's right now," Val said.

"I doubt it," Gordie said.

Alice obsessively scrolled through Izzy's phone. "I'm texting Ahmed again." We had been scanning the street for the sumo wrestler, but so far, no sign. I'm on St. Mark's. U still here?

No response.

"I wonder who Molly is," Val said.

"Molly, like the drug, Val," Alice said.

"Oh."

We sat on the steps of the naked doll store, keeping our eyes peeled for Ahmed and trying to figure out the next stop on our fruitless journey.

"I need a nap." Jean said what we were all thinking. We agreed to rest a little and resume our search after dark. Part of me hoped we wouldn't resume our search at all, because I wasn't sure I was ready to wander around at night, when the lizards came out of the shadows.

When we got to Gordie's brownstone, I took a shower and dabbed the monster tail and put on my leprechaun T-shirt and soccer shorts. I drew the hunter-green paisley drapes and crawled under the supersoft sheets of the corner guest bed, just before Gordie slipped in. He closed and locked the door and pulled off his T-shirt and khaki shorts. He stood for a second in his polka-dotted boxers, and suddenly I no longer needed a nap.

A while later, I left Gordie curled up like a wombat and tiptoed down to the den, where Jean was sitting at the window, drawing a black-and-white cityscape.

"That is so good, Jean. I'm jealous of your brilliance."

He wiped a clump of residue off the page and stared out the window. "I don't know if it's brilliance. It's more like lunacy. I get ornery when I'm not doing art."

I watched him add line after line to make the outlines of buildings, then bring the buildings to life.

"Do you think we'll find her?" he said, pausing to look at me.

"I don't know. But honestly, I don't want to go inside another trap house ever again. I still think about the scabby arm of this guy who was lying on a mattress in that disgusting living room."

He nodded. "Isn't it bizarre what your mind decides to latch onto?"

"Yeah. It is." I thought of *his* face flat against the shards of honey jar and gravel.

Jean turned the page of the sketch pad. "See this?" It was a black arm, reaching out of a block of ice surrounded by penguins and fish jumping out of the sea.

"Whoa. That's amazing."

"It's kind of messed up, actually."

He turned the page and showed me the same black arm, reaching out of a tree trunk. A giant butterfly with the face of a girl rested on the palm of the hand.

"I was nine when we had the earthquake. People ran around looking for family. I left the house and wandered toward my school. There was one section where everything was just leveled." He smiled. But it was one of those *This is so awful I don't know how to say it* smiles. "I saw something sticking out from under a windowsill that had sunk into the rubble. I realized it was a man's arm. I wanted to help him, so I pulled and pulled with both hands."

"Oh, Jean."

"Yeah. It took me years to convince myself that it hadn't been my father's arm I was pulling."

I didn't move. I wanted him to feel like he could talk if he wanted to talk. He flipped the page to another arm, reaching up to a waterfall dropping from the sky.

"I decided this will probably end up being my college portfolio. This is who I am, part of me, at least."

"It's incredible."

"There are hundreds of these. I'm hoping someday I'll feel like I can stop."

I sat quietly as he finished the beginnings of his cityscape and nearly gasped when he held it up. "Jean, it's beautiful. And I thought you were all about the smiling masks."

The sounds of the city were amplified at night. So, it seemed, were the garbage pile smells and the aroma of rich spices coming out of the Indian restaurants. I was careful to check in every few hours, to make sure Mom and Dad had a perfectly false sense of security. The last text sealed it: All the crew tuckered out. I think the Central Park Zoo was enough excitement. Going to bed. Love you guys. Ugh. Bad. Bad. Bad.

Dad texted back a picture of Grandma Sullivan with a milk mustache.

We made our way back down to St. Mark's Place and loitered in front of a hookah shop, pretending to be deep in conversation. Ahmed still hadn't texted back, so our only hope was the asshole homeless kids with the asshole homeless dogs the Walt Whitman guy had told us about.

At some point, I decided it would be a good time to tell everyone about Ella's mom. Since that first night when she had gone out in the limo, she had posted photos of herself buying an ATV for her new boyfriend, more expensive tequila, and a road trip to some Louisiana casino.

"Now we know why nobody dropped money into her Neighbor-Care fund," Alice said.

"I feel awful that we sent that canary, and that Ella has two lizard parents. It just sucks."

"Sadie, we didn't know. And how could we have not tried, after what you went through with that baby?" Val said. "I don't regret it at all."

"I do think we need to reconsider our strategy," Gordie said. "The care package model might be too risky."

We all agreed.

"Damn, you'd think it would be easier to dole out a bucket of diamonds." Jean nodded toward a man pushing a stroller full of empty cans. "I mean, there's no shortage of need."

"Street urchins, nine o'clock." Val pointed to a group of seven or eight chain-wearing, cigarette-smoking, biker-booted kids bouncing down the street with their leather-collared dogs and their Bob Marley rainbow hats in the ninety-degree heat.

"Come on. I'm done sitting on my ass," Alice said. She wove through a line of cars waiting at the red light.

The "street urchins" congregated on the steps of the naked doll store. They eyed us suspiciously as we approached. I didn't blame them. We didn't make sense. I had foolishly changed into my Taylor Swift concert T-shirt Dad said I would wear until it died because it cost him fifty-five dollars. I hadn't even considered wearing something tougher.

"Dude, we're looking for a smack house near Fourteenth," Alice said to a skinny guy with thick black eyeliner and divots the size of quarters in both ears.

"Why are you asking me? That's obnoxious," the guy said. He had a southern accent.

"Look. I don't have time to fuck around. Some homeless guy told us there was a pack of asshole street people with asshole dogs who hang around St. Mark's Place that give out tips in exchange for money." Alice put her hands on her hips and got close to his face. "I don't know you. I don't know if that homeless guy was full of shit. I'm appealing to the human side of your grubby ass. Might you know of a smack house off Fourteenth Street called the nest?"

Divot Ears called over his friend, a doe-eyed girl who didn't look a day over fifteen. She had a lime-green bruise under her eye and a puppy squirming in an open Whole Foods reusable bag.

"Hi, puppy." Alice smiled at the puppy. The girl eyed us.

"This chick is looking for a smack house off Fourteenth called the nest." Divot Guy laughed and they all started laughing. "She says she'll give us money."

"How much?"

"Wait a second," Jean said. "Like we're going to hand you cash so you can make up addresses. Do we look like damn fools?"

The girl laughed. "Yes."

"Fair enough," Jean said. "But if you want money, you need to take us there."

It was all so bizarre, like a scene from a badly written play.

"How much are you offering?" the girl said. "Fourteenth is a long street." She was clearly the ringleader of the skittish group. It appeared that beneath the grime and the metal face accessories and overuse of army prints, their gang was as mismatched as ours. "You know the dealers eat kids like you," she said matter-of-factly. "They'll stuff you into a meat grinder and eat you on a bun with aioli and pickles." I could tell by the way she talked that the girl was raised refined. She reminded me of Izzy.

"We'll take our chances," Alice said, sounding impatient to see if this weak lead took off.

They moved in a pack, with their collared dogs and duffel bags. We followed behind like awkward first graders boarding the big-kid bus. I tried to make small talk with a girl who clearly wanted nothing to do with my Taylor Swift T-shirt ass.

"Kind bar?" I offered.

"Whatever," she huffed. But she took the Kind bar.

The alleged smack house off Fourteenth was a run-down apartment building with black residue thick like tar streaking the once-white walls around the barred first-floor windows. The gang of urchins led us past the building quickly, then turned the corner.

"I don't want anybody seeing us with you," the ringleader girl said, staring at me. "These people have Uzis and shit."

I did not like the sound of that. The shrink's trap house had been scary enough, and that was just a bunch of trash bags and needles on a pizza box. I wanted to turn around, walk back to Gordie's, and permanently abort the mission. I was getting more uneasy by the minute with the situation we had gotten ourselves into.

"Where's the money?" Divot Ears held out his hand.

We all looked at Gordie. I had my bank card and an old Metro-Card with one ride left.

"I can't believe we're paying these people to take us to a smack house," Jean whispered to Val and me. We hung back while Alice and Gordie negotiated.

"I've got twenty-three bucks," Gordie said.

"I want fifty bucks," Ringleader said.

"Or what?" Alice said.

"Or Evan will hit you with his nunchucks."

Evan was five seven and about ninety pounds.

"What if I just buy all you guys pizza on my credit card?" Gordie said. It was slightly amusing that I was standing in the middle of New York City with Gordie Harris, who was negotiating with street kids to get them to play neighborhood smack-house tour guides. Shay would die laughing.

"Do you have any clue how many idiot Good Samaritans give us half-eaten pizzas? I want sushi. The good kind." The girl knew what she wanted.

"And soba noodles," some other guy chimed in.

We ordered the sushi and soba noodles and stood around in Union Square with our street thug acquaintances near the chess players and the Hare Krishna people, who had not moved since before we took our naps. The humidity was brutal, even after the sun set over the noisy, sticky city. My feet throbbed to the beat of the chanting and the flute sounds. Blisters had formed where my flip-flop straps hit my toes.

"What in Jesus's name have we gotten ourselves into?" Val whispered. "My mother will have my ass. You don't understand. She will beat me with a broom if she finds out I'm hanging out with street people. This is just wrong."

"Hey, Kardashian chick," Divot Guy called to me. I couldn't tell if he was going to hit me or hit on me, but I went anyway. "The nest is a very screwed-up situation. Get your friend and get the hell out."

"What kind of situation?"

"I'm not even going to go there."

I almost said *You seem like a nice kid. Come with us. My dad is an ice cream man. He'll help you*, but I didn't. I knew I couldn't help any of them, any more than I could help baby Ella, who, it occurred to me, could easily become one of these street kids someday.

Gordie came back with two huge bags of Japanese takeout. Our tour guides grabbed the bags and walked away.

"Geez, they could have at least said *thank you*," Gordie said loudly in their direction.

We strolled past the nest building. A stick-figure woman with mottled skin—white as glue—and hair that looked like she cut it all off herself smoked a cigarette on the front stoop.

We loitered on the corner until Alice finally took the lead.

"I'm going up to the door. You all hang out here."

"Hell no," Gordie said. "We are not going to have a repeat of last time. We're all going."

Alice pulled on her hair and stomped her boot. "Listen, you guys need to let me do this. Just stand near the door."

We stood near the door like a bunch of parents waiting for their kid to trick-or-treat.

Alice buzzed. She buzzed again.

"What?" a man's voice said.

"I'm here to get Izzy."

"Fuck you. She's not coming out."

"Fuck you. Yes she is." Superhero Alice was back.

Nobody moved.

Alice buzzed again. She held down the buzzer.

"I will shoot you in the fucking head," the guy screamed through the intercom.

"Send out Izzy."

"Izzy owes me forty-five hundred dollars. Bring me forty-five hundred dollars and you can have her."

Alice stormed away and we all followed.

Back at our spot around the corner, I said, "Alice, this is insane. These people have Uzis." My heart was beating so hard I felt it in my stomach.

"Alice, I have some money saved. I can take it out." I couldn't believe Val was offering money.

Alice made a *WTF* face. "No, Val. Just...no."

We stared at our shoes. We watched a cab whiz by. Finally, Gordie said, "I'll get the damn money."

"God. No. We're not negotiating with terrorists. Let me think." Alice's face was flushed. Her hands were balled up at her sides.

"If they won't let her out, how is she going to get the money?" Val said meekly.

"Oh, for fuck's sake. Why are you so stupid? Why don't you go to another sweet fifteen party at the church, Val? You're driving me crazy," Alice yelled. Val shrank against the bricks behind her. "She's probably going to have sex with some disgusting guy, okay? Lots of disgusting guys, maybe."

And then Alice puked. She knelt down and puked all over the brick wall. The puke splashed on my blistered feet.

Val turned away and held her head in her hands. Tears dropped to the ground.

Jean and Gordie froze in horror.

I waited until the retching stopped and handed Alice and Val each a tissue from Alice's bag, then wiped my feet with more tissues.

We all inched away from the vomit and stood against the wall for a long time.

A group of twentysomething gadflies, the kind who blew into the Hamptons and expected everyone to hold the doors for them and part the seas so they could eat a meal, stopped in front of us to decide whether or not to Uber to their stupid party. They were loud and obnoxious and I wanted to trip them and stick them with medieval bone daggers.

"Gross. It smells like barf," one of them said before they scurried away.

"Okay, last idea," I said. "I'm pulling out all the stops." I reached back to unbutton the back pocket of my shorts. I dug down to the bottom of the deep pocket, pulled out a perfectly shaped yellow diamond, and held it up between my thumb and forefinger. I had forgotten about the in-case-of-emergencies canary until that very moment.

Alice closed her eyes and rocked slightly. For a second, I thought she was going to pass out.

"We are not giving anything to anyone," Alice said calmly. "I'm sorry I yelled, Val. And I'm sorry I puked." She took a deep breath. "This was a stupid idea. I can't believe I dragged you guys into this bullshit." She closed her eyes again, marched down the block, and sat on the steps of a brownstone.

"We're done," she said. "I'm going to fix this right now."

Alice texted Izzy's parents from Izzy's drug phone. She told them the address and that their daughter was with dangerous people armed with Uzis, so they should call the police. She signed it, Good luck. —The Unlikelies.

Everything moved in slow motion for a while. I noticed a heap of garbage that had been ripped open and left exposed. I noticed a phrase somebody had spray-painted across a sidewalk square: *the gilded life*. My feet hurt. Every step was a struggle.

Alice marched in front of us, staring down at the phone. Gordie and Jean followed. Then me, the pitiful limper, then Val, arms crossed, heart bruised by Alice's words.

"Guys, can we stop a minute?" I summoned everyone to a dark storefront. The streets were still hopping with drunken college kids, who had probably just moved into NYU for the semester.

Gordie stopped. "What's wrong?"

"I can't walk."

Out of nowhere, Jean threw up his arms. "Can you stop whining about your damn feet? I can't take it."

I was exhausted and in pain and more scared than I had ever been. And Jean's comment filled me with fury. I took a step back. "Oh, I'm sorry I'm whining, Jean. Why don't you hide in your sketchbook and draw some dead arms, you freak?"

His eyes got wide. And then he left before I could take it all back. He bolted down the street and texted Gordie that he was taking the Long Island Railroad all the way to the end and could Gordie drop his stuff when he had a chance?

I felt like I wanted to puke on a brick wall.

❧ TWENTY-SIX ❧

GORDIE HAD BEEN excited to wrap up the Izzy rescue in a timely fashion so he could have a night alone in the brownstone guest room with me.

That wasn't happening. It was late by the time we got to Gordie's, and I collapsed on a bed with Val for a few hours before Gordie woke us all up to go home.

Val was furious at Alice. Furious Val still smiled, but she walked around with her arms crossed in front of her. Alice was mad at the world. She locked herself in one of the rooms and didn't emerge until Val and I were in the car and Gordie threatened to leave her in New York. Jean, of course, was gone. Because of me. I couldn't tell anyone what my comment even meant, because I didn't want to betray Jean more than I already had.

The car trip home was full of awkward silence. Alice's parents called to tell her Izzy had been found, hallelujah, she was safe and sound, but *Oh dear, what a mess that it had all unfolded on the New York news stations.*

I texted Jean SORRY no fewer than fifty times. He never responded.

The buildings and the billboards blurred by as we drove through Queens. I couldn't separate the images that rushed through my mind, elbowing one another for space. I thought of the people we called street urchins, but somebody else called sisters, brothers, children, friends. I wondered how Izzy felt when the police showed up. Was she scared? Was she relieved? Or was she just pissed they were taking away her drugs again?

Our eyes were glued to the social media headlines: MYSTERIOUS GROUP BUSTS HEROIN RING; THE UNLIKELIES NAB ELUSIVE DRUG NETWORK. Unlike the East End cops, the New York cops had no problem telling the media about us and our text to Izzy's parents. By the time we reached Val's, the bust was on every major tristate online network.

"I want to see Jean," I said to Gordie.

"I don't think that's a good idea, Sadie. Just let him have some time."

"Gordie, please stop at Jean's."

"No, Sadie. I'm beat. I need sleep."

He dropped off Val, who waved weakly and walked toward her building without looking back. I hoped she wouldn't go looking to Javi for comfort. I hoped she would stay strong.

"We never did find that ornate gate or the gargoyle, huh?" Gordie said right before we pulled up to Alice's.

"Yeah, right? That was a clusterfuck of a wild-goose chase I started," Alice said. "Thanks, Gordie. You're awesome." She leaned over and kissed his cheek. And that left the two of us.

"Are we in a fight?" I said.

"No, Sadie."

"Do you know how bad I feel?"

"I know. Everybody was unhinged. Let's go home, sleep, regroup, and we'll talk tomorrow, okay?"

"Tomorrow?"

"I don't know? Later?"

"Whatever you want." It was all unsettling. Gordie was right. Everybody was unhinged and it felt awful.

Mom was pulling weeds when Gordie dropped me off. I climbed out of the backseat and grabbed my stuff from the trunk. I almost took Jean's stuff, too, so I could hold it hostage and force him to talk to me.

"How'd it go?" Mom briefly looked up from the flower bed below the mailbox.

"Great. It was a little overstimulating for some of the people, but everybody had fun."

I was a liar with a monster tail. I felt disgusting all the way to the core of my soul. I stood in the shower for over an hour, head down, eyes fixed on my purpling foot blisters. At one point, I nearly blacked out from the steam and the thoughts that I carried with me—dark, overwhelming, shameful thoughts.

If I had been a different person, maybe it would have been enough to say, *We found Izzy. Izzy is safe. Everything worked out.* But the images hung in my mind like ornaments on a tree. And the anger dug a hole in me and hatched, and I was all clogged up with images and anger, and a nagging fear that Jean wouldn't forgive me and the Unlikelies would disband forever. And a nagging fear that Gordie Harris didn't like me anymore.

I dabbed ointment on the foot blisters and put on my soft cotton robe. I sat on the bed, with all the fans blowing on me, and stared at my phone. I had to try again. Jean, I am so sorry I said that. I was stressed out and I got pissed when you called me a whiner and it just came out. Our friendship means SO much to me. Please forgive me. Sadie.

And then I fell asleep.

I woke to the smell of garlic and the sounds of dishes clattering. I was starving.

"Well, well, well, look who it is." Dad put his paper down and stood up from the kitchen table to hug me. I wanted to cry. "Tell me about the trip."

I didn't have the energy to search for lies. "It was so hot. Look at my feet."

"Oh, man, you need to wear better shoes when you're walking around."

"Woody, do you want salad?" Mom licked sauce off a wooden spoon.

"Nah, just give me the good stuff."

I could hear the news guy's voice from the living room. "Here's a bizarre story out of the East Village. A drug operation has been outed by a mysterious group calling themselves the Unlikelies." I casually grabbed a section of Dad's paper and wandered over to the couch.

The building near Fourteenth Street was sectioned off, accessorized by yellow tape, bustling with police and reporters. They showed footage of people being taken out late at night in handcuffs. At the very end, before they cut back to the reporter, I saw Izzy. She looked like how I had imagined a heroin addict would look. She no longer looked anything like Neigh from Girl Scouts. It broke my heart.

According to the news, the nest was a movement, an insidious barter system where desperate young addicts went to exchange sex and stolen merchandise for drugs. And the main headquarters, which had eluded authorities until the Unlikelies' tip, was in a grungy building off Fourteenth Street. By the time Izzy's parents got there with their lawyers and their hired security, multiple agencies had pulled out nearly a hundred minors, including Izzy, and twenty-seven lizards.

It was a lizards' nest.

The shellacked news guy turned to his coanchor. "This Unlikelies group has established itself as an anti-trolling, anti-bullying network on the Internet. Its reach extends as far as Scotland and Singapore. It appears the group has now taken to the streets," he said.

"Really? So it's like a group of vigilantes, of sorts?" the coanchor said.

"Seems so."

I texted Gordie, How did I just see we've been anti-trolling in Scotland and Singapore?

Remember I was developing a program to sniff out troll and bully threads and hit them with our avatar? Mission accomplished. (Working on translating to other languages.)

You're a genius!

Really? I thought I was nerd boy.

That was it. No *I have to see you.* Nothing. And not a word from Jean.

Me: Do you want to hang out?

Gordie: Can't. Stuff going on at home.

Me: Are you sure you're not mad at me?

Gordie: I'm sure. Talk soon.

Me (to Jean): Please. Please. Please. Please. Talk to me.

Jean: Silence.

Val: I just wanted to tell you guys they are talking about the Unlikelies on the Today show. I cannot believe this.

I turned the channel and caught the very end of the segment. They were talking about the nest bust and how we were taking down troll mill chat rooms all over the world with the avatar. It was so weird to see the masked Civil War soldiers, to see *us*, on national TV.

I FaceTimed Val. "I am stunned right now."

"How are we all over the world?"

"Gordie figured out a program that sniffs out troll bully language and slaps the avatar on the threads. His genius nerd boy ass is figuring out how to translate the software, or something like that."

"That's much more efficient than dropping off care packages," Val said.

"I like the care packages," I said, biting into a day-old bagel. "Hey, are you going to forgive Alice? Because I need us back together. I have anxiety."

"I already forgave Alice. I'm a very forgiving person, Sadie."

"So why isn't she responding to our texts?"

"I think she's in a bad place."

"Let's check on her later," I said. "Hey, Val?"

"Yeah?"

"I miss *us*."

"*Us* will be back, Sadie. We're just all taking a little break."

"I don't like little breaks."

"Clearly." She laughed.

"You okay?" I said.

"You'd be proud of me. Javi texted to see if I wanted to talk and I ignored it."

"I *am* proud of you. Love you, Val!"

"Love you, too, *mi amiga*."

I was glad to get back to the farm stand and the regulars and even the city people with their white pants and expensive shoes. Daniela laughed when a lady with a gravelly voice and oversize sunglasses held up a bunch of sunflowers and asked me *how much* in Spanish.

"I don't speak Spanish," I said flatly.

I delivered lemonades to the farm stand guys and was exchanging my hummus and carrots for their doughnut holes, when an old Lincoln town car showed. I nearly passed out because, for a second, I thought it was Mr. Upton.

It was Sissy.

I left the rest of the hummus with Papi and rushed out to the car. Sissy felt like my only living link to Mr. Upton, and my relationship with the old guy had gone from *The peach is fine—stop inspecting it* to *Thanks for nominating me as a homegrown hero* to *I guess I'll unlock the suitcase and make amends for your dead lizard* to *What the holy hell am I supposed to do with a heaping pile of yellow diamonds?*

"Sissy! It's so good to see you. The farm stand hasn't been the same without you guys." I greeted her with a big hug and she filled me in on her life. Mr. Upton had been true to his word, and Sissy received an inheritance from his will. She had taken her kids and grandkids down to Trinidad for a wonderful family reunion.

"I wanted to check on you and see how you're healing. How are you, my dear?" She ran her fingertip over the monster tail, now mostly covered by my growing bangs.

"I'm good. Thank you for asking." We moved under the shade of the willow tree. "Oh, Sissy, wait. I have a treat." I ran into the farm stand and brought out a container of wild blueberries, the ones that come out only two weeks a year.

We ate berries and talked about Trinidad and my parents and some of the regular customers, and then I just said it. Because I was a balloon, so full of secrets, so ready to bust open, I couldn't keep it in one more second.

"Sissy, I really need to talk to you about that suitcase Mr. Upton gave me."

"You got the suitcase. Good. I wasn't sure if you made it up there yet."

"Oh, I made it up there. And I have to tell you, there was some valuable stuff in the suitcase. As in loose diamonds."

"Really?" Her eyes got wide.

"Yes. And when I visited the hospital, he asked me to figure out a way to redeem his evil father's bad deeds with the contents of the suitcase, and it's a little overwhelming." My throat got tight and the tears welled up. "I really want to do the right thing."

She stared at me and closed her eyes and shook her head.

"What is it, Sissy?" I had no idea what I had done.

She opened her eyes and said, "That old codger."

"What?"

"That old fool has been trying to get other people to redeem his evil father's bad deeds or some nonsense for decades."

I was confused. "He has?"

"Yes. Old lovers, friends, guys from the Rotary, me. We all told him, 'Stewy, you're a good man. Get over it.' But he couldn't, so he tried to get other people on his guilt wagon."

"Oh." I thought I had been special, that he had picked me because I saved Ella, because I was a do-gooder.

"That old codger knew what you had been through and he guilted a teenager into doing his dirty work?" She stood in front of me and held me by the shoulders. I couldn't stop the tears from flowing. "You listen to me," Sissy said. "Whatever was in that suitcase is yours. Stewy left gobs of money to everyone and their brother, myself included. As frugal as he was when he was alive, he's making up for it on the other side. And I promise you, he's resting peacefully."

"Okay."

"You do what your heart tells you to do, not what you think Stewy would have wanted. You know why?"

"Why?" I wiped my cheeks.

"Because you'll drive yourself nuts. *He* didn't know what he wanted. How could you?" She laughed. "Oh, Stewy. The surprises keep on coming."

I felt better instantly. Like Sissy had taken me, the overinflated balloon, and gently let some air out, just enough, so I could feel relief. I still had no idea what we were going to do with all those canaries, but I felt much less pressure to get it right.

I drove myself to Willie Ng's therapist. My parents trusted I wouldn't skip the appointment and lie about it, after I admitted I sort of enjoyed going. I tried to figure out what I most needed to talk about as I drove through the back roads, sipping lemonade and listening to Alice's angry playlist.

There was so much to process: The *Today* show. The bullshit promise I made to Mr. Upton. The tension I was feeling with Jean.

Gordie texted me while I sat in the stuffy waiting room. Just saw Today show clip. Damn. I'm good at what I do. Would you like to have a proper date tomorrow night?

Yes, please.

The therapist was wearing the same stained T-shirt as the first session, except there was a new coffee stain above Mickey Mouse's ear. He flipped through his pad, cleared his throat, and smiled.

"How's the sleeping these days?" He jumped right into it.

"Actually, getting better."

"And how about life? What's been going on?"

"Can I ask you about something unrelated to the incident? Like, interpersonal?"

"Absolutely." His face lit up.

"I've been having issues with one of my friends. I said something really hurtful and I don't know how to fix it."

He looked through his pad. "Is this Shay?"

I had forgotten I told him about Shay and how I had thought she was blowing me off when she was actually pretty miserable at tennis camp. Now he was probably going to write, *Sadie is one of those pain-in-the-ass high school girls who always has drama with her friends.* I hadn't actually talked to Shay since the CVS conversation. But I knew it was going to be okay from our happy emojis and Miss you and Talk soon texts. It hit me that I needed to talk to Shay, clear the air. Apologize for walking around being mad at her—which I probably did only because it was easier than missing her.

"Uh, no. A different friend. Anyway, I don't feel comfortable getting into the details. I just need advice on how to get my friend to answer my texts. He won't even let me explain myself."

"Is this a romantic interest?"

"No. Just a guy friend."

"Without knowing the full story, I suggest you give it time, and allow your friend to cool off a bit. Sometimes people need that. Then reach out again, maybe not via text message, as sometimes texts can be misconstrued."

I said "Okay," but I didn't have the patience to let Jean cool off anymore.

"How does that sound?"

"That makes a lot of sense."

We spent the rest of the session talking about the incident. I admitted I was sick of the incident. I didn't want to talk about it, think about it, dream about it, or write about it ever again. I just wanted to snap my fingers twice and make it disappear.

"So finish up that letter for the victim advocate for next session, and we can stop talking about the incident. What do you think about that?"

"Yes, definitely," I said.

As hot and cold as I was about my trips to the therapist, I always left feeling better. I also always left feeling hungry.

I sprinted out of there and ordered from our favorite Chinese place.

While I waited in the parking lot for the food to be ready, I decided to call Shay.

"Shay?"

"Hey."

"I'm sorry. I'm so, so, so, so, so sorry about not being a good friend."

"It's okay, really. I loved my care package. The cookies were all broken, so I put them on my ice cream."

"Can we try to be normal again?" My voice cracked.

There was silence on the other end.

"I have to tell you something, Sadie. I remember what happened with Gordie Harris at CVS."

"Okay?"

"I had a basket full of incriminating shit. Like tampons, yeast infection medicine, I don't even know, but Gordie Harris was trying to talk to me and I freaked out and ran away. I promise you, Sadie, I had no clue what he was saying. When you mentioned it, I had to search my brain. But anyway, I'm really sorry. I was all kinds of mortified."

"Oh my God, Shay. I totally understand."

Then Shay began to cry.

"I've been really sad, Sadie. I can't deal with all these people out here, and it felt like you just moved on with Pooch and those guys. I don't even know what happened with us. I feel so empty."

"Shay?"

"Yeah?" She blew her nose.

"I think I pushed you away because everything was changing and it was stressful and I was probably mad at you for leaving."

"I get it. Believe me."

"And there was a reason I brought up the Gordie Harris thing."

"What reason?" She sniffed and blew her nose again.

"Gordie isn't gay. And I've been hooking up with him." And then I started laughing.

"Shut up."

"I know."

I ate vegetable fried rice with a plastic spoon at a table in front of the Chinese restaurant window as flies buzzed around me. I bit into an egg roll and suddenly felt the urge to find Jean and talk to him in person. It was more than just wanting to repair the cracks in the Unlikelies. I had grown to adore Jean with his beard and his sketching and his quirky one-liners and passion for life despite everything he had endured.

I wove through the Tiny Art Camp parking lot searching for Jean's van. When I didn't see it, I took a chance and went to his house. It was starting to get dark and his tree-lined street was quiet, almost eerie. I parked in front. There were no lights on, no signs anyone was home. I climbed through the tangled bushes, shimmied against his neighbor's fence, and tiptoed behind the house. A single light shined through the blinds in Jean's room.

I'm outside your window, I texted. I waited a few seconds and then tapped on the glass. I waited a few more seconds and tapped harder.

Jean pulled the blinds apart and peered out. It was still light enough for him to make out my grinning face. I waved. He shook his head, opened the blinds, and pulled up the window.

"What the hell are you doing?" He was not amused. "Do you know what would happen if somebody like me tried this shit?"

"A short, bearded person?"

"Are you just going to keep pissing me off?" He didn't crack a smile. "What is it, Sadie?"

"I really only want to talk to you for a minute. Please, Jean?"

"Fine. Whatever."

I crawled through the window and landed on his bed.

The room was cluttered with sketch pads and masks in various stages of completion. Jean was doing what Jean did, escaping the world in his art room.

"You don't have to talk. I just want to tell you that there is no excuse for saying what I said."

He sat on the desk chair turning a chisel over and over in his hand.

"I never shared those drawings with anyone before you. Not even Umi." I watched his hands move as he talked. "So, yeah, it felt pretty shitty when you said what you said."

I stood in front of him, sick to my stomach as the full awfulness of what I had said enveloped me. I felt my lip tremble.

His face softened.

"I guess I shouldn't have yelled at you for whining about your nasty feet," he said.

I smiled, still not 100 percent sure he was offering an olive branch.

"Did I ever tell you that my great-grandmother, also named Sadie Sullivan, had both her feet burned off in a fire while successfully saving seven children?"

Jean laughed. "You are such a pain in the ass, Sadie Sullivan junior."

"Can you please forgive me? I am so, so sorry." I picked up a carved mask painted black and white. "And this panda bear mask is freaking adorable."

He wiped his hands on his pajama bottoms and took my hand. He hugged me and then we took a selfie of us smiling cheek-to-cheek and texted it to everyone.

Val texted, Aww. So sweet.

Gordie texted, Um. Why is my girlfriend in your bedroom, might I ask?

Alice didn't text anything at all.

As I was leaving, this time through the front door, Jean said, "Oh, and you've told us about your great-grandma burning off her feet no fewer than a million times."

"Good. As long as you know."

I watched TV all night with my parents, something we hadn't done in a long time. Between Shay back-to-normal texts, and group texts (most of them joking about my "hookup" with Jean, all of them ignored by Alice), and Can't wait for tomorrow Gordie texts, I scrolled through chat rooms literally flattened by our avatar. Gordie had figured out how to code the "sniffing" so it could tell the difference between *My mom is bitching at me* and *Taylor is an ugly bitch*. He even took down the book trolls, the ones who thought it was cool to bully fictional characters. *OMG. Hermione is SOOOOO annoying* was replaced with five masked Union soldiers. BAM.

The craziest part was that other people were creating copycat avatar masks to take down bullies, assholes, and trolls all over cyberspace. There were articles popping up about chat rooms full of bullies being driven out by people posting *Come to the light* over and over and over again. Kids who were struggling talked about how *You're one of us now* just appeared on their social media pages out of nowhere.

I almost felt bad for the bullies and the trolls, the gadflies and the ruffians, sitting alone in their rooms, banging their keyboards in utter frustration.

When Dad turned on the eleven o'clock news, a caption read THE UNLIKELIES REACH THE EAST END.

"Wait, I know that girl," I said. It was Meghan Rose Sharp, the one who always laughed when people were mean to Greg O., the one who thought it was hilarious when Greg O. hit himself out of humiliation, the one who received one of the very first asshole care packages.

The news lady with the bleach-blond bob stuck a mic in Meghan Rose Sharp's face. "They left a package on my deck a while ago. There was a candy necklace in it and a note that said *choose kindness* or something like that, signed the Unlikelies. My mom wouldn't let me eat the necklace in case it was tainted with poison. It wasn't in any sort of packaging."

"What a dumbass," I mumbled.

"Is she a friend of yours?" Dad asked.

"No."

"Have you been following this Unlikelies story? It's all over the place. They're some sort of vigilante network. They uncovered a huge drug operation in the city."

"Yeah. It's pretty cool."

My heart raced. I said good night and ran upstairs.

Meghan Rose Sharp is on the news talking about the care package. They're coming out of the woodwork, I texted.

Val texted back, We were on the Today show. They're gonna come out of the woodwork!

TWENTY-SEVEN

ALICE'S DAD ANSWERED the door when I showed up unexpectedly at eight a.m. on Saturday with breakfast sandwiches and coffees.

"Sadie, hi. Alice is still sleeping."

"Sorry I'm here so early. I have to work, but I wanted to check on Alice. She hasn't been answering our texts."

He held the door open. "We think all the Izzy stuff is finally hitting her hard. We've been letting her sleep, but, honestly, it's time to get her up. Go ahead. Just yank the comforter off her."

"Uh. Okay."

I ran up the stairs and burst into Alice's darkened room. She was all the way under the covers. "Alice, it's me. Wake up, Pooch."

"Hey."

"I have breakfast sandwiches and coffee. How about we go to the duck pond for a quick little morning walk?"

She said yes.

She threw on leggings and an old T-shirt, grabbed her vegan bag, and climbed into the passenger side of the Prius. As I drove away, I noticed her dad watching us through the living room curtains.

"I apologized to Val," she said, between sips of coffee. "What I said was awful. I hate that I said those things."

"She's forgiven you. She knew how stressed you were. We all have our moments of awfulness."

"Sorry I haven't been in the mood to text. I was mind-bendingly tired. It's a good thing you're getting my lazy ass out of bed."

I didn't know if it was the long sleep or the strong coffee, but Alice was in the mood to talk. I told her about my visit to Jean's room and my talk with Sissy.

"So I guess anything goes now, huh?" she said. "Canary party."

"Actually, I feel more paralyzed than ever. I mean, I think this is a decision I have to figure out myself. I've been trying to get you guys to figure everything out for me, just like Mr. Upton tried to pawn it off on his friends."

"You'll do the right thing, Sullivan."

Alice told me Izzy got shipped to Utah. Her dad wanted to send her to Oman because it was a Muslim country and she might have a tougher time getting drugs. But her mom worried about the hot weather and was afraid that if Izzy did get her hands on drugs, she'd be thrown in prison. "These conversations seriously happened. In my kitchen," Alice said. "After a lot of Bloody Marys."

Izzy's mom said she didn't want to continue living in a community that judged her and shunned her daughter and made them all look like "trailer trash," so she found an apartment near the rehab place and left Tanner to fend for himself with his dad, a nanny, and a new puppy. Puppies were notorious consolation prizes.

The duck pond was nearly empty when we got there. We took our coffees and breakfast sandwiches and sat on the grass near Jean's dreaded pack of ducks. Alice pulled a letter out of her bag. "Here, read this while I eat."

The letter was written on Hello Kitty stationery with a green felt-tip pen.

> *My Allie Belle Poocher,*
> *You know how much I adore you, right? How did we get to this place? How did I get to this place? I wanted to be a dancer. And a waitress (remember?). I wanted to go to college in Boston. I hope I can do even one of those things. I hope I can get clean. I'm not there yet. That's a start, right? Saying I'm not there yet. But I'm going to keep trying. You, my sweet Allie, are always the branch I grab on to when I'm floating down the river. And no matter what happens, I'll never forget that.*
> *I love you so much, my Allie Belle Poocher.*
> *Neigh*

"That's good, right?" I said, folding the letter and tucking it in Alice's bag. "It is a good start."

"She gave that to me seven months ago."

"Oh."

Alice laughed. "I don't think I ever told you...Izzy and I had a secret brick. We kept money under it so we'd always be ready when we heard the Woody's Ice Cream music. We'd run down to that brick and dig around in the dirt for change." She stopped talking then. It was as if that one memory dislodged something so painful there was no place for the pain to go.

I held Alice's head in my lap while she cried and cried and trembled with grief. I stroked her spiked hair and played with the silver studs that lined her ear. A couple walked by our spot near the pond and I gave them the *My friend is having a hard time* smile and they understood.

When she was done, Alice looked at me and wiped her eyes with the back of her hand and said, "I lied, Sadie. I do feel bad about killing Hector with the voodoo doll."

I didn't want to leave Alice on her porch with swollen eyes and a guilty conscience, but I had to go to work.

Daniela was there before me, which was a rare occurrence. "Limonada!" she said when I walked out back to help fold boxes.

"Hey, give Papi and those guys a chance. They're cool."

"We have nothing in common." She made a face.

"What are you doing tonight?" I said, smiling.

"I'm parenting, like I do every night. But obviously you want me to ask you what you're doing. What are *you* doing tonight, Sadie?"

"*Me?* Oh, just going on a date."

I stood in the spot where the incident happened, where my whole summer changed course, and felt all fluttery at the thought of being alone with Gordie Harris.

Hannah S. caught me off guard. I was filling the flower buckets with the hose when she snuck up behind me.

"Hi, Sadie, what's going on?" She had a strange look on her face.

"Not much. Just watering the flowers. How are you?"

"Good. We're going down to the beach tonight. Do you want to come with us?"

"Thanks for the invite, but I have plans. Do you want a free sunflower?" I held out the sunflower.

She took it. "Soooo. When were you planning to tell me about Gordie Harris?" Now the casual *Just stopping by to say hi and invite you to the beach* made sense.

I stared at Hannah. "There's nothing to tell. A bunch of us have been hanging out."

"It all adds up now," Hannah said, as if all the mysteries of the universe were instantly solved. "No wonder you haven't been at Shawn's. Gordie is so not a Shawn Flynn party guy."

"Yeah. He's way too cool for that," I said.

It seemed like for better or for worse, our fate was sealed. Sadie and Gordie were a rumored couple.

Senior year could begin.

There were a ton of texts waiting for me after work.

Turn on channel one, Gordie texted. A spin-off group calling themselves Ebenezer is asking radical religious groups to lay down their arms and join the movement.

Val: Why didn't we think of that?

Spin-off groups were taking down hater sites with armies of masked avatars, demanding kindness, urging renegade tipsters to join the Unlikelies.

It was good in a weird way and weird in a good way. And it was exhilarating.

Mom always had a way of making me tell her things. She'd get me when I was distracted, like when I was watching a show or trying to figure out what to wear. She'd slip in a random question nonchalantly and I'd let my guard down and tell her something. Then she'd hold it against me for the rest of my life.

Once I let it slip that Shay had HPV. I was unaware HPV was a sexually transmitted disease. I thought it had something to do with her yeast infections. So after the slip, Mom would say things like *Maybe if Shay's mother didn't play tennis so much she wouldn't have that HPV*, or *Maybe if Shay's parents didn't attend so many fund-raisers, she wouldn't have that HPV*. That was always said in Farsi. All of Mom's judgy statements came out in Farsi, unless, of course, she was saying them to Grandma Sullivan.

I had to avoid Mom because I had become a bomb, packed full of wires and chemicals and tiny traps. One lit Mom-match could blow bits of secrets all over the East End. And they weren't *that HPV* kind of secrets. They were *trap house, cyber vigilante, we weren't with the Turtle Trail people in New York, I'm falling for Gordie Harris* kinds of secrets.

A slow drizzle fell on the roof and bathed the flower beds. We sat in our usual chairs with our plates of sautéed mushrooms and lamb.

"I'm thinking of going vegetarian," I announced.

Mom laughed. "That's crap," she said.

"Why is that crap, Leila? She can go vegetarian if she wants."

"Animals were put on this earth for us to eat."

"Really, Mom? Do you ever think about the baby lamb that died so you can grow your ass?"

"Lamb doesn't grow my ass. Ice cream grows my ass."

"Don't blame me for your ass," Dad said. "Which I like, by the way."

Mom smacked Dad's leg. "And what are you going to eat for dinner?" she asked me. "Mushrooms?"

"Alice eats lots of stuff and she's a vegetarian."

"What's next? An earring in your nose? Maybe green hair to match the vegetables?" Mom stabbed a hunk of lamb with her fork.

Dad laughed and changed the subject. "Let's see a movie tonight." He wiped the sauce off his whiskers with a leftover Fourth of July paper napkin. "We haven't done that all summer."

"I kind of have plans."

"Oh." I saw the *My little girl doesn't want to be with her old dad anymore and it hurts like hell* expression.

"Tomorrow?" I smiled my *I still love you so much, Daddy* smile.

"Tomorrow's good."

I showered and shaved, put on lotion and makeup, dabbed the monster tail, and stuck a little butterfly barrette in my slightly grown-out bangs. I wore my favorite blush-pink dress with silver sandals and the diamond studs Grandma Hosseini gave me when I turned sixteen. And I slipped out of the house before Mom could ask me why I was trying to look pretty.

The Range Rover pulled up exactly on time, a first for Gordie Harris. I ran out just as it began to rain hard.

"Sadie," Gordie said, drawing out my name. "You look amazing."

"Thank you." He squeezed my hand and didn't let go until we got almost to Montauk. Gordie backed into a gravel lot behind a wall of sea grass.

We sat in the car and waited out the rain, talking about Gordie's "stuff going on at home," which had to do with Frances and her cancer and that it was worse than they had hoped. I felt like an idiot for bothering him with *Are you sure you're not mad at me?* texts when he truly was dealing with real issues.

"Keith is sensitive, and when he gets upset, he regresses, so we have to be careful how much we tell him," Gordie said, still holding my hand. "But we have a solid plan."

"Great. What is it?"

"We're going to adopt Keith and Frances. We'll have an adoption ceremony and everything to make it official. That way my parents will be Keith's legal guardians, and he doesn't need to perseverate about Frances until the very end."

"What's *perseverate*?"

"Worry."

"Got it."

"Of course, my mom is planning an adoption ceremony that'll be bigger than most weddings. You guys are on the list."

"Aww. That's going to be sweet."

"Yeah."

He pulled away a bit and stared at me, and tucked my hair behind my ear. He traced the monster tail with the tip of his finger.

"So what do you want to do?" I said, staring back.

He laughed. "Stay here."

"Why?"

"I have a little surprise."

The rain had moved out to sea, and I waited, my eyes focused on the craggy trees in front of me, while Gordie opened the back and moved stuff around.

"What are you doing?"

"Don't look."

If it had been Seth, the wild groping would have been wrapping up and we would have been on the way back to Shawn's.

"Okay, come out."

It was still light behind the dark storm clouds, and streaks of sun dropped down over the whitecaps. I jumped out and walked around to the back of the Range Rover. Inside, Gordie had arranged a pile of blankets and pillows and tiny LED tea light candles on a tray with a thermos of hot chocolate and a pie dish covered in foil.

"You cleaned out your car for me?"

"I did. Let's hope we don't need a shovel."

"Or a metal detector."

"Or a metal detector," he said, laughing.

We crawled in and lay on our sides facing each other. Gordie took off the foil from the pie dish.

"Do you want some cobbler?" he said.

"You made me cobbler?"

He said, "I told you I owed you for those kickass biscuits. The peaches are kind of mealy now, so I went with blueberry."

He handed me a fork and I took a bite. It was delicious.

We poured the hot chocolate and Gordie held up his cup. "Here's to things worth waiting for."

I touched my cup to his.

"And to that auspicious moment when the Hamptons Hoodlum got booted from the homegrown heroes luncheon," he said.

"I actually met that girl," I said. "She's having a hard time, so let's not call her that anymore."

"Hey, you know how at the homegrown heroes luncheon, when people were saying where they wish they were and I was being all mysterious?"

"Yeah."

"This is where I wanted to be. With you," Gordie said, leaning in to kiss me.

"Are you serious?"

"And can I tell you something even more embarrassing?"

"Yeah."

"I have spent the past three years playing the most ridiculous game." He paused and looked at me. "So, I always try to sit strategically in class so I can just make out the top of your pants, where, if I'm lucky, your shirt will ride up a little and I'll get a glimpse of your underwear."

I slapped his arm. "Oh my God. You little perv."

"I'm totally a little perv."

"How often did you see my underwear?"

"Not often enough."

"I need longer shirts."

"No. No, you don't. Your underwear is the reason I'm probably going to be valedictorian. No joke. Sometimes I'd be like, *Screw it. I'm not going to school today. I'm going to stay home and play my harmonica.* But then I'd think, *Wait, what if today's the day I get to see Sadie Sullivan's underwear and I'm home? Can't take that chance.*"

I covered my face with my hands. "Mortifying. And creepy."

He looked at me with an *I'm thinking about your underwear right now* expression.

"Did you have a favorite pair?" I raised my eyebrows.

"The purple ones."

"You're kind of turning me on right now." I moved my lips close to his.

The fluttering.

"You kind of turn me on all the time," he said.

His shirt found its way to the front seat and the electric candles scattered all over the place and Gordie's hand found my black underwear—the ones I never, ever wore to school—and his mouth found my mouth and it was all incredible.

We pulled the blankets up and I snuggled against him. I told him all about Shay, that I had finally had a good talk with her and things were much better. He told me he was glad because nobody on this planet is perfect and Shay was probably suffering post-inseparable-senior depressive disorder.

We didn't talk about the Unlikelies or what happened in New York or what I was going to do with my promise to Mr. Upton. We didn't want to sully our perfect night with things that were too intense for almost-seniors to deal with.

"So what's going to happen when school starts?" I said, eating another heaping forkful of cobbler.

"Like, as in with you and me?"

"Yes. As in with you and me. Do you intend to be the couple who holds hands in the hallway or the couple who sneaks around in the bushes?"

Gordie kissed my blueberry-stained lips. "Whichever gives me more access to you and your purple underwear."

"Okay, good. Because Hannah S. already seems to know about us."

"I don't care who knows about us, Sadie." He slid his hand up my shirt and gently held the back of my head as he moved toward me and kissed me long and hard until he finally stopped and said, "Sexy Sadie."

"Okay, that's weird," I said.

He laughed. "That's a Beatles song."

We lay in the dark with a new bout of rain hitting the car roof. Gordie held me in his arms and the world felt good and safe and hopeful again.

❧ TWENTY-EIGHT ❧

THE PRESS COVERAGE of the Unlikelies had shifted to everybody trying to guess who we were. One news network decided the Unlikelies had originated in Manhattan and was probably somebody with connections to the East End of Long Island. Thank you, Meghan Rose Sharp.

Our offshoot, Ebenezer, was all over the news.

"Since when have you been interested in news?" Mom called from the kitchen, where she sipped tea and read a fall flower magazine.

"Shh." I turned up the volume. The news guy with the hair plugs and overly white teeth was interviewing two women in their early twenties wearing Alice-style print skirts and tank tops.

"Are you the Unlikelies?" I held my breath, afraid they would claim our baby.

"No. Not at all," the glossy-haired girl with glasses said, looking directly at the camera. "The Unlikelies inspired us to create Ebenezer, you know, as in *Scrooge*, because Scrooge was misguided and then rehabilitated after he had an epiphany."

"So what exactly is Ebenezer's mission?"

"We are encouraging young people who might be drawn to fundamentalist and fringe groups to join us." Glossy-Haired Girl stared into the camera again. "There are better ways to make your mark. As the Unlikelies say, 'You're one of us now.'"

The news guy stuck the mic in the other girl's face. "Do you know who the Unlikelies are?"

"No. But we're all Unlikelies now, right?"

The guy continued interviewing them until a commercial break.

Damn, they were good, Jean texted.

Who's our spokesperson? Gordie texted.

You, Jean texted.

Nah. I nominate Sadie.

You're biased cause you're banging her.

I'm right here, I wrote.

Val wrote, Is this really happening?

All because of a couple of candy necklaces for assholes.

Alice? Is that you? Val wrote.

Gordie wrote, She's back!!!!!!

I went to Alice's that afternoon. I had something to show her. I hoped it would make her feel better. When I got there, Alice was lying on her front lawn with a blue-gray puppy curled up on her stomach.

"Who's this little guy?" I whispered. The puppy stirred when Alice got up, but she stayed asleep.

"This, Sadie, is the best consolation prize my parents could ever give me."

"She's yours?"

"She's mine." Alice held the puppy up to her cheek. "It took my best friend being shipped off for heroin addiction to finally get a puppy, but she's all mine."

"What's her name?"

"I don't have one yet. That's a very important decision." Alice took a picture of me holding the puppy and texted it to everyone.

We went up to Alice's room. "I have something to show you." I took a folded copy of a newspaper article out of my back pocket and handed it to Alice. I sat next to her on the bed, and we read Hector's obituary together silently.

> Charles Adam Sands, 19, died of a heroin overdose Saturday in a Queens bathroom. He was the son of Mary (Lewis) and Arthur Sands and brother to Lily, Maeve, and Sydney, his three "baby bunnies," as Charles called them. Charles loved baseball, chocolate-chip pancakes,

Christmas, and visiting his grandparents in Arizona. He also loved to sit with his cat, Paisley, on his chest while he watched fairy movies with his sisters. Charles got sick the first time he tried heroin at a party, when he was fifteen. His family adored him and spent every moment of every day trying to help him get away from heroin. But heroin won.

Alice threw the obituary on the floor. "Why are you showing me this? Are you trying to make me feel worse?"

"No. Alice, look at the date. Hector died on July seventh," I said gently. "All that time you were looking for him, he was already gone. He died before you even started poking the poppet."

Alice sat back on the bed and held the puppy. She didn't say anything, but I could tell by the way her forehead relaxed a little that she felt better. We put the puppy in her crate and listened to her cry for Alice the whole way up to the attic. The altar was pretty much the same as it had been the last time I was there, but the room was slightly cooler.

"How do you want to do it?" I said, gathering scraps of fabric from the floor.

"Let's do it the way we did the lizard's suitcase."

"That sounds good."

We pushed all the dolls and candles and books and scraps into a big black garbage bag, and Alice went back to her puppy while I went straight to the supermarket, chucked the whole voodoo collection into the dumpster, and drove away.

By the time I got home, half the damn world had changed their Facebook profile photos to our masked Union soldiers or one of the spin-offs, including Gordie's mom, baby Ella's mom, and the insufferable Meghan Rose Sharp.

Jean: We should be getting royalties for this.

Gordie: It was only a matter of time before this entire thing became convoluted. It's like Einstein and the nuclear bomb.

Nobody knew what he was talking about.

❧ TWENTY-NINE ❧

WHAT WAS SUPPOSED to be movie night with Dad turned out to be movie night with Dad, Mom, both grandmas, Mr. Ng, and Willie Ng. They purposely chose a movie that didn't have sex scenes, because of Willie's "issues." They neglected to consider my issues and chose a movie with multiple brutal, bloody assault scenes.

A few times, I caught myself finger snapping. That was when I decided to focus on the popcorn and chocolate-covered raisins. Grandma Sullivan seemed a little too into the movie. She swatted my hand every time I tried to check my phone. By movie's end, the good guys finally took down the dirty cop, although I felt like the Unlikelies could have taken him down in thirty minutes.

After the movie, we walked to the pizza place, except for Willie, who claimed he had someplace to be.

Mr. Ng wanted to treat.

"Put your money away," Dad said.

"Put *your* money away, Woody. I've joined the Unlikelies," Mr. Ng announced.

"Isn't that something?" Dad said. "That an underground movement of Good Samaritans is going viral because of the Internet? Although my buddy in Syosset was complaining the precinct phones are ringing off the hook. Renegade tipsters turning in drug dealers, sex traffickers, secret polluters, dog-fighting rings."

"It's probably a scam," Grandma Sullivan mumbled.

"What'd she say?" Grandma Hosseini asked Mom.

"She thinks that the Unlikelies is a scam."

Grandma Hosseini gave Grandma Sullivan a thumbs-up. "That's what I thought, too," she said in Farsi.

You know you've made it big when Grandma Hosseini and Grandma Sullivan accuse the Unlikelies of being a scam, I texted everyone.

"She's texting her boyfriend, Gordie," Grandma Sullivan said with a mouthful of pizza.

"Gordie's gay, Ma," Dad said.

"He's not gay." Grandma Hosseini spoke perfect English when she felt like it.

I cleared my throat. "Soooo. I have an announcement."

They all stopped midchew.

"I kind of discovered Gordie isn't gay. It was all a mix-up. And then I discovered we like each other." They stared at me.

"Told you," Grandma Sullivan said.

"Wait a minute. I let you do overnights with this punk and he's not gay?" Dad's face went purple. "I can't believe that little shit pulled this."

"He didn't pull anything. He's a perfect gentleman, okay? He's a really good guy and you don't even have to threaten to cut off his penis and serve it on a cone with sprinkles."

Mr. Ng choked on his soda. "You said that, Woody?"

"That was supposed to be a man-to-man talk between Seth and me. Kids today are pricks."

Mom took a sip of water. "Stop cursing, Woody." She looked at me with an *I'm really skeptical about everything* expression and then surprised us with "He's going to be valedictorian. We'll take him."

"No more overnights," Dad said sternly.

We finished eating in virtual silence, except for the giant belch that erupted from Mr. Ng.

That night, I had an epiphany about the promise I made to Mr. Upton.

We hadn't all been together since Jean ditched us on the New York street corner. After work and nonsense and drama and family commitments and no fewer than seven thousand texts, the five of us were finally meeting.

But this meeting was all business.

We gathered on Jean's girlfriend's dock in sweatshirts and jeans on the first cool night of the summer.

Alice took the purple collar off the unnamed puppy and dipped her tiny paw into the water.

"I feel like Sissy has given you an out, like you can really do whatever you want with the diamonds," Alice said.

"Canaries," Val said.

"Okay, we're sitting on a dock. Nobody can hear us. I think we can safely call them diamonds." Alice threw a half-eaten rice cracker in the water.

I opened my Woody's Ice Cream tote bag and took out four small packages wrapped in brown paper and tied with yellow ribbons.

They tried to cut me off with jokes and speculation, but I held up my hand.

"Let me just get through this," I said, lining up the packages on the dock in front of me. "This was my promise to Mr. Upton. And it's my decision. So here's what I've decided: Most of the diamonds will go into a safe-deposit box until exactly four years from now, when I will summon you all back to share what you've learned about life and money. Hopefully, we'll all have more wisdom after college and I will take it all into consideration and have my answer about what to do with them. That being said, the one rule is that if any one of us is in danger of not finishing college because of money, we dip into the diamonds, no questions asked."

"That's awesome, Sadie," Alice said.

"Except that's probably not going to be you or Gordie," Jean said, flicking Alice on the arm.

"Oh, please, Gordie could get disowned any minute now," Alice said.

"That's it," I said. "Pretty simple. Oh, and these are your end-of-the-summer care packages." I handed each of them a wrapped box. "You can open them."

Each box contained the same three items: a candy necklace to remember how it started, a tiny plastic lizard to remember why it started, and a miniature stuffed Raggedy Andy, a tribute to our creepy doll friend.

"Where did you find this, Sullivan?" Jean said, holding up his Andy doll.

"Online. They were very reasonable," I said.

Alice leaned over to hug me. We fell over, and soon we were a pile of Unlikelies with one adorable nameless puppy.

We knew that diamonds, as changeless and prized as they were, had limits. They couldn't ever really begin to redeem the lizard's evil deeds, any more than they could bring Hector back to his family, or guarantee that Izzy would never crave heroin again. They couldn't make Javi nicer or take away Frances's cancer or make baby Ella's parents love her the way she deserved to be loved.

The truth was, we didn't need college to know that there would always be lizards. There would always be diamonds. And there would always be people willing to start unlikely revolutions.

When Gordie dropped me off, he walked me up to the porch, where my parents were sitting under blankets listening to Springsteen.

"Springsteen again, huh? Good choice," Gordie said.

"He's the Boss," Dad said.

"Yes, he is."

"So I'm guessing we'll be seeing a lot of you?" Dad said.

"I hope so." Gordie smiled.

"Good." Dad stood up and gave Gordie one of his firm thumbless handshakes.

Before bed, I texted Jean and Val and Gordie and Alice. As soon as you're home, go someplace private, take scissors, snip Andy's crotch, and stick your finger up in there.

Excuse me? Val wrote.

Just do it.

I pictured Mr. Upton's ghost laughing with me as my friends dug into the seams of their miniature Andy dolls and extracted two yellow diamonds each and a tiny rolled scroll.

Each scroll simply said *Do something noble.*

Val's Andy doll had a second scroll and a second pair of diamonds. That scroll said *For Javi's medicine.*

But Javi's an asshole, Val texted.

Then it will be our last asshole care package.

They all graciously accepted the canaries. That night, I didn't wake up once.

Daniela must have told the farm stand guys it was my last day of work because they showed up with candy and flowers and a handmade card that said *Gracias, Limonada!*

I hugged them and got teary-eyed.

"I can't believe you're abandoning me," Daniela whined. She worked the farm stand until it closed after Thanksgiving. I wanted to say, *You abandoned me for Candy Crush months ago*, but there was no point.

"Thank you for being so good to me that day. What would I have done if you weren't there to catch me when I went down?"

She laughed. "It was my pleasure. God, that seems like so long ago."

"Doesn't it? Give the kiddo kisses for me. I'll visit," I said.

"I'll save the good pumpkins for you."

I walked out to the spot where the incident happened.

When I thought of *him*, I thought of the same sound bites: the screaming and cursing, calling me an *A-rab*, slamming down the basket, the liquor breath. I wondered if maybe, in some deep place where a flake of love floated inside him, he had wanted to take Ella away to the mythical Hamptons where rich people sip liquid gemstones on marshmallow yachts, but somewhere along the way, the demons got him and extinguished the instinct to give his baby a better life than he had.

Whatever his intent, he was a lizard now. I realized I could help Ella by keeping *him* away from her. I needed to write that letter.

I sat at the coffee shop with my laptop, my *Guide to Northeast Colleges*, a caffeine buzz, and a good frame of mind. I opened a blank page and wrote my letter, the letter that would be presented to the judge, the letter that would possibly help determine *his* sentencing. I wrote about the incident and how terrifying it was and how it left me with blood in my urine and spleen pain and broken ribs and a bruised forehead and a scar on my face. The scar was still there. The headaches were still there sometimes. I had bad dreams. I had night terrors. I got nervous when a car pulled into the parking lot too fast. I got nervous when I smelled liquor on someone's breath. I got nervous when I saw a baby crying. (I left out the part about stalking Ella's entire family on Facebook. That just made me look pathetic.) The incident left me a little broken. It also left me humiliated. People made fun of me, judged me, made me feel bad about myself. I was afraid that if *he* got out of jail, he'd come after me. I was even more afraid of what he'd do to his baby girl.

Those things were all true. They were what needed to go into the letter. But they weren't the lasting effects of the incident. The lasting effects of the incident started with Mr. Stewy Upton nominating me as a stand-in for Alexis Ahern.

"Here, Mom. It's done." I handed her the letter. She read it and reread it and smiled, which seemed inappropriate.

"Why are you smiling?"

"Because you laid it on thick, and I think it's going to influence the judge to get that bastard in the balls."

"Weird, Mom. You've been hanging around Dad too long."

My mother got out her meticulous file of bruise photos, a rainbow of ugly Sadie faces and monster tail poses.

"Gross, Mom."

"We're not entering a beauty pageant, are we?" She got her phone off the counter. "One more for luck."

We went out to the garden, where the hydrangeas were browning a bit and the chill had killed the daylilies. "Don't move." I held my hair away from the monster tail and Mom took too many pictures.

I didn't want to look, but I did. It was there, as it always would be, curled and trying to look cute. It had gotten slightly lighter, more flesh-toned. "Better than it was, honey," she said. "And after all that complaining, you're done. Remember that when I suggest you get going on the college applications."

"Will do, Mom."

I was in the mood to clean my room and purge my summer shit and get ready for school. I stood in the doorway, staring at the origami cranes hanging haphazardly from corner to corner. In one long tug, I pulled them down.

Every last one.

❧ THIRTY ❧

GRANDMA SULLIVAN WAS fine creeping around the neighborhood in her Toyota Avalon in daytime, but after sunset she was all squints and panic. *I can't see! I can't see, damn it!*

"Take Grandma to get the lotto tickets," Mom said, giving me the *I have a migraine* sign.

I was in the middle of a virtual tour of Pepperdine with Shay and her very awesome roomie Eleanor from Detroit. The other two roommates were book troll gadflies, but Shay and Eleanor from Detroit were two sweet peas in a pod with their friendliness and unending quest for fun. Shay had left the hellish tennis camp behind her and was starting anew.

"*Here comes the sun,*" I sang.

"What?" Shay said.

"She's singing the Beatles," Eleanor said. And I liked her even more.

Even though Grandma Sullivan couldn't see at night, she was still perfectly capable of backseat driving all the way to the convenience store so we could buy her lotto tickets.

"Turn left up ahead. It's a shortcut," she said.

"I'm going the way I like to go," I said.

I waited in the car for a while and finally decided to go into the store to see what was taking her so long. That was when I literally collided with Seth and D-Bag. It took me a couple seconds to process Seth's grinning face. I almost turned and ran away. Then I saw D-Bag's T-shirt.

"Speak of the devil. We were just talking about you."

I ignored Seth and stepped in front of D-Bag. "Where did you get that T-shirt?"

"This? It's the Unlikelies. Have you been living under a rock?"

"I know what it is. Where did you get the T-shirt?"

"Online."

I couldn't believe D-Bag was standing in a convenience store, holding a Red Bull and wearing a T-shirt with *our* five masked Civil War soldiers, *our* avatar printed on the front.

I shook my head and started to walk away.

Seth grabbed my arm. "You're that bitter? You can't even say hi?"

I took a deep breath. "Hi, Seth. How was your summer?" I said with my sweetest Sadie Cakes voice. I stared at the T-shirt. Some self-serving online loser was making money off our movement.

"It was good. I'm just packing for college. I guess you were too busy with Gordie Harris to answer my texts."

"I'm sorry, Seth. I really, truly hope you have the best four years of your life." I reached up and gave him an awkward hug. "I have to go."

I left the store and fumbled with the Prius keys. Grandma Sullivan was already in the backseat. The last thing I wanted to do was cry in front of my grandmother, but I couldn't help it.

"What's wrong, Sadie?"

I reached for the tissue box. "Nothing, Grandma. I was just freaked out to see Seth."

"The new guy is better looking. You can tell Seth will be bald by the time he's twenty-five. Good riddance."

That was Grandma Sullivan's best attempt at consoling me.

"Thanks, Grandma."

"Don't waste any more tears on that slob."

But the tears weren't over Seth. They were tears of rage. The Unlikelies was our thing. It was built of our goodwill and pure intentions, and it had degenerated into a freak show on the news and a T-shirt business catering to the poseurs and wannabes, including a kid who purposefully referred to himself as *Douche Bag*.

I dropped off Grandma and her tickets and rushed home to Google the Unlikelies. There it was—an online store with hats, T-shirts, sweatshirts, bumper stickers, mouse pads. I forwarded it to everyone and sank into the chair in the corner with my Flopper and a stomach full of fury.

Gordie was right. He had said it was only a matter of time before the whole operation became convoluted. And now there was nothing any of us could do to stop it.

Early the next morning, I tiptoed to the basement to dig my leprechaun T-shirt out of the dirty laundry. I stopped in front of the family photo wall. Great-Grandma Sullivan watched, smiling her goofy toothless smile.

"Don't judge," I said out loud. "I need my damn shirt."

I wondered what Great-Grandma Sullivan's life would have been like if she had kept her feet but left the children to die. They weren't her children. They weren't even any relation to her. Would she still be smiling in that picture?

I picked up egg sandwiches and coffees and got to the duck pond in record time.

"Why do we continue to meet in a place that makes me uncomfortable?" Jean said. "Next time we're meeting on a massive spiderweb, Val."

"Great, Jean. Let's do that," Val said, patting the blanket she had laid out under a tree. Jean sat next to me. He had a fedora on and was clutching a duck-fighting baseball bat.

Gordie rolled in just after we finished our sandwiches and his.

"You ate my sandwich?" He looked wounded.

"Can I just say how irritated I am that a random kid from our school was wearing our avatar on his shirt, and some amoral asshole is profiting off our idea?" I said.

"Sadie, we're all pissed. As soon as I saw the coverage all over the place, I knew it was coming. It's bullshit," Gordie said.

"Maybe we should just go public," Val said. "We'll call everyone out."

Alice lifted her finger and held it in the air. "Under no circumstances will we ever go public."

"So do we just let it go fully corrupt?" Jean said. "Like walk away?"

"We didn't really have a grand plan to begin with," Alice said. "We helped Greg O. with his website, dropped some care packages, and started anti-trolling on Val and Jean's school slam page. That's it."

"Clearly it has evolved, Alice. Do we walk away or do we do something?" I didn't know the answer. I just wanted to protect all the good things we started without the nonsense.

We lay back on the blanket and stared up at the tree branches, heavy with late-summer leaves. Nameless Puppy jumped on our stomachs and licked our faces. Finally, Val sat up and smiled her *The wheels in my brilliant and abnormally productive mind are turning* smile. "I've got it."

We used up the rest of Jean's sketchbook and half of another. We spent hours on the blanket in the middle of the duck pond park while the puppy chased away oblivious ducks and gutsy squirrels, bloated from the fruits of summer.

And then we were finished. And we were exhausted.

"What do you think we would have done if all this hadn't happened?" Gordie said as we walked to the cars.

Alice laughed and heaved her bag over her shoulder. "Been really friggin' bored."

Dad had chicken and corn on the grill when I got home. I was three days into vegetarianism so I ate the corn with a side of hummus and pita while Mom sneered and told me I was going to die of protein deficiency.

We settled into our chairs on the porch and watched the fireflies struggle to keep up with the hum of the cicadas. It smelled like fall.

After dinner, Dad and I took the ice cream truck over to Gordie's for our special group date.

"Hey there, Mr. Valedictorian." Dad was embarrassing.

Gordie jumped in the truck. "Woody, turn on the music. This is awesome."

Dad turned on the music, and Keith and Zoe ran out of Gordie's house.

"Woody! Woody!" Keith ran up to the window. "Wait, I have to get money."

"No, you don't, Keith. This one's free. And I have a little surprise for you." Dad opened the side door. Keith and Zoe climbed in front. And away we went. We picked up David and gave him a hat to match the new ones Dad had stuck on Keith's and Zoe's heads, and we drove all over the East End, playing the music, serving the customers, eating excessive amounts of ice cream.

Gordie and I sat on the floor in the back, facing each other, legs crossed, knees touching.

He licked his lips and that was all it took. I raised my eyebrows and ran my fingertips over his bare legs. He shook his head, and his eyes said, *You can't pull this shit in your dad's ice cream truck.*

"Last, but not least," Keith called from the front.

"Last, but not least, buddy," Dad said, pulling into Turtle Trail Recreation Center.

Dad did have the best job in the world.

Is it up yet? Alice texted. Gordie and I were in my stuffy room working on our secret project. Mom had pulled the *I'm going to set some clean towels on your bed because I want to make sure you're not having sex even though the door is open* routine.

Yes. Just finished, Gordie texted.

He sat back in my chair in the corner. I lay on the bed playing with Flopper's tail, feeling nervous and excited.

"Don't judge," I said when I caught Gordie staring at me. "Flopper's gotten me through some rough times."

Gordie had changed our avatar to a link. The link took people to a statement with the intentions of the founders of the original Unlikelies.

It was our manifesto.

We are the founders of the Unlikelies. We started
this movement to disrupt the cyberbullies and high
school assholes, the ones who make life much less
enjoyable for the rest of us. Then we moved on to
turning in the keepers of the underworld, the ones
who get young people addicted and leave them
for dead. And that was all good. Except that you
all became fixated on trying to figure out WHO we
were, and you ignored WHAT we stood for. And then
we didn't even know what we stood for.

So we had to pause and think. Pause and think,
people.

Pause and think.

We stand for kindness. That sounds cliché. But we
can't help it. We stand for kindness. We believe in
sticking up for people who are being mistreated
online, in person, wherever. We believe in sticking
up for people we don't even know. And before you

change your Facebook photo to our avatar or buy a T-shirt some asshat sold to make a quick buck, pause and think: What have YOU done today to stick up for someone? What have you done to stick up for yourself?

We stand for bravery. We need to step in and help our friends and classmates who are struggling with addiction and depression and all the things you may think you're immune to. You're not. We believe in being brave and speaking up and speaking out and turning in the traffickers, the dealers, the soul stealers.

And we stand for respect. Respect our planet. Yeah, it's simple. But we all need to do better. Respect the person to your left. And your right. Respect yourself. Because you matter. And by the way, go, Ebenezer! You guys rock!

Do something noble. You're one of us now.

—The Unlikelies

Gordie closed the laptop and motioned for me to sit with him in the chair.

"I wonder if any of this will rub off on our dysfunctional class-mates," I said.

"We'll see soon enough."

"Do you think we did it right?" I whispered as I lowered myself onto his lap.

"Well, you know what they say." He smiled.

"What do they say?"

"If you see something, say something."

"Good one, Mr. Pause and Think. Pause and think, people."

Val: What now?

Jean: No clue.

Alice: Sleep until school starts?

Me: There's a carnival tonight.

And that was where we went. We ate loads of cotton candy and bit the hard, glossy shells off the candied apples and smeared one another's faces with the powdered sugar from the fried dough. We rode the Ferris wheel, over and over again, and tried to win giant stuffed animals but failed miserably, probably because the games were rigged. There were a few annoyingly long lines and two of the rides were broken and Alice found a long black hair in her raspberry slushie.

But other than that, it was amazing.

✣ ACKNOWLEDGMENTS ✣

I would like to send a lifetime supply of Woody's ice cream to my editor, Lisa Yoskowitz, and my agent, Sara Crowe. You are my dream team and I will sing your praises to the ends of this earth. Giant, bottomless sundaes go to everyone at Little, Brown and Hodder, especially Lisa Moraleda and Jane Lee for your loveliness and professionalism.

A care package filled with gratitude goes to the following people for sharing professional wisdom and, in some cases, very personal anecdotes on everything from heroin addiction to police response scenarios: Dale Hernsdorf, Brian Preleski, Jared Shaw, and my husband, Michael Firestone (who definitely knows what a spleen is). And thank you to the Hamptons teens (especially K) who thoughtfully answered all my questions. Your musings on real-life issues shaped this book.

Mile-long candy necklaces go to the following people for your support: Callista DeGraw for being my first (and very special) teen reader (again); Laurie Uhlig, Alex G., Grace S., and Lisa Berman (for your fandom); my Barnes and Noble Canton buddies (for reminding me to walk so I don't get a DVT); Jen O'Dea (for the sleepovers); The Pandas (for being the best critique group ever); my "Sweet Sixteen" and other author friends (for your commiseration and encouragement); and Denise Alfeld, Eleni DeGraw, and Wendy Avery (for being my other dream team).

If I found a suitcase full of diamonds, I would give it to you—Dad and Kay, Mom and Fred, Jen and Tim and Devin, and Lindsay and Andrew—not just because I love you guys, but because I know you would use it to do something noble. My family has taught me there are countless ways to give back, to do "good," to fight lizards. Note: Val's migrant school-supply program was modeled after my father Ray Lenarcic's similar program, one of many he has created to make Herkimer County, New York, a better place.

Hugs and love to Lauren Firestone for giving Sadie her name, and to Emily Firestone for coming up with the original title. And thank you, Grandma P. and Pop Pop Firestone, for entertaining the girls in the Hamptons so I could work.

Michael Firestone, you deserve another thank-you for being far more wonderful than any love interest I could write. You are living proof that "instalove" is real. (And it's spectacular.)

That saying "Friends come into our lives for a reason, a season, or a lifetime" is true.

I had the opportunity to celebrate the *Loose Ends List* launch with my "lifetimers" in NYC and Little Falls, New York. Both events were snow globe moments I will never forget. Thank you, lifetime friends, for your loyal and essential presence in my life.

And finally, I experienced two unforgettable "seasons" many years ago. One took place during the summer of 1990 in an apartment overlooking Geneva, New York's Seneca Lake. The other took place in 1994 at a Manhattan bar called Sullivan's. Some of the people I hung out with during those "seasons" are dead. Some have disappeared. Some I talk to often. But they all remain with me. We shared the thrilling experience of being young and free and adventurous. Those unlikely friendships, however fleeting, have stayed with me. Those unlikely friendships inspired this book.

If you know someone struggling with addiction, you don't have to go through it alone—talk to someone you trust and/or learn about available resources through organizations like drugfree.org. And if you're looking to make an "unlikely" impact in your own community, volunteering with reputable nonprofits is a great place to start.

TURN THE PAGE TO START READING
ANOTHER ONE-OF-A-KIND NOVEL FROM
CARRIE FIRESTONE

AVAILABLE NOW!

-&o ONE o&-

WHEN GRAM CALLS, I ignore it. Lizzie and I are at Starbucks waiting for Kyle and Ethan to get out of lacrosse practice. We're working on our Loose Ends lists, and they're just getting good. I scroll through mine while Lizzie sticks her straw into another iced tea lemonade. It's uncomfortably hot for May.

One. *Save enough lifeguarding money to pay for a road trip.*
      Last year I blew all my money on a stupid designer bag that now has ink all over the inside.

Two. *Have an alone day with each of the E's.*
      I love my three closest friends deeply, but those girls glom onto one another like puke under a toilet seat.

The noise, the drama, and the differing opinions can be maddening.

Three. *Learn how to cook an entire meal to perfection so I can survive on my own.*

Mom bakes constantly, but she doesn't cook. And Dad's Thanksgivings are amazing, but most nights we get hummus and lentil chips. I want my uncle Wes to design a menu and teach me to cook from scratch.

Four. *Discover a new constellation.*

Dad and Jeb and I have been studying the sky since we were curled-up marsupials wrapped in Dad's sweatshirt. Jeb enjoys stargazing because he's a stoner. I like it because I appreciate vastness, and it's the only thing I have in common with Dad.

As much as my friends make fun of it, my astronomy hobby helped me get Ethan last winter during a sledding party. I have a well-known weakness for team captains, and I had been eyeing Ethan since he landed that esteemed lacrosse title, beating out Lizzie's precious Kyle. I jumped on the sled behind Ethan, and we flew into a snowdrift. I wrapped my legs around his, and broke the silence with, "Look, it's the Big Dipper. Isn't it cool?" He looked up, and I kissed his cheek.

I pointed out four constellations that night before he kissed me back on the lips. It tasted like beer and watermelon gum, but I had snagged Ethan, the hottest captain of them all.

Five. *Rewatch all the eighties movies during a weekend marathon,* preferably with Abby, since she's the only other one willing to eat massive amounts of junk food without complaining about fatness.

Gram calls again.

"It's just my grandmother," I say. "She's probably at Saks. She hates my graduation dress and won't give up on trying to find me a better one." I take a swig of iced chai. "Okay, I have a few more loose ends and then we can finish with something big."

"Isn't a road trip big enough?" Lizzie also missed out on the doomed road trip last summer, after her dad found out about a certain topless selfie. Gram says Lizzie leaves nothing to the imagination, which is pretty ironic coming from an elderly woman with a library full of VHS porn.

Six. *Find a drive-in movie theater somewhere in Connecticut and watch from the car in my pajamas.*
I plan to do this with my friends because Ethan will just try to bone me again.

Seven. *Let Ethan try to bone me again.*
The first time was a disaster. Ethan had an "accident" the second we got into his twin bed. I try not to dwell on the details, but it was gross, and his apologizing no fewer than five thousand times annoyed me so much I had to leave. Now he's insecure and telling me it happened because I'm so pretty.

As irritating as he is sometimes, I'm staying with Ethan for now because he's firmly in my social circle and it would take way too much energy to avoid him all summer.

Eight. *Prepare for City Living.*

My phone vibrates. Gram.

"God, my grandmother gets obsessive when she's shopping." I ignore again.

"She is so funny," Lizzie says. "My grandma watches *Wheel of Fortune* and goes to Target when she needs an adventure."

"Yeah. My grandmother gets mud wraps in remote jungles when she needs an adventure," I say. "You should see her boyfriend, Denny. He's my mom's age and wears diamond rings on both pinkies."

"I can't stand jewelry on men," Lizzie says.

"This guy is drippy diamond rich. Actually, Drippy is a good name for him." I grab Lizzie's phone. Her list is pretty conventional. *Learn how to do a proper shot. Lose ten pounds.*

"Lizzie, this is more like a to-do list. You're so boring."

"Maddie, I've been trying to do a shot for months, and it always comes out my nose. Perfecting my shot technique is definitely a loose end."

"Okay, but please get rid of *lose ten pounds*. You're already skinny, and that's a waste of a good one."

"Hey, you wrote *change hair color*. That's equally lame."

"I crossed it out. I do need an edgier look for New York, though.

I was thinking of going strawberry blond." I wrap my unruly Medusa curls into a bun.

"No way. That would totally wash you out. My stylist says blue eyes, light skin, dark hair. Keep it brown."

"Your stylist lives in Connecticut," I say as my phone vibrates. It's a text from Gram. I need to talk to you right away. It's urgent. My stomach sinks. Gram has never texted me before. I run outside to call her.

"Gram, what's wrong?"

"You don't return my calls now? Are you too popular for your grandmother?"

"You just freaked me out. You never text me."

"You wouldn't answer your phone. I happen to know that thing is glued to you at all times."

My heart is still racing. "Can you not do that again, please?"

"So what are you doing that's so important?" Gram says.

"I was making my Loose Ends list."

"What's a Loose Ends list? Sounds fascinating."

"It's a list of the things I never got to in high school that I want to do before college."

"Like blow jobs?"

"Oh my God, Gram. You're disgusting."

"So, I need you all to come to my place tonight at seven sharp."

"But it's Friday. I have to drive everyone to a big party." Gram knows I'm the permanently designated driver of a powder-blue minivan.

"Hon, I have something important to share, and I need the

family here. Somebody else will have to drive your bimbo cheerleader friends." There's a strange urgency in her voice.

"You're making me nervous." Gram always has surprises up her sleeve, but she usually blurts them out before she can build any anticipation. "Did you call Mom?"

"I got your father. He said they would be here. I had to bribe him with Indian food and theater tickets, mooch that he is." Gram thinks Dad is a weird, socially awkward freeloader and that Mom ended up with him because she has the emotional fortitude of a newborn panda.

She's kind of right.

It's a good thing I haven't had to rely on my parents for much more than stargazing and shoe shopping. Gram takes care of everything. We shop, eat out, visit museums, take amazing trips, and meet famous people. Once, just to piss off Dad, Gram got her board member friend from the planetarium to give Jeb and me a private show.

Gram always delivers. So I will play her little game and go to her mystery meeting.

"Fine, Gram. I'll be there. Can you give me a clue?"

"No." She hangs up.

"I have to go into the city." I grab my stuff and hug Lizzie good-bye.

"Wait, what are you talking about?" Lizzie yanks my T-shirt.

"My grandmother needs us for some surprise announcement. I have a feeling she's engaged to Drippy."

"Why do you have to go into the city for that? Even the college people are coming to this party." Lizzie's whining. "Can you at least come later?"

"I have no idea when I'll be back. This is bizarre, even for her."

-ಓoಐ-

I find Rachel, my neighbor and former best friend, watching TV in our living room. Our mothers have been friends since we were in utero. Mom spends her afternoons at Rachel's house drinking while Bev eats. They accept each other unconditionally and dwell in the underworld of the American housewife, sipping cocktails, eating cupcakes, and watching prerecorded episodes of Kathie Lee and Hoda.

My friendship with Rachel became a struggle in fourth grade. My Barbies were not compatible with Rachel's LEGOs. We tried. We even built a LEGO yacht for the Barbies, but they just couldn't get comfortable.

By seventh grade, I had found Lizzie, Remy, and Abby. We dressed one another up like Barbies, and called ourselves the E's because our names ended with the *E* sound. We group texted and had sleepovers, studied together, and made appearances at all the parties.

There was no place for a Rachel among E's.

Of course, our mothers were devastated. They labeled me a snot and Rachel a victim of exclusion and bitchiness. So we sat them down one afternoon, when they were all tanked up on gin and banana bread, and explained the situation.

"Mom," Rachel started, "I am not a victim. I have friends. Most of them are boys, but that's because boys are the only ones who get my computer games. Maddie and I need to go our separate ways right now. We will always be friends, but our interests are diverging."

"Good word, Rach," I said. "I promise we'll reverge—"

"Converge," Rachel interrupted.

"Converge, when we're adults and have children and our interests don't matter anymore." And that ended that. We still hang out, just not in public. Rachel is a stargazer, too, because she's obsessed with *Star Trek* and always on the lookout for alien life-forms.

"Rach, Gram's up to her old cryptic tricks." She looks up from her box of donut holes. "She wants us all to go to her apartment tonight for an announcement."

"Maybe she's getting another tattoo." Rachel knows Gram.

"I hope not. I saw her ass a couple weeks ago, and the seahorse is sagging like someone whacked it with a flyswatter."

Dad comes up from the basement. "Astrid wants us at her place in two hours. I'm guessing she's going to announce her engagement to that Denny."

"The one with the pinkie rings?" Rachel wiggles her pinkies.

"I was thinking engagement, too," I say. "I'm calling him Drippy from now on. Can you imagine the wedding? Who gets the bigger diamond?"

Mom comes downstairs in a perfectly pressed dress, with her full makeup face on.

"Here, Rachel, take these to Bev." Mom takes a picture of cinnamon scones on a tray for her Pinterest page and wraps the tray in plastic.

I text the E's: Family emergency. Can't drive. Will try to meet you later. I ignore the flurry of responses. My friends aren't used to me bailing before a party. Ignore. Ignore. Ignore. The E's are panicked chickens with no head.

-ɛ₀ TWO ₀ɜ-

JEB MEETS US in Gram's lobby. He's a sophomore at Pratt, an art school in Brooklyn, where he listens to angry music and paints twisted crap. He looks ridiculous in his skinny jeans and silver hoop earrings.

It's even hotter in the city, and Dad is more sweaty and disheveled than usual. Mom gives Jeb a heaping bag of groceries and hugs him like she's welcoming him back from two tours of duty.

"Mom, stop. I saw you last week." Jeb has little tolerance for Mom. He should be nicer to her. The woman spends half her life baking him cookies.

"Nice to see you, too, Jeb," Dad says.

Mom's sister, Aunt Mary, walks in with my twin cousins, Brit and Janie, who are back from their first year at college. Brit is a whiny, homely brat who has nothing better to do than stalk Janie and me online. Janie is an honorary E because of her name and because she's funny and fun and fascinatingly urban.

"I guess Mother isn't getting enough attention," Aunt Mary says. We cram into the elevator. Aunt Mary is Brit in thirty years. Her black cloud of negativity nearly suffocates us all on the ride up to the penthouse floor. I don't blame my uncle for leaving her.

The elevator opens into Gram's living room, which is sleek and pristine with white furniture and painted white floors. There are color-coordinated collections on the walls, the shelves, and the tables, gathered from all corners of the globe, and each attached to a different adventure. Only Astrid North O'Neill would set a carved Swiss music box next to an Argentinian peyote jar and a Chinese oracle shell, all because they share a shade of eggplant.

Mom's younger brother, Uncle Billy, pours white wine. His husband, Wes, gets up from the piano.

"Baby girl, look at you." Wes kisses my cheeks. He's tall and dirty blond and ruggedly handsome. Janie and I never quite understood how Wes fell for our skinny, sullen, four-eyed uncle.

"Where's Gram?" I ignore another text from Abby.

"We have no idea. Titi says she's staying locked in her room until everyone gets here," Wes says. Gram's housekeeper walks out of the butler's pantry carrying a tray of macaroons. Aunt Mary pulls her aside and berates her with whispers. Titi shakes her head repeatedly, sets down the cookie tray, and escapes to the kitchen.

Brit is texting and completely ignoring Great-aunt Rose. Granted,

Aunt Rose tells the same ten stories over and over again, but Brit could at least have the decency to pretend she's listening.

"I'm assuming pinkie ring Denny isn't here yet," Wes says.

"I've renamed him Drippy," I say.

"You'd think Billy could find something to say to his own damn family." Wes nods toward Uncle Billy, who is sitting on the piano bench studying *The Wall Street Journal*. "I mean, make an effort at least. Look at Aaron charming the pants off Mary."

Dad nods enthusiastically as Aunt Mary makes a face. Dad has no family to speak of—he was an only child, and his parents are dead. They were antisocial, so Dad barely knows his relatives. This is my whole family, for better or for worse.

"Do you like Brit's outfit?" Janie says, stuffing a macaroon into her mouth.

Wes laughs a little too loudly at Brit's ensemble of pleated, high-water khakis and metallic gladiator sandals.

Titi rings a little bell and instructs us to go into the library. She slides the fake bookcase wall in the living room to the right, revealing a hidden passageway where we used to act out all kinds of Anne Frank, Underground Railroad dramatizations. I follow Janie into the library, where Gram's longtime lawyer fidgets with a stack of papers. We sit in a semicircle of chairs arranged in front of the desk.

"Eww." I elbow Janie and point out the lawyer's crusty scalp.

Gram walks in and stands behind the desk. She pauses for a moment, taking in the visual of her entire family seated before her.

"Okay, Mother, what's up?" Aunt Mary breaks the silence.

"Hello, beloved family, and thank you for coming." Gram welcomes us like she's giving a speech to a foreign delegation.

"Where's Denny?" Aunt Rose calls out. "I hear you two are getting married."

"Oh stop, Rose, for God's sake." Aunt Rose looks wounded. "Give me more credit than that. I was only seeing that buffoon because he had great opera seats. I told you after Martin died I would never marry again, and I won't." She shakes her head. "Now, listen. I called you all here for a reason."

"What's the reason?" Aunt Rose yells. Wes stifles a laugh.

"Rose, let me speak." Gram beckons the lawyer to join her. She links her arm through his. He towers above her petite frame.

"Okay, here I go. Kids, I brought you here because I'm sick. Well, I'm basically dying. I have pancreatic cancer, and in case you don't know, that's one of the bad ones."

My stomach drops. A thick lump forms in my throat, and I can't breathe.

All the blood exits Aunt Mary's face. "Why are you telling us like this?"

"Mary, I wanted to tell you all at the same time. I just found out a couple weeks ago. I needed time to make some big decisions."

We sit, motionless, until Dad breaks the silence. "Well, thank God we're in the best city in the world for medical care," he says. "We'll get you into Sloan Kettering this week. My buddy is a top-notch oncologist there."

"I don't want to see your friend, Aaron. Could you just let me say what I brought you here to say?" She takes a deep breath and smiles. "I've booked us all on an eight-week cruise. It leaves right after Maddie graduates." She looks at me. "I'm still working on finding you a dress, by the way."

I can't tell if she's trying to be funny, if all of this is a sick Gram joke.

"Mom, we're not going on a cruise. We need to figure out treatment options," Uncle Billy says.

"There are no good treatment options. I'm not sitting around some hospital room with fluorescent lighting, stuck to a chemo drip for the last few months of my life. I've booked the cruise. It's done."

"What makes you think we can drop everything and take a cruise?" Aunt Mary raises her flinty voice. "You are not thinking clearly."

"Well, let's see. Aaron's a teacher, you and Trish are homemakers, a term I use loosely, and the kids have summer break. Wessy and Bill can turn over the business to the staff for a while. I'm thinking very clearly, dear."

The air is trying to get into my lungs, but it can't get past the growing lump.

Gram returns to her spot behind the desk and clears her throat. "Okay, where was I?" she says. "Oh, yes: I'm dying. And I want to take you on a cruise. Don't worry, it's not one of those tacky, all-you-can-eat buffet ships. It's a lovely ship, state of the art. And all the passengers are dying, or accompanying someone who is dying."

"Well, that's terrible, Astrid," Aunt Rose says.

"No, Rose. It's not terrible at all. We, the dying, get to plan the entire voyage. We get to customize it to satisfy our final wishes. Maybe we'll tie up some loose ends around the globe or add a few items to our bucket lists." Gram winks at me. I fake smile back. "The best part is while we're at sea, and when I'm ready, I will go to my private cabin where a trained physician will inject me with potassium and a sedative. Then I will go to sleep, and you charming people will see me off."

CARRIE FIRESTONE
is the author of *The Loose Ends List*
and *The Unlikelies*. A former New York
City high school teacher, she currently
lives in Connecticut with her husband, two daughters, and their pets.
She invites you to visit her online at
carriefirestoneauthor.com.